ERASING

RAMONA

Peggy Rothschild

ERASING RAMONA is a work of fiction. Names, characters and events are ALL products of the author's imagination. Any resemblance to actual events or people living or dead, is entirely coincidental. Real places in this novel may be used fictitiously.

ISBN-13: 978-1512013580

ISBN-10: 1512013587

ALSO BY

PEGGY ROTHSCHILD

Clementine's Shadow

For Richard

ACKNOWLEDGMENTS

Once again, my sincere thanks go to
The Sunday Morning Writers
– a smart, talented, perceptive group –
who read this manuscript in its many
iterations and shared their insights:
Ann Brady, Anne Riffenburgh, and
Howard Rosenberg.

One
November 1984

Where the hell was I? My mouth tasted like sour cherry and a jackhammer pounded somewhere behind my eyes. We must've kept partying after Billy's gig. But where? Here? I freed myself from the tangle of sheets. "Billy?" My voice sounded hoarse and thin. Leaning against a bedpost, I pulled on jeans then fished through the pockets for my vial of pills. I shook out a Xanax and swallowed it dry. A dark sleeve poked from beneath the bed. Shivering, I turned my sweatshirt right-side-out and yanked it on. After struggling into socks and ankle boots, I looked out the closest window.

Gray sky loomed above rolling hills dotted with sycamore and sequoia. Definitely not San Francisco. Was I back in Mill Valley?

Which one of Billy's friends lived out here? I turtled my icy fingers inside my sleeves and stepped into the hall. A wide staircase led down. "Billy?"

Nothing looked familiar – not the tiled entryway, the gilt-framed family portrait, nor the heavy wood shutters covering the windows. When I reached the first floor, a faint hum mixed with the tick of a clock, but the place still felt abandoned.

A door stood open on the far side of the entry. "Billy?" I covered my nose. "Oh, man. You been eating refrieds again?" I stepped inside. A cast-off shoe sat near one of the sofas. I rounded the end of the six-foot sectional and stared.

Dried blood webbed the carpet. Three bodies lay snared in the rust-brown strands.

A man and two women. The right quarter of the man's head was gone; white spurs of broken bone poked through the remains of his brain. A wide red-black halo stained the neck of his navy shirt and the surrounding tan carpet. The low buzz I kept hearing wasn't coming from inside my head: flies feasted on the gore. One of the woman's eyes remained open, but there was no question she was dead. A bullet had left a bloody hole in the center of her forehead. Some of her insides spilled through a long gash across her belly. The second woman's eyes were closed, her pink turtleneck splotched with blood.

My stomach lurched. I covered my mouth and backed away, unable to tear my gaze from the sight. My heel bumped against something. I forced myself to turn. A little boy lay curled on the carpet, like a sleeping cat. The boy from the painting in the foyer. But blood covered his Spiderman pajamas. I tried to scream, but no sound came out. Bile burning my throat, I turned and ran.

I pinballed down halls and through spacious rooms, but didn't find a living soul. I ran until I found the backdoor and stumbled outside. On the concrete patio, I doubled over, sucking air. Tears blinded me and a sob burst through my clenched teeth. Had Billy done this? Did he kill those people? No, he couldn't have. No matter how loaded Billy got, he never went code red on anyone.

But those poor people must have screamed. And the screams would have been terrible. Did I ignore them? I stared at my hands, but tears blurred my gaze. I wiped my eyes and looked for signs of blood on my skin and clothes. I couldn't have helped someone do any of those terrible things, could I? Still, my heartbeat became a little less frantic when I saw dirt instead of blood crusted beneath my nails.

But why did I wake up inside the house? Why didn't I remember anything?

I staggered to one of lounge chairs alongside the swimming pool and collapsed. The wind sent a leaf skittering across the concrete. I jumped then wrapped my arms across my stomach and started rocking. A vague image shimmered in the shadows of my brain. Six or seven people piled in the back of a van. All of us coming back from Trash's gig in San Francisco. Billy had said something about needing to see a guy in Mill Valley after the show. But I couldn't remember if the others drove all the way out to Mill Valley with us. Hell, I couldn't remember anything else about the ride.

Another image flashed: Sex with Billy. I stared at the dark second story. We went to a room upstairs. Then the two of us split a 'lude and drank some sweet wine before we ran outside to skinny dip. When the message from the bitter cold of the water reached my soggy brain, I'd screamed and climbed out of the pool. Billy had pulled himself from the water then doubled over, laughing at me. The two of us raced inside, grabbed towels and blankets, and wrapped them around our shivering bodies. In the upstairs bedroom, we washed down a mixture of pills with peppermint schnapps. After that my memory remained blank.

I looked down at the pool. Something floating in the water caught my eye.

Oh God. Another body. A caftan covered most of the dark shape, outlining legs and rear end. For several moments I stared at the spot where its head should have been. It was gone. Then I understood: The water didn't look opaque because a layer of fog blocked the sun. The water was stained with blood. I closed my eyes, but when I opened them again, the scene remained unchanged.

I needed to call the police. But I didn't want to go inside the house to find a phone. I searched through my pockets for my vial of pills, poured out two Quaaludes and another Xanax and swallowed the mess dry. What should I do? Go back inside or find another way out of the back yard and knock on a neighbor's door? But how was I going to explain my presence here to the cops? I resumed rocking back and forth and waited for inspiration to hit.

Shadows edged my vision, darkness creeping through my head like San Francisco fog. My body swayed. I tried to grab the lounge chair but my hand refused to follow my brain's command. The last thing I saw was the ground rushing toward me.

Two
June 1994

I knew lies. A good liar built their story on facts, giving a solid foundation to their falsehood, while less skilled fellows scrambled to avoid the truth. But one lie was never enough. Before too long, you had to shore it up with another. Then one more. And soon the lies had grown like an onion, one layer wrapped around the next. And, if you tried to slice through to the truth, everything fell apart.

If you asked any liar, I imagined they'd all say the same thing: They had a good reason for that first lie.

How I wished I'd told Rob the truth last night.

The sun's heat pressed against my shoulders as I ran down the sidewalk. If only I'd been more brave. But when I saw that ring, my brain froze up. How many lies could I own up to and still be the person Rob said he loved? Like a sputtering engine, one thought droned on: But, but, but....

I'd fix this. I'd tell him today. I checked my watch. Not now. I only had forty-five minutes until I had to be at the garden shop. But, after work, I'd call Rob and ask him to come by. This wasn't an out-in-public sort of conversation.

Sweat ran down my nose. I wiped away the trail and turned the corner onto my street. With my apart/ment just over half a block away, I slowed to a walk.

It wasn't that I didn't love Rob. For the first time in years, I had someone in my life I couldn't stand to lose. But I couldn't say yes until I came clean with him. In spite of the day's warmth, my fingers grew cold. I started walking faster. Last night, after telling me to call him when I knew what I wanted, Rob had left. I needed to act fast or risk losing him forever.

A pickup truck rumbled past, exhaust overwhelming the scent of the gardenias edging the sidewalk. I pulled my T-shirt over my nose to block out the fumes. In the distance, a familiar gray-haired figure caught my eye. I squinted against the morning sun. My neighbor was limping toward the far corner and a busy four-lane street.

Oh God no.

I sprinted down the sidewalk, hoping I could get to her before she reached the curb. About ten feet from my target, I called out.

"Mrs. S. Mrs. S. Over here. Behind you. It's Suzy."

The petite woman turned back from the brink of the busy intersection. Mrs. Stegman's expression remained blank.

I fed her more clues as I ran toward her. "From down the street." I pointed back the way I'd just raced. "I live next door to you."

The cloudy look cleared. Mrs. Stegman smiled. "You bring in our trash barrels."

"Right." I sucked in a couple mouthfuls of air and wiped my palms against my shorts. "Where you off to?" I tried not to stare at her ensemble of pink flannel nightgown and carpet slippers.

"To see Berta. I heard she's sick." Mrs. Stegman raised a liver-spotted hand to show me a can of peas. "When people are sick, you bring food."

I forced a smile. The odds of Mrs. Stegman making it across the four lanes of traffic to Berta's house were less than zero. "That's nice. But, I heard Berta's got a doctor's appointment this morning. Maybe we should get you home. Then you and Mr. S. can call Berta later. See if she's ready for company." No way Mr. Stegman knew his wife was out wandering the street.

"Oh." She looked at the can clutched in her bony hand.

I touched her shoulder and nodded in the direction of her house. To my relief, she turned around without complaint.

When we reached the driveway to the Stegmans' one-story bungalow, her husband raced from the backyard, his white hair tufted up like a cockatiel's crest. "Annie. Where were you? I searched everywhere..." He peered at me over his glasses. With a visible effort he erased the worry from his face and turned to his wife. "Well, no matter. You're home now. Why don't you go inside and sit in your chair? I'll make you a cup of tea."

We watched in silence as she climbed the two steps to their front door, then Mr. Stegman turned to me. "Where was she?"

"At the end of the block. She wanted to take some food to Berta."

His face paled. "She's never wandered from the house before. I don't know what I'm going to do." The muscles along his jaw bulged. "All I did was answer the phone. When I hung up, she was gone." Mr. Stegman cleared his throat. "Thank you." He nodded then followed his wife inside.

Though there were chunks of my life I'd love to forget and one chunk I was afraid to remember, how much history could a person lose before they became someone else? I turned up the path to my in-law unit. Halfway to the front door, the blare of the TV reached me. My stomach flip-flopped. Rob had come back. I ran up the walkway to the porch but froze with my hand on the doorknob. If he had come expecting an answer, what was I going to do? We needed time to talk, time I didn't have right now.

I took a deep breath and opened the door.

"Hey Suzy-Q. Good run?" Kicked back on the sofa, Rob's attention stayed focused on the screen. Dressed in a T-shirt and jeans, heavy work boots propped up on the coffee table, his pose appeared relaxed. But though his tone was light, his voice didn't hold its usual warmth.

My breath came in short puffs, but not from the run. Sweat popped out along my hairline – also not from the run. I toed off my shoes, parked them next to the door mat and took a deep breath. "What's up? Work get cancelled today?"

"Nah. I was on my way in when I heard about this on the radio. Your place was closer. I wasn't gonna miss seeing it." He waved a well-muscled arm toward the TV.

"Seeing what?" I dried my face with the hem of my T-shirt.

"O.J. Simpson's on the run. I think the guy's flipped out." Rob looked over his shoulder at me. "Don't worry. It's not pics of his dead wife or anything gross." He shook his head. "The guy was supposed to turn himself in today, but snuck out of his lawyer's house instead. Now he and some friend are leading the cops on a low-speed chase. The thing's totally bizarre. Give it a look."

When the story broke about the murders, my nightmare ran three times while I slept instead of the usual single showing per night. "I'll pass." My pulse rate slowed to normal.

The blue velvet ring box wasn't sitting on the table; Rob hadn't come for my answer. I walked behind him and kissed the top of his head, then continued on into the narrow kitchen to rinse my face. The cool water felt good dripping down my neck. I blotted myself dry with a paper towel then pulled off the elastic ponytail holder and freed my hair. The phone shrilled and I headed back to the living room. After last night's awkward conversation, I doubted Rob felt at home enough to answer my phone.

"Look at this." Rob pointed at the screen.

Several cop cars trailed a white SUV. Stories about the stabbing deaths had hit the airwaves Monday. By Tuesday, the killings were the focus of every news show. I had done my best to avoid articles or broadcasts about it.

The phone rang again. I grabbed the handset and turned my back to the TV. "Hello." No one spoke, but the line wasn't dead. "Hello?" I repeated.

"Miranda?"

The voice sounded cracked and frail. A part of me reeled; she had saved my number. "Mom. Hi. Everything okay?" She didn't answer. Was that a sniffle I heard? "What's wrong?"

"Your father's dead."

"What?" My knees wobbled. I leaned against the sofa back.

"Your father's dead. I'd like you to come to the service."

"You okay Suzy-Q?" Rob circled the sofa to stand beside me.

I covered my free ear. "What happened?"

"He had a heart attack. A massive coronary. In the fifth game of a set at the club. He charged the net then collapsed."

"Oh God." My chest felt tight. The TV broadcaster's voice clamored on. I covered the mouthpiece. "Turn that off." I gestured at the screen with my chin. Rob hurried back to the coffee table and fumbled through the newspapers for the remote.

"Yes, well..." My mother's voice trailed off.

When the silence stretched long enough that I felt sure she had finished talking, I spoke again. "You really want me to come up?"

"Most everyone in Mill Valley will attend the service. I think you should, too. While you're here, we can handle a few matters."

Dad was dead, but I didn't want to go home and face the past. I glanced at Rob hovering off to the side. I had to go. I needed to go. It was time. To figure out what the hell happened all those years ago. If I didn't, I'd never be able to move forward. "Okay." My heart hammered so loud, I raised my voice to drown it out. "I've got to make arrangements to take a few days off." I wound my finger through one of my curls and pulled until my scalp protested. Focusing on the pain helped calm me. "I can probably be on my way in a couple hours."

"Good. Now, Miranda, I want you to pack something appropriate." Mom's voice picked up strength as she made her way onto more familiar footing. "Nothing gaudy, please. Think somber, tasteful and somewhere between knee- and mid-calf length."

"Right." Leave it to my mother to give me fashion tips for Dad's funeral. "I won't get there until late."

"If you like, I can make a reservation for you at the Mill Valley Inn."

A familiar twist wrenched my gut. After more than a decade, I still wasn't welcome to stay under my parents' roof. I took a shaky breath. "Fine. That'll be fine."

"I'll tell them to expect a late check in."

My throat felt as if it was clogged with rocks, but I managed to get out another, "Fine."

"Come by the house tomorrow at 9 a.m."

"Sure. I'll be there." I hung up then covered my mouth with both hands.

Rob touched my arm. "What's wrong?"

I dropped my hands to my side. "My dad's dead."

"Ah Suz." He rested a warm palm along the back of my neck. "I'm sorry, honey. You're going home for the service?"

"Yeah."

Rob touched his forehead to mine, his warm breath smelling of cinnamon and apples. "Are you sure you want to go? It's not like your family's close."

"I know. But he's my dad." My throat constricted. "Was my dad."

Rob's arm circled my back. "You never talk about either of them. When's the last time you were up there?"

"Ten years ago."

"Listen." Rob straightened, one hand gripping each of my shoulders. "I'll go with you."

Uh-oh. Worlds colliding. Could Rob feel my shoulders stiffening? I couldn't do this right now. I looked away, my gaze landing on the blank TV screen. "That's sweet, but... it'll take Mom a few days to get the service together, which means I'll be gone maybe four days. There's no point in you missing that much work."

"I don't mind."

Why hadn't I told Rob the truth last night when I had the chance? I was way too twisted up inside to tell him now. And if I let him come up north with me, he'd do a full-on freak out when he saw how I had lied to him. Better to piss him off than let that happen. "No." I steeled myself and stared into his deep green eyes. "It's going to be tough enough seeing my mom after all this time. I can't be looking after you, too."

He took a step back, a deep crease marring his forehead. "Jesus, Suz. I want to come along to take care of you. Not the other way 'round. You never let me help you."

I wrapped my arms across my stomach. "I can't do this right now."

"You never can." Rob eased my left hand free then stroked my palm with his thumb. "Look, I've made it clear how I feel. What I want. And I've been waiting two years now for you to start counting on me. To show me you trust me. I think that by now, I'd rate a visit home. You ashamed of me? Think your mom's gonna look down at me 'cause I work construction?"

"The truth?"

He nodded.

"Yeah. But she looks down on me, too. That's not why I don't want you to come. I need to travel light for this. Please trust me and leave it at that."

Rob released my hand. "Sure. But we need to have a talk when you get back." He walked to the coffee table and picked up his keys. When he reached the front door, he turned and looked at me. "Sorry about your dad. Drive safe." He nodded, then the door closed with a crisp click.

Had I done it this time? Driven Rob away for good? That wasn't what I wanted. I trusted Rob more than anyone in the world. More than I had dared trust anyone since...leaving Mill Valley. When I got back, I'd tell him everything. After Dad's funeral. After I had a chance to face my past and get some answers.

Dry-eyed, I collapsed onto the sofa. A small photograph of Dad and I sat on top of the TV. The picture had been taken on my first day of school. With his slicked back hair and dark suit, Dad looked handsome and dignified while I'd looked a little like Raggedy Ann. I couldn't believe he was gone. My stomach churned. When was the last time Dad held me? Age ten? The photo blurred as my tears fell. I stood and started pacing.

Dad was dead. I hadn't seen him in eleven years and now I never would again. I wanted to say goodbye, to go to his funeral. And Mom was all alone now. This might be my one chance to fix things between us. To grab the last bit of family I had. But, if I wanted to move forward with my life, I couldn't go back home without visiting the one place I never wanted to see again. I shook my head, refusing to give in to the familiar stab of fear.

In less than seven hours, I'd be in Mill Valley. The scene of my major disasters and failures. And my biggest nightmare.

Three

I rubbed the metal fob on my key chain while giving the apartment a final once-over. Though I hated to admit it, even to myself, I was afraid to face my mother. My lone remnant of family. She must have loved me at some point in time, but I wasn't sure she ever liked me. No, I needed to stay positive. We hadn't talked since I was seventeen. A lot could change in ten years. I certainly had. And we needed each other now. The knots in my stomach tightened. I suspected I was more nervous about seeing Mom again than the possibility of crossing paths with the Mill Valley cops.

But in the decade since I ran from Mill Valley, the cops had never knocked on my door. There was no reason to think a quick trip home would put me on their radar. Even so, I couldn't picture this trip going well. I patted the pockets of my jeans and checked my purse for extra Kleenex before grabbing my overnight bag and stepping outside. With a sigh, I locked the front door and scuffed my way to the sidewalk.

When I reached the curb, I unlocked the trunk of my Celica and looked up. Wispy clouds meandered overhead. "This is a bad idea." Great. Now I was talking to myself. After stowing my bag, I leaned my hands against the warm metal and took a deep breath. Then I climbed behind the wheel and began the four hundred-mile drive home.

Fridays brought out the heaviest traffic. The northbound 405 freeway would be a slow and go until Mulholland. I spun the radio dial, but all the stations were full of O.J. Simpson's low-speed car chase. "Dammit." L.A. freeways had elephantine memories, continuing to snarl long past the original incident that sparked the traffic jam. O.J.'s adventure was going to add at least a couple hours to my drive.

By the time I reached the Richmond-San Rafael Bridge, it was almost midnight. My eyes burned from too many tears and too many hours behind the wheel. In nine hours, I would face my mother. I corkscrewed one of my curls around my index finger and pulled. My stomach felt like I had swallowed a box of nails. I took a couple deep breaths. Though 'picturesque' was how most folks described Mill Valley, I couldn't imagine relaxing here. I rolled off the freeway at Richardson Bay and turned onto Miller Avenue then fumbled for the heat knob. I had forgotten how fast temperatures dipped here at night, even during summer.

As I passed the triple arches that announced the entrance to Tam High, a violent shiver ran down my spine.

Before leaving home, I'd called the Mill Valley Inn to cancel the reservation my mom made. While I didn't know the exact price, the place was way too rich for my budget. Though I wasn't about to tell that to Mom.

A horn blared. A driver revved past as I continued to crawl along the block, trying to get my bearings, one eye out for the Cozy 8 Motel. Within ten minutes I spotted the sign. Still in business. Its vacancy sign glowed red, turning a portion of the white stucco exterior pink. The utilitarian-looking building formed a large U around a blacktopped 'courtyard' and was anything but cozy. But the price was right. After pulling into the lot, I sat for a moment, working up the nerve to leave the safety of my car and commit to a stay in my old hometown.

The air outside smelled of pine and saltmarsh. My gut unclenched a bit at the familiar scent. I pulled my luggage from the trunk, took a deep breath then strode across the asphalt to the lobby door. A tinny bell rang when I pushed it open. The dark-haired girl behind the check-in desk didn't react. I walked to the counter. She still didn't look up. I took advantage of her inattention to study her glossy cap of curl-free hair. The one time I cut my hair that short, it had looked like my scalp was covered with copper springs. I put down my bag and put my hands on the counter. The clerk's attention remained focused on a paperback splayed in front of her. "Hi. You have any rooms?"

It took at least twenty seconds before she tore her gaze from the page. When she lifted her head, the look in her large brown eyes said my question bored her beyond belief. "We got nothing but rooms." She blew a pink gum bubble.

After I gave her my credit card and signed the necessary forms, she pushed a key across the counter. "You're on the second floor. Outside and to the right." She resumed reading before I slotted my credit card back inside my wallet.

I shouldered my bag and headed back outside and located the staircase. The wooden stairs could've used a coat of paint, but then that seemed true of most the Cozy 8. My room wasn't anything fancy, but at least it looked clean. It smelled of Lysol and lemon, and featured a queen size bed, antique-looking TV, and a window with a view of the building's other wing. I threw my bag on the bed then went in search of the mini bar.

There wasn't one.

"Perfect." I flopped onto the quilted bedspread and rubbed my eyes. Probably for the best there was no bar. Otherwise, the odds were good I would drink until drunk and, in the morning, face a high bill to go with a crashing headache. Though worn out by the long drive, I suspected anxiety would make sleep hard to come by. After showering and pulling on a fresh T-shirt, I climbed into bed. When I closed my eyes, memories of my father circled, finally lighting on the tennis lessons he gave me and his frustration at my timidity when charging the net. The first time I served him an ace, disbelief then anger flashed crossed his face, before he grinned at my success.

Always one with high standards, I wound up disappointing him often, making for more bad memories than good.

I rolled onto my back, letting my thoughts float. Though the demands of his law practice filled his days, Dad was the one who taught me to drive. More than one lesson ended in yelling and tears.

The image of his clenched jaw and twitching hands popped into my head. I only saw him that over-the-edge once. But the sight had burned itself onto my retina. That was the night he walked in on me having sex. With the very boy he had forbidden me to see. Let alone allow inside the house. Forget about broken camel backs. That final straw ripped out his heart. Raw fury shook Dad's frame as he kicked me out of the house, out of his life.

I shook off the memory and pictured Rob's green eyes, his crooked smile. The way he belly laughed when something struck him as funny. I missed that laugh. I hoped I would hear it again after I got back to L.A. After we had our talk.

When I fell asleep, I sweated through my usual nightmare then jerked awake. A long sleepless stretch followed and I tried reciting passages of favorite books from memory until I finally nodded off again. Awake again at 6 a.m., I gave up and climbed out of bed. I pulled back the curtain on the room's one window. The sun hadn't yet shouldered through the morning fog, leaving the sky a cottony gray and purple.

My face-to-face with Mom was in three hours. The day promised to be a long one. Too antsy to stay cooped up, I pulled on jeans, T-shirt and tennis shoes then grabbed a sweatshirt jacket from my bag.

Outside, the combination of damp air and the smell of Douglas fir felt familiar as an old friend. I climbed down the staircase to the parking lot, zipping my sweatshirt. The Cozy 8 didn't look like it was doing a bang-up business; less than half the parking spaces were full. Inside the lobby, a new face greeted me at check-in; the bored-looking girl replaced by an acne-scarred young man. Someone had hosed the place with air freshener and the small reception-area smelled like a mad arborist had crossed a pine tree with a bottle of fabric softener.

"Um, hi. Uh, can I help you?" the clerk said between bites on a well-chewed thumbnail.

"Yeah. You got a continental breakfast?"

"Um, yes." He turned, knocking over a stack of brochures with his elbow. His face reddened as he stooped to pick them up. Once the tri-folds were back in place, the clerk set a laminated map on the counter and tapped a highlighted square with his index finger. "Breakfast's served here in the Nook. But it doesn't start until 6:30."

"Thanks." Too long to wait. I needed to move, burn off some edginess. Back outside, I scoped out my surroundings. The motel sat about two-and-a-half miles from the traffic circle that marked the entrance to downtown Mill Valley. I turned toward town. It felt good to be in motion.

Other than the flat coastal area and marshland where the town butted up against the shore of Richardson Bay, Mill Valley occupied a series of narrow wooded canyons on the southern slopes of Mount Tamalpais. The rich smell of the redwoods tickled a memory of crouching behind a tree at our old house, hoping the kid who was 'it' wouldn't find me. Then the rush of triumph when he yelled, "Olly olly oxen free," signaling it was safe to come out of hiding; I had won. That was the thing I needed to hang on to: Not all memories of this place were bad.

Sequoia and sycamore trees shadowed the roadway. From the surrounding hillsides, alders and cottonwoods rose on the steep inclines. I breathed the homey smell of pine along with the sharp tang of eucalyptus. At this hour, traffic was light. Though the odds were low anyone driving by would recognize me, I still fought the urge to turn my face away from the road. Seeing people who knew me was unavoidable. And not the problem. I focused on my surroundings, hoping to keep my mind busy enough to crowd out the images from my last time in Mill Valley.

Near downtown, the street narrowed. I remembered how trapped this wooded place made me feel as a teen. While the towering trees looked beautiful, their looming darkness cramped my world. I grew to see their rising trunks as huge bars that locked me in.

I was sixteen and stupid when my dad kicked me out. And in love.

"Billy Bang." Speaking his name aloud made my stomach twist.

Four

In spite of taking a brisk walk, butterflies still battled it out in my gut as I drove to my old house. The Celica's tires crunched up the gravel drive. Trees rose on either side, casting pockets of shadow. The driveway was longer and steeper than I remembered. By the time I pulled under the white porte cochere, my palms and armpits felt swampy. Two other cars sat out front: a black Mercedes and a maroon BMW. I glanced at the stone façade then turned toward the juniper bushes edging the drive. Small birds darted in and out of the greenery, breaking the silence with their warbles.

Though we moved six times before I hit my teens, this was the most commanding of the homes we lived in. But I had never liked it. The place was too big, too cold, and too easy to feel lost inside. It also held too many ghosts. My hands started to tremble. I clutched the steering wheel. Any remaining butterflies flitting inside me surely drowned in the flood of stomach acid that came as I remembered the last time I was here: January 5, 1984.

On that visit home, I showed up after Dad left for work. A cold, wet day, the hard driving rain didn't slack off during the long bus ride from San Francisco. Though I'd told Billy I was going to Mill Valley to retrieve my winter clothes, a part of me hoped Mom might ask me to come back. I had trudged from the bus stop, six endless uphill blocks, my socks and tennis shoes squishing with each step. My sweatshirt felt like a cold wash rag as I stood trembling in the driveway, lashed by the wind and rain. Several minutes passed before I worked up the nerve to climb onto the porch and knock.

My mother had opened the door within seconds. Ten months had passed since we last saw one another, but she looked unchanged. As usual, not a single ash blond hair was out of place and her lips were pursed into a tight moue of distaste. But she didn't seem surprised to see me on her doorstep. I suspected she had watched from the dining room while I stood shivering in the rain. "Mom."

Dressed in a powder blue cashmere twin set and gray tweed skirt, she could have stepped right out of *Home and Garden* magazine – in spite of her frown. The smell of Chanel perfume and Earl Grey tea wafted towards me. I had forgotten how the combined scent always drifted alongside her.

She crossed her arms before she spoke. The frown wasn't limited to my coming by uninvited. She hated being called 'mom.' Once I outgrew 'momma,' she coached me to call her 'mother.' But I'd rebelled.

"Miranda. I wasn't expecting company. What do you want?"

"Can I come in?"

"I think you know your father wouldn't approve of that." She continued to stand, arms crossed, blocking the doorway, in the pose I always thought of as 'The Interrogator.' When I was in single digits, she would adopt that stance to grill me. Now, though she lacked the authority, her disapproval remained.

"Right. I wanted to get a few of my things. My old hiking boots. My ski parka."

"Your old things? We gave everything to the Women's Club for their rummage sale. Almost a year ago."

A dull pain burrowed through my chest. "I haven't been gone a year. You gave my stuff away right after I left? Right after you kicked me out? Couldn't wait to get rid of the traces, huh?"

My mother shifted her gaze toward the stormy sky. "Your father thought it best. You chose not to live by our rules. You knew what that would mean. It's not as if we didn't give you ample warning."

"What about my other stuff?"

"What other stuff?"

"My records? My tapes? Photos? My stuff."

Mom shook her head then stepped back. "I think you'd better leave. Goodbye Miranda."

The door closed in my face – a refined rejection. No scene. My mother didn't believe in them.

I dried my palms on my jeans as I tried to shake off the memory. This visit was about mourning my father and, hopefully, rebuilding a relationship with Mom. But my twisting gut wasn't optimistic. Mom had always been a master at taking shots at my too-thin skin. Much of what happened between us was my fault, but she played her part, too. Still, I had disappointed my parents over and over again – and they didn't know the worst of it.

I felt hollow and sick that Dad was dead. Or maybe the sick feeling eating at me came from the fact I wasn't more torn up about his death. Or at least as torn up as I thought I should be.

The pomegranate tree to the left of the driveway was in flower. As a teen, I'd counted the days until gray streaked the blood-red fruit, signaling it was ready for picking. I had loved tearing open the hard shell, digging out the garnet-colored seeds with juice-stained fingers. I reached up and plucked one of the narrow leaves. Mealy bugs covered the underside, sucking the life from the foliage. I crushed the leaf, along with its parasites and dropped it to the ground.

My knock on the heavy front door sounded muffled, but my mother hated it when visitors used the brass knocker. After a brief wait, the door was opened by a plump blonde in a black dress. She looked about fifty. That and the diamonds hanging from her ears put her in the 'friend of Mom's from the club' category.

"Yes? May I help you? Are you with the florists?"

"No, I'm Miranda. Marion's daughter."

"Oh." A small frown creased her forehead. She glanced at my tennis shoes then looked at my blue jeans and knit pullover. "Please, come in, won't you? I'm Gwen Hardesty. I'm a friend of your mother's." She brushed a microscopic piece of lint from the sleeve of her dress. "Do you plan to change here?"

I followed Gwen into the high-ceilinged foyer, the smell of roses heavy in the air. "Change what?"

"Your clothes."

While what I wore wasn't up to country club standards, I didn't think a visit home required more formal attire. I wrapped a curl around my index finger then pulled it taut. "Why would I change?"

Gwen pursed her lips and massaged the fingers of her right hand. "Well, dear, you can't plan to wear that to the funeral."

I stopped walking. "The funeral's today?"

"Of course."

"Mom didn't say it was today."

"Well, I'm sorry, dear, but it is."

"That's fast. I know Mom's organized, but I can't believe she got everything arranged already."

Gwen continued to frown. "The service is set for 10 a.m. Do you need to run back to the Inn for your clothes?"

"Uh, yeah." I started toward the door as a thought hit. An acid wave crashed against my stomach lining. One day was too fast to get together the kind of funeral my mother would want. "When did Dad die?"

Gwen retreated a step, as if to distance herself from Marion's crazy daughter. "Well, dear, Del died Monday afternoon."

Five days ago. Mom waited four days to let me know my father died. I guess I should feel lucky she let me know at all. I turned and walked out to my car.

Five

At 5:30 p.m. I walked into The Deuce and waited for my eyes to adjust to the dim lighting. The snug neighborhood joint looked half-full. Not bad for a Saturday evening in sleepy Mill Valley. Spotting no open stools at the bar, I moved toward the room's outer rim and found an unoccupied table. Some natural light came in through the two street-side windows, but I chose a seat in comfortable gloom. I leaned my elbows on the table and waited for a cocktail waitress to find me in the crowd. My hands shook. I fisted them to make the trembling stop.

Funerals sucked. No getting around that. I hadn't gone to that many of them. Six. Maybe seven. But my father's funeral blew. Blew with chunks. I closed my eyes and took several deep breaths, listening to the mix of canned music, conversation and ricocheting pool balls.

"A beverage, miss?"

The Irish lilt got me to pop my eyes open. For a moment I thought I gazed at an oversized elf. The drink waiter towered from a height of at least six-foot-five, his golden hair, pointed chin, green eyes and dimpled smile promising more than a pot of gold. I resisted the impulse to look at his feet to see if he wore shoes with curled up toes. "Yeah. Vodka tonic. With a twist."

"Right away, miss."

His servile words didn't match the gleam in his eyes as his gaze raked up my legs then journeyed on to my cleavage. I bet the guy's ability to undress female patrons with a glance brought him beaucoup tips. Or a lot of complaints. With my red-rimmed eyes and twitching hands, I doubted his appreciative smile was genuine.

The waiter turned away, but after he gave me at least fifteen seconds to check out his rear view he turned back again and smiled. "My name's Sean and I'll be happy to serve you. You let me know if you're needing any wee thing."

"Just the vodka tonic."

"Right away, miss."

After one more survey of my breasts, the giant Elf sauntered toward the crowded bar. I watched his retreat, tugging on the strands of hair I'd coiled around my finger. My gaze drifted upward. The toilet seat guitar still hung on the wall above the bar. It was nice to know that after more than a decade, Charlie

Deal's musical creation remained on display. Good things could stay the same.

Over the sound system Dee Dee Ramone gave his rapid fire count of "One, two, three, four." My heartbeat quickened. Before the first chord was struck, I knew the song would be *Rockaway Beach.* At fifteen, this had been my favorite Ramones' song. My shoulders and spine relaxed as my head started to bop along with the driving beat. Say what you will about their musical ability or – as my parents used to say – lack thereof, the Ramones knew how to make a body move.

But every Ramones' tune ran way too short and in less than two minutes, the song was done and an overblown pop number oozed through the air. With nothing more to distract me, my thoughts turned back to my meeting with Mom.

When I had re-entered the house after a quick trip to the Cozy 8 for an even speedier change of clothes, I found my mother sitting on the living room couch, dressed in black, cradling a teacup. The curtains over the floor-to-ceiling windows were still drawn, making the wood paneled room look even gloomier than I remembered. A chill ran up my arms. Mom raised her gaze from the steaming brew and stared. I felt her assessing my ensemble, taking in my black fake leather pumps, midnight blue stockings, my a-tad-too-short navy dress and the cable-knit sweater draped over my arm. At five-foot-eight, I stood half-a-foot taller than her, but she always managed to make me feel small. When Mom's visual survey reached my large black leather-look purse, she sucked in her cheeks like she wanted to spit. But my mother never spat. She shook her head then took a sip of tea.

"I guess I shouldn't have expected anything more."

I went for the high road and ignored her dig at my outfit. "Why didn't you tell me Dad died five days ago?" Okay, so I didn't make it all the way to the high road.

Mom ignored my question and stared at me. "I see you still haven't managed to tame your hair. I suppose I should be grateful it's no longer purple."

My fingers were already tugging at a curl before I realized it. I returned my hand to my side then shrugged. "So you say."

She raised one well-groomed eyebrow. "'So I say?' And what, pray tell, is that supposed to mean?"

Good. A question was loads better than a polite cut-down. "Why didn't you call me when Dad died?"

"I did call. You're here, aren't you?"

I sighed then tried again. "Yeah, but you called me yesterday. Dad died on Monday. Why didn't you call me sooner?"

Mom brought her cup to her mouth, but didn't sip. "Your father was a very important man. I had a number of people I needed to contact. His death affected a great many."

Bull's eye. She got me, though I tried not to show it. My mother didn't think I was one of the 'great many' affected by his death. Maybe she was right. He'd been absent from my life for more than a decade. Maybe losing him affected his friends and acquaintances more. The damp weight of depression settled on my shoulders.

"Miranda, don't slouch. Remember you're not only representing yourself at this funeral. You're representing the family. Representing your father."

The morning went downhill from there. Before climbing inside the limo that would ferry us to my father's funeral, Gwen Hardesty pulled me aside. "I don't know if your mother told you, but there'll only be a graveside service." Gwen rubbed the swollen knuckles on her right hand.

"Is that something Dad wanted?"

"Since Del wasn't what you'd call religious, Marion thought it more appropriate to just do the graveside service. At Fernwood, of course."

"Of course." Fernwood, the go-to cemetery for the rich and powerful of Mill Valley.

Gwen seemed to sense something amiss in the mother-daughter bonding process and positioned herself between Mom and me in the limo's roomy backseat. The three of us rode in silence through a series of tree-lined winding roads to the cemetery. When we drove through the cemetery's entrance, I started crying. This was real. Dad was dead. I looked past Gwen. Mom sat dry-eyed, staring ahead at the back of our driver's head, a frown twisting her mouth. Mom didn't like scenes. And that included crying in public.

I wiped my face and took a shuddering breath. My landlady always swore a tried and true way to stay calm was to study your surroundings. To focus on the external not the internal. I stared out the window, eyeing the different monuments as we continued along the winding road. In business since the late 1800s, Fernwood had an air of history and finality.

Once in our appointed spots in the first row of folding chairs under the white cloth canopy, tears blurred my vision again. I looked away from the coffin and wiped my eyes. Beyond the broad expanse of lawn dotted by heritage oaks and bay trees, sprawled the valley and surrounding hills. It struck me as sad that my father wound up in one of the most park-like spot in town, when he couldn't appreciate his surroundings. Though he had never been one to stop and smell the roses.

A man in a charcoal suit set a large spray of gladiolus near the head of the coffin. Gwen patted Mom's arm though Mom didn't seem to notice. Voices murmured as mourners settled themselves in the rows behind us.

A gruff male voice drifted past. "He was the best player in his age division. This year's tournament will be a walk-away for Dennis Fabrini."

I wondered if the speaker was one of the important people in Dad's life who got notified about his death before me. I resisted the urge to turn and console him and the country club on their loss. I tried to tune out the conversational threads weaving through the crowd. The raised rosewood coffin with its gleaming brass fittings looked beautiful. My throat ached. I imagined Dad's body moldering inside that pretty box, like a sick gift. I closed my eyes, pictured his face. Frowning. Scowling. I tugged on one of my curls as I tried to imagine him smiling or laughing, but couldn't get his features to cooperate.

A look he used to give me fluttered through my brain. When I was five or maybe six, playing with my dolls or out running around in the yard, I sometimes caught Dad watching me. Posture erect, head cocked to the right, he appeared for all the world like a bird trying to catalog or classify what type of critter I was: Dangerous or tame? But when our eyes met, he would wave and turn away.

Now I couldn't help but wonder what he had seen in me in those unguarded moments.

A soft-spoken man led the graveside service. His voice choked with emotion as he talked of Dad's many charitable pursuits.

Since Dad wasn't religious, Mom must've made a big donation to leave the guy so moved. But the person he spoke about was a stranger to me. The father I knew was short-tempered and unforgiving. Had he changed as much as I had in the last ten years?

At the point when the service passed the length of a simple loving tribute, the chairman of the Chamber of Commerce rose to speak followed by a mucky-muck from the Mill Valley Tennis Club. Next came a woman from the Ladies Auxiliary who read a poem which ran on eight or nine verses. I lost track somewhere amid the "rainbows after a storm." From the ill-timed meter and awkward rhymes, I suspected she was the poetess.

After ninety long minutes, the service ended and the casket was lowered into the ground. Tears blurred my vision as I added my shovelful of dirt to Dad's grave. Mom accepted a few sympathetic hugs then straightened her shoulders and marched across the grass toward the limousine. Gwen and I exchanged a look. Then, with a shrug, Gwen trod after my mother. I turned and stared at the hole in the ground. My knees weakened and I felt a matching hole hollowing out my insides. For most my life, I had felt on my own – at least emotionally. But in the face of Dad's death, I felt a new kind of alone. I wiped my face dry then trailed behind Mom and Gwen. Once settled on the cushioned backseat, the cortege caravanned back to my parent's house for a buffet lunch.

At the lunch, Mom paraded me in front of an array of 'important' people – members of the Country Club, former business associates of my father's, members of the Chamber of Commerce, the women's club, and two dozen Eagle Scouts. The reason for the presence of so many Eagle Scouts eluded me.

"Miranda, you remember Beverly and Ralph Duffy?" Mom said as she maneuvered me beside a gray-haired couple. Mrs. Duffy's eyes went wide and she grabbed her husband's arm. Mom pretended not to notice the woman's reaction and barreled on. "No? You attended Tam High with their daughter Rhonda. Or was it Rachel? I get confused which one of the girls was in your class." None of their names meant anything to me. I nodded at the couple but that only seemed to alarm the woman further. What was her deal?

Mr. Duffy interceded. "I believe Rhonda was in the same class."

"How's she doing?" Mom said. "Isn't she in public relations?"

I studied my mother while tuning out their response. She made small talk as if this was a cocktail party, not her husband's funeral. I wondered if her behavior stemmed from her need for control or if it signified something else.

While Mrs. Duffy's body language said she viewed me as something potentially contagious – and not in a good way, like laughter – at least my brief conversation with her husband landed within the range of the normal. In comparison, at least twenty people reacted with shocked expressions when I was introduced as Del's daughter. It took a few go rounds of stuttered condolences before I got it: My parents hadn't mentioned my existence to any of their friends from the post-1983 era. That still didn't explain Mrs. Duffy, but for all I knew, she greeted every new face with horror.

After the introductions were completed, Mom excused herself and joined a covey of older women. Gwen Hardesty stood slightly apart from the crowd, near the buffet table, looking lost. Her expression brightened when I joined her. "How are you doing, dear?"

"I've been better." Across the room my mom still worked the crowd like a champion.

Gwen nodded. "She's an amazing woman."

"Right. Manners always at the ready."

Gwen rested a plump hand on my shoulder. "I know your mother appears indomitable. But she still needs you."

I gave her a tight smile.

Gwen cleared her throat. "So, dear, were you able to avoid the ruckus at the Inn?"

Loath to let my mother know I couldn't afford the Inn – even through such a sympathetic-looking channel as Gwen – I said, "What ruckus?"

"You didn't hear? You don't know what happened?" Her eyes lit up.

Good thing I decided not to tell Gwen I had booked a room at the Cozy 8. She obviously enjoyed a good gossip. "No. What?"

"Oh, it was awful. I heard all about it from Stella Goyette. Her brother came in for your father's funeral. Gordon Goyette. You know him?" I shook my head and she resumed. "Of course he and his wife were staying at the Inn. It's the one place in town I ever recommend. Which is what makes this all so shocking."

I resisted the urge to roll my eyes. Instead, I aimed for a look of polite interest. "And, that was what?"

"Well, dear, this awful man struck one of the desk clerks. He wasn't even a registered guest. If you can imagine." Gwen accepted a glass of claret from a passing waiter, but I demurred, afraid if I started drinking, I might not stop. The time for a good long drunk was later, away from my mother's judging eyes. Gwen took a sip then continued. "Gordon was in the lobby when the whole thing happened. This man walked to the reception desk, said something to one of the young girls who work there. Then he grabbed her and hit her on the nose."

"At the Inn?" I couldn't picture any unpleasant scene – let alone a violent one – playing out there.

"I know. Inconceivable. The Inn's an institution. Gordon said there was blood everywhere and the girl was sobbing. The poor thing's nose was broken."

"Why'd the guy do it?"

"Who knows? Probably her drunken boyfriend. Girls date the most inappropriate men these days. Even girls from good families." She shrugged. "Something I simply can't understand."

My face grew warm. Had Gwen heard about my inappropriate boyfriend?

"Imagine. Gordon said the brute shoved two people out of his way when he left."

"He punched her then walked out? No one tried to stop him?"

"Well, you know, Gordon has that tricky knee of his. So he couldn't do anything. He said that everyone was too shocked to react." Gwen shook her head. "I can't believe something so ugly could happen at the Inn. You're lucky you missed it."

"Right."

As awkward as I felt at both the graveside service and reception, at least there were other people around to provide a needed buffer zone between Mom and me. Once the guests left, Mom's artificial politeness cracked. She turned to me, teacup in hand, her eyes red and hard as nail polish. "Well, that part's done. We've one more hurdle to get over then you can go."

Nothing like getting dismissed from your former home. "What hurdle?"

"Lloyd Jenson. Your father's lawyer. He'll be back in about ten minutes. To read your father's will."

"Oh." I wrapped a curl around my finger and started pulling. It had never occurred to me that I would be mentioned in Dad's will. He wasn't someone who had dealt well with disappointment, meaning: Dad hadn't dealt well with me.

I followed Mom into the study where a crew of rent-a-waiters cleared away the detritus from the reception. She settled into the Queen Anne chair and smoothed some nonexistent wrinkles from the skirt of her dress. I avoided the two nearby Eames chairs. An oft-touted 'feature' of the room during my youth, I had grown to hate their rosewood veneer. Instead, I sat on the far side of the room in my grandmother's homey maple rocker.

"Whoever's cutting your hair needs to go back to beauty school. Or are you still cutting it yourself?"

I rocked instead of answering.

"With your bone structure, you should get it straightened. I'm sure that would be a better look. Maybe get it colored, too. Take out some of the brassiness."

My cheeks grew warm. I took a deep breath and reminded myself Mom had just lost her husband. Four days before she bothered to tell me, but still... I started rocking faster.

"Must you make that noise?"

The chair made a rapid-fire squeak with every move of its wooden rockers. I brought the chair to a stop and thought about shifting to another seat then resumed rocking. "I guess so." By the time Lloyd Jenson arrived, Mom's jaw looked clenched so tight I didn't see how she managed to still sip her tea.

Mr. Jenson reminded me of a bark beetle: Broad shouldered and bandy legged with a full head of hair that had been sprayed or gelled – and dyed – into a shiny black shell. His dark pinstriped suit only added to his bug-like appearance. He scuttled into the room, gave my mother a peck on the cheek, nodded at me then strode to my father's desk. Without asking permission, he made himself at home amongst my father's things, moving aside the heavy rose quartz paperweight along with the gold pen and pencil set. It seemed as though he was calculating the value of each item as he cleared it from his work area. The lines running from Mom's nose to her mouth deepened. Mr. Jensen did a fair job of pretending not to notice the tension in the room as he continued making himself comfortable. He spent a couple minutes sorting through a stack of papers then removed his gold-rimmed glasses and gave them a good polishing with his handkerchief before clearing his throat. He nodded at Mom then turned his gaze toward me.

"Your drink, miss. Vodka tonic with a twist."

My giant Irish elf returned with a very cool, very tall beverage in hand. The man knew how to pour a generous drink. He brushed against my fingers as he handed me the glass then smiled. "Been having yourself a tough day, have you?"

He was good. I had to give him that. His charming manner almost came across as natural. I watched his eyes as I lifted the glass to my lips and sipped. I couldn't tell if he was working me for a higher tip or if I looked vulnerable enough to come across as an easy lay. "No, not tough," I said. "Peaches and sunshine all day long."

"Then you're the lucky one, aren't you, miss." He winked then turned and strutted back toward the bar.

By the time I downed my third vodka tonic, the giant elf was looking pretty good. I watched him wend his way across the crowded floor of the bar. But I was no cheater. Talk about a sure-fire way to end things with Rob.

Rob. How many times had he told me I needed to open up and trust him? This was the first relationship since Billy where I wanted to open up. But... I had told him so many lies already. Would the truth drive him away? I tugged on a curl and shook my head. I didn't even know what the truth was. And that needed to change.

When I finished my drink and stood, the floor seemed to tilt. I grabbed the table until I got my legs under me. I couldn't blame my wobbliness on wearing high heels. The third vodka tonic was a mistake. It'd be a huge mistake to drive. I dropped enough cash to cover my bill, plus a twenty percent tip, then tottered back to the pay phone mounted near the restrooms. I smiled when I saw the number for the local cab company felt-tipped onto the wood panel above the phone. I dropped my coins into the phone and dialed.

Six

"Where to?" The cab driver coughed. His gravelly voice made him sound like a pack-a-day smoker.

A hack with a hack. I plunked my purse by my feet, settled into the back seat then met his gaze in the rearview mirror. "I want to drive around for a while."

He shrugged. "It's your money."

My money. Right.

It's not every day that you get disinherited.

Disinherited. *Dis,* indicating negation, lack, invalidation or deprivation. The opposite of inherit - To come into possession of; possess. To receive property from an ancestor or another person by legal succession or will. And in biology, the process of genetic transmission of characteristics from parents to offspring.

Did my father spend time puzzling over how his genetic contribution towards my making went awry? It's not like I was always a disappointment to him. Once upon a time, he held big hopes for me. When I started talking in two-word sentences at eighteen months and three-word sentences a few weeks later, he told everyone I would be a Rhodes Scholar. I read my first word, 'cat,' before age two and soloed my way through a first grade primer by the time I was thirty-six months old. By then he upped my potential to rocket scientist or Surgeon General.

I can't remember a time when I wasn't fascinated by words. It wasn't the way they sounded, but their construction that drew me in, the why and how of them. Like how, by dropping the 'm' in 'meat' – a change of a single letter – a word could morph into a related concept, while dropping the 'm' in 'team' altered the word entirely. In my hunger to understand, I began reading Webster's Unabridged Dictionary at age eight. I didn't realize that remembering what I read was unusual. My dad figured I would graduate college while still in my teens.

At age six or seven, my mom hauled me to San Francisco where I was tested by a woman with lots of moles and a droopy right eyelid. At the time, I didn't know what the tests were for, but over the years the fact that I was gifted got hurled at me whenever I failed to live up to my parents' expectations.

My parents' dreams for me died a little bit at a time. I showed little interest in science and always excelled in English so they shifted their plans for me. I would become a lawyer, perhaps a justice on the Supreme Court, writing briefs and defending the Constitution of the United States. They were even open to the possibility that I might become a great novelist. Perhaps Poet Laureate.

I still remembered the day I stopped writing. For years I'd kept a journal, jotting down my hopes, thoughts, and observations. Then one day when I was fourteen, I opened my journal and realized I wasn't writing my thoughts and feelings because I wanted to. I wrote in my journal because my parents expected me to. They bought me the beautiful leather-bound books for that purpose. One every three months. I stuffed the current journal into the back of my closet and went about pursuing a failing grade in English Literature.

Jesus, but I had been a pain in the ass. It was a wonder Dad mentioned me at all in his will.

A strange sensation, getting disinherited. But the strangeness wasn't about the money. Or rather, about not getting the money. I never expected Dad to leave me anything, except perhaps a strongly worded message telling me to shape up. No, it felt strange to know my father spent so much time thinking about how he could excise me from his life, cutting me out like some form of malignant cancer. But with the removal scheduled to take place after he was dead – when I couldn't bother him anymore. Not only that, he spent money on this legal surgery. I had no doubt he paid Lloyd Jenson a hefty fee to get the job done right. My initial assessment of Jenson's likeness to a bark beetle turned out dead on. The man thrived by living off the stressed and weakened, burrowing below the surface, spreading infection, and creating a canker that ultimately rotted away their host's core.

Five thousand dollars. I shook my head. To my father, I'm sure the amount was an insult. To me, it equaled what I had managed to save over the past ten years. The $5,000 was mine, with the stipulation I make no additional claims against his estate. I was fine with that. But I did find it strange how smart Dad was about me. The man didn't know the worst of the things I had done. No one did. Yet he knew me well enough to want me out of his life. I couldn't say I blamed him.

I rolled my head against the vinyl seat then stared out the window. The sun had set but a corona of peach and vermillion still lit the horizon. The beauty of the quiet valley felt like a sick joke.

Over the past decade, I had made a lot of changes. No drugs except booze and, with the exception of this trip, in restrained amounts. I made sure to get plenty of exercise, flossed after meals, and donated to charity – even when money ran tight. I gave time to good causes and tried to look out for the little guy. I wanted to become someone I could feel proud of. Though still ashamed of my past, I felt comfortable with myself now. But Dad never met the 'new' me. He only knew 'back then' me. And the 'back then' me had more than a few problems.

Ten years ago, I felt sure Dad didn't have a clue about the drugs. But now I realized how unlikely that was. Though often preoccupied by work, he didn't become the senior partner in a leading law firm without reading the people around him. The last two years I lived at home, I surrounded myself with a fuzzy buffer of stonedness. Between the pot and the downers, my tepid grades sank to drowning level and my 'snot-nosed attitude' – as defined by Dad – evolved into an 'I don't give a shit' attitude.

Oh yeah, he knew what I was up to. At fifteen the drugs helped me get through the day. I told myself I had everything under control, staying clear of the quick addictives like coke, speed and heroin. Wound way too tight for any kind of upper, the last thing I needed was something to ratchet me up another notch. But I loved the Quaaludes, codeine and Xanax – my personal party-pack favorites. By the time I turned fifteen, I spent more time stoned than straight. But even now, I would still say I never had a bad trip. Dozens of bad arrivals, yes, but no bad trips.

But I learned the hard way that letting myself get lost in that fog held more kinds of danger than I suspected.

"Want me to circle through downtown again?" The cabby's raw voice brought me back to the present. A pinched **V** between his eyes was visible in the rearview. That furrow told me he thought me more than a bit nuts.

"Yeah. No. Take Blithedale to the 131 and head north."

"Okey doke, lady."

I rolled down my window a couple inches. Curls blew across my face and I pushed my hair back. The scent of charcoal and chicken wafted in from someone's barbecue.

The cab driver swore then jerked the wheel and I fell against the door. Brakes squealed behind us and the smell of burning rubber masked the aroma of cooking chicken.

"Idiot. Driving a station wagon like he's Mario Andretti. Did you see that knuckle-head Smith? Asshole almost sideswiped my cab. An accident like that goes on my company record. Even if it's not my fault. Damn moron."

I righted myself. The driver lit up, the smell of cigarette smoke drifting back. Most the time cigarettes no longer appealed, but every now and again, the smell got to me. The cabby's cigarette smelled damn good. I checked my watch: 8:10 p.m. Traffic was heavier around here than I remembered. At least twice as many cars filled the road and they went about fifteen miles faster than they used to. But, in spite of the cab driver's near miss, traffic still wouldn't be labeled heavy by L.A. standards: the cars moved and no one blocked the intersections. Traffic thinned as we got farther north, and the redwoods grew more numerous on the outskirts of town. The cab's headlights spilled across the city limit sign. I sighed. I knew our destination. I leaned forward and gave the cabby directions. He remained silent, making no comment about our goal until we parked in front of the sprawling home.

The plaster-fronted house sat atop a small rise, one wing obscured by Douglas fir and redwoods. The arched entrance with its dark wood door was visible, as were the boards that covered one of windows flanking the entry.

"Goddamn kids. Little punks keep breaking the windows." The cabby opened his window and spat.

"Nobody lives there?" I wrapped a curl around my index finger and pulled the strands taut.

"Nah. Not since, you know... I heard some rich guy bought the place from the victims' relatives. They live Back East. That was seven, maybe eight years ago. The guy was going to fix the place up, but nothing's happened. Every now and again I get a passenger saying they've seen lights on during the night. Like the place is haunted or something. Me, I think people remember what happened and get worked up. Either that or the wiring's gone to crap. You ask me, they should burn the goddamn thing down and start over." The cab driver turned in his seat for a better look at the mansion. "I didn't figure you for one of the looky-loos. Most the folks I bring here, they want to ride straight to the house. No dilly-dallying. Like they can't wait to get a peek at the place where it went down." He looked through the clear protective panel that separated us. "I had a couple a year ago who were writing some kind of true crime book about it. Everybody's always interested in the unsolved ones. The gory ones, too. But who the hell would want to read about something like this?"

I didn't want to talk about it, but he sounded like he expected some type of response. "I don't know."

"World's going to hell in a handcart, if you ask me." He turned and stared at the house again. "That murder was the county's bloodiest. For all I know, it may've been the worst ever in the state. Except for maybe that Manson freak. I read they cut off the head of a two-year-old kid and threw it in the swimming pool. Sickos."

He had his facts wrong, but I didn't correct him.

"Those writers I mentioned? Said they had a new slant on the murders. Most folks said those killings happened because some sicko was obsessed with the guy who wrote *1984*. Me, I never read that kind of crap. I figure, life's tough enough without reading some weirdo's ideas about how the country's falling apart. Tell me something I don't already know. But these two thought it might've been something else. A kind of ritual killing. Like a cult. You know, like that Jim Jones freak. They said there was evidence that the ones that died were doped. Like they were so doped they didn't know what was happening. Until too late. Or maybe they never knew at all. Just woke up dead. But, I can't buy that story. I mean, please, how could anybody – even a sick-in-the-head Jim Jones kind of asshole, pardon my French – chop off some little kid's head?"

He scowled at the house then looked at me in the rearview. "What brings you out here?"

A patch of scalp had started to ache from me pulling on my hair. But my lie was ready. "I've got family in the area. When I was a kid, we used to visit. This older cousin would drive me and my other cousins here. Scared us to bits. Told us an entire family got killed here. I used to have nightmares about the place. Thought seeing it again as a grown-up might make the nightmares go away."

"Hell, I never got brung here as a kid and I get bad dreams about the place."

Seven

The image of the house began to fuzz over. I blinked back the tears. "I'm ready to go to my motel."

The cab driver retreated into silence as he resumed driving. I closed my eyes but still saw the façade of the Spanish-style home. Vodka-flavored bile rose in my throat. I swallowed hard then opened my eyes and stared out at the dark landscape. I had hoped seeing this awful place might give me some answers, but all it did was spur the same horrible images. The ones that had haunted me for ten years. Even though I hadn't been back in a decade, I saw the house every day already. Oh sure, sometimes a good twelve to sixteen hours slipped by with me too busy to think about it. But then came the night. The terror-soaked night. I saw that house every night.

Tuesday afternoon. November 13, 1984. That was when the bodies were found. The date the Orwell Massacre was discovered. By that point, the people in the house had been dead for days. I didn't know how many days exactly or what the coroner determined in the end. But since I had seen them four days before anyone sounded the alarm, I knew everyone had been dead at least that long.

When I woke up inside that big beautiful house, I'd swallowed a Xanax then went downstairs looking for Billy. Instead of Billy, I found six bodies.

Dumb luck the codeine I was hooked on back then gave me a chronic stomach ache. Because of the pain in my gut, I hadn't eaten for over twenty-four hours and had nothing to upchuck when I found the blood-soaked bodies. One piece of evidence I didn't leave behind. One that might be part of the reason I didn't wind up in prison. That and the weird November cold snap.

When I woke on the cold pebbly concrete by the swimming pool, the sky was starlit. Hoping it was all a bad dream, I'd sat up and stared at the inky surface of the swimming pool. Even in the dark, I could make out the shape of the headless body. I found my voice. "Oh God, oh God, oh God."

How in the world could I call the police now? What could I say? That I woke up earlier in the day, found the bodies, then went to sleep for six or eight hours before bothering to call? How could I explain why I was there? How I got there? I couldn't claim to know the owners. The police would never believe I had nothing to do with these killings. I wasn't sure I believed it either. My hands might be free of blood, but I certainly hadn't done anything to stop the killings.

"I'm sorry," I said to the body in the pool. I retreated inside the house, wiped the doorknob with the sleeve of my sweatshirt. I didn't know where all my fingerprints might be, but wasn't going to leave any more of them.

When I reached the room with the little boy's body, I averted my gaze and said, "I'm sorry," again. In the next room, I edged around the three bodies and said, "I'm sorry" one more time. Then I found my way to the front entry, cracked the shutter on the adjacent window and peeked out. The street appeared empty. I leaned my forehead against the door and took a deep breath. All I had to do was walk out and not look back.

A loud buzz like static from a TV set pulled my attention. "Billy?" No one answered. I turned, wrapping my arms across my chest before following the noise. Part of my brain screamed at me to get the hell out of there. But I stayed, hoping the sound would lead me to Billy. A swarm of black flies circled a wet-looking jacket. I stumbled across the marble entryway. "Oh no." Billy's black jeans jacket. Rimed with blood. Weak-kneed, I walked toward the archway ahead. "Billy?" My voice sounded thin and rusty, but still too loud. The buzzing of the flies remained the only sound besides my thumping heart. I crept through the dark doorway into a high-ceilinged room. A pool table sat in the center with a bar and juke box against the far wall. "Billy?"

The buzzing grew more frenetic. I slowed my pace, fearing the worst.

I found it.

Black vest and torn white T-shirt. Blue jeans with the threadbare knees and the black and white checkered Van's sneakers. From the clothes, I knew the body belonged to Billy. That was all I had to go on.

There was a bloody stump where his head should've been.

"Oh God, oh God, oh God." I ran back the way I came. In the entryway I slid on something and landed on my knees. I scrambled up then grabbed the shiny piece of metal I had skidded on. Billy's silver chain – now broken – and his dead brother's dog tag. Billy always wore the medallion around his neck.

Oh God, Billy's neck.

Hot tears streamed down my face. I stuffed the chain and the dog tag into the pocket of my jeans, grabbed the front door knob with my sleeve then let myself out. Face pointed down to avoid prying eyes, I walked away.

Eight

Bloody bodies wove through my dreams, along with Billy's severed head begging me to come back and help him. When I crawled out of bed at 8:20 a.m., pain throbbed along my brow ridge, but the sick feeling hovering in my gut had nothing to do with the too many vodkas I had downed at The Deuce the night before. My jeans still lay crumpled on the floor with my tennis shoes and T-shirt. Exactly where I tossed them while making a quick change for Dad's funeral. I fished inside the pockets of my jeans for my key chain and the dog tag Billy used to wear. I had carried it for nine years. When key chains broke or wore down, I shifted the dog tag to a new key fob. My current chain held keys to the garden shop, my apartment, my landlady's house and garage, my Swiss army knife and the dog tag. Over the years, the tag had become a talisman; I rubbed the metal rectangle when worried, I rubbed it when good things happened. Such a part of the fabric of my days, it was rare for me to stop and read the words inscribed there. But I read them now: Williamson, Grady, followed by a series of numbers.

Billy was the first boy I ever had sex with. That first was also the first time I saw the dog tag. Billy told me he never took it off. He didn't explain that fact right away, we were too caught up in the need to pull off clothes, to touch, thrust, clench. But afterwards, sprawled on the floor of my bedroom, a location chosen not in the heat of the moment but because the springs in my mattress squeaked and might wake my parents, I had fingered the silver piece of metal centered on his sweat-wet chest.

"It was my brother's," Billy said, his voice rough. "He got drafted when he was eighteen. Then they sent him into the jungle and lost him. I was eight. He was my hero."

"He died there?"

Billy turned his head towards me, his bleached blond hair bright in the light from my bedside lamp, a new hardness in his hazel eyes. "Grady was MIA. His captain reported him as a deserter. That damn lie broke my mom's heart. For three years, rumors about Grady hung over our house. Neighbors gave us funny looks, not talking full voice, but still loud enough for us to hear. Coward. Yellow. A runner. We knew what they thought. Then the Army admits Grady's dead. That he got killed in an ambush."

"I'm so sorry." I felt lame and inadequate. Nothing in my sixteen years' experience gave me the kind of wisdom I needed.

"Yeah. So was the Army. Sorry. Sorry my ass. Telling us Grady wasn't a deserter, but only after we learned he was dead. That put the nails in Ma's coffin. When we first heard Grady deserted, she changed. Stayed in bed a lot. Then when we found out he was dead, she gave up. Went full-on zombie."

"Jesus."

Billy continued as if I hadn't spoken. "My old man, he was so damn proud that his son died serving his country. After years of living in shame with his kid called a deserter, he could finally feel proud of Grady. Proud of him because he was dead." Billy sat up then grabbed his jeans. He pulled a hard pack of Marlboros from the back pocket and lit up.

My parents slept two rooms away – a fact that was never far from my mind once I snuck Billy into my bedroom. I jumped up, opened the window then emptied earrings from a ceramic box and gave the bottom half to Billy for an ashtray. The action made me feel stupid. Worry about burn marks on the carpet or my parents smelling cigarette smoke remained the fears of a child compared to what Billy was talking about. "I'm sorry," I said again though nothing I could say would change anything.

"I knocked out two of his teeth."

The abrupt change of course left me confused. "When you were kids?"

"What?" Billy took a long drag then squinted at me through the smoke as he exhaled.

"You knocked out two of your brother's teeth when you were little?"

"Hell no. Grady could've whipped my ass any day of the week he wanted to. And believe me he did. Lots of times." Billy shook his head. "I meant my old man. I knocked out two of his teeth."

Still confused and now cold, I pulled the heavy orange and brown comforter from the bed and wrapped it around my shoulders. "Why?"

"Because he was proud Grady had died. For his country."

"Oh." I worked out the time frame then looked at Billy. His mouth was drawn into a tight line, his eyes stormy. "But, you were what, eleven?"

"Twelve. By the time we learned Grady was dead. But I didn't have the reach to tap my old man then. So, I waited."

"For what?"

"For my sixteenth birthday."

"What happened then?"

"He wished me happy birthday and I told him to go to hell. Then I popped him one in the jaw. I can still feel the crunch of his jawbone under my fist." Billy cradled one hand inside the other for a moment then shook his head. "It wasn't gonna bring Grady back, but it made me feel a little better."

I scooched closer to him. "What did he do? After you hit him?"

"Kicked me out. Told me if I ever showed my face again, he'd beat the living crap out of me then have me arrested for trespassing."

"Jesus." I rested one hand on his bare thigh, his skin hot beneath my cold fingers.

"So, I took off. But not until I grabbed this." He lifted his brother's dog tag off his chest. "He was always the bravest person I knew. They tried to take him away from me. But I took him back."

I stared at the dog tag. Well-polished from use as a worry bead, the metal now warmed in my hand. Grady went missing at age eighteen, his body returned home three years later. Billy had the tag for close to seven years and I had held it for another nine. Of the three of us, I had carried the tag the longest, three times longer than Grady wore it.

If Grady had lived, he would be forty-two. If Billy had lived, he would be thirty-two. Was Billy's father still waiting for his younger son to come home someday?

I needed to hear a friendly voice. My landlady Cleo remained one of the few who knew the ins and outs of my family relationships. But it was way too early to call a night owl like her. And, with the way my last conversation with Rob went before I left, calling him seemed like a bad idea. I walked into the bathroom, turned on the tap full blast and sluiced cold water across my face and neck. In the mirror, bloodshot eyes looked back at me. It never felt right, me being the one who survived.

Coming home was a huge mistake. This town held too many bad memories and not enough answers. Too much guilt lurked in the shadows. But I couldn't leave yet. I had to find a way to spark my memory. Besides, I had made a promise to Mom's friend. While Gwen and I hovered beyond the buffet line at yesterday's reception, she had asked me to help her and Mom sort through some of Dad's stuff. I agreed so Gwen would think ours a normal family. Mom didn't need emotional support from me for any of the tasks ahead. But she did need my help maintaining the façade of normal family life which she presented to the world.

The idea of Mom and me repairing our relationship while I was back in Mill Valley had been nothing but a fantasy. I longed to blow off helping, stuff everything into my bag and run back to L.A. But I couldn't. Years of making appearances at company parties, Women's Club lunches and a wide range of business-related events had me too well-trained to feel okay about ditching out on an obligation. My dad was dead and Mom didn't expect much in the way of help from me. This might wind up the sole thing she let me do for her.

Gwen had set our start time for after lunch, leaving me with four hours to kill. The wired crawly-skin feeling I hated got me pacing. After adding four minutes of wear-and-tear to the beige motel carpet, I tied back my hair, took two aspirin then pulled on jeans, T-shirt and sweatshirt jacket and went out for a walk.

Cool and overcast, it would be another hour before the sun burned away the mist. Perfect for a fast-paced walk. I strode north on Miller, amazed at the number of cars starting out on the San Francisco commute. Near downtown, I spied my car parked across the street in The Deuce's parking lot. After I burned off a bit more nervous energy, I'd go retrieve it. I stared at the bar's facade. When I lived here, The Deuce felt big and important. Now I saw how small it was. Kind of like a metaphor for life in Mill Valley.

Back when I was in high school, this was the route I always took after the last bell rang. Eager for my first glimpse of Billy, my pace and heartbeat sped up as I drew close to The Deuce. Billy would lean against the wall between the octagonal windows, waiting for me. At the first glimpse of his white-blond hair and torn white T-shirt, I'd break into a run. I shook my head and turned away. Billy's imagined face always turned into Billy's remembered corpse.

Traffic thinned near downtown. In a gap between oncoming cars, I jogged across to the north side of Throckmorton. I needed to stop thinking about Billy. It was bad enough the nightmares hit when I slept, there was no need to revisit them during the day. I studied each storefront I passed and tried to recall if it was a new shop or one that had lined the street when I was in my teens. The brick front of the Italian restaurant appeared the same, as did the exterior of the theatre with its posters of coming attractions. After six blocks, when the street climbed and curved and the area became more residential, the new versus old shops led by a four-to-one margin. Ten years had brought a lot of changes to town. The place looked more upscale than in my youth, but would still be deemed 'quaint' by most visitors. When I reached Old Mill Park, I crossed the street and began to walk back toward the small downtown.

"Spare some change?" a scratchy voice called out. An older woman sat cross-legged on the sidewalk, slumped against the stucco façade of the Mill Valley Mercantile, a shopping cart packed with plastic bags and crushed cans parked by her side.

I felt the pockets of my jeans before remembering I had left the motel with only my room and car keys. I shook my head. "Sorry, I don't have any money on me."

"Ramona?"

The sound of that name rippled the hair along the back of my neck. "What?"

"You're Ramona, right? You used to go with Billy Bang."

My heartbeat ratcheted into overdrive. No one called me that anymore. The name was part of a life I buried ten years ago. I stared at the woman's face. Grime darkened the lines in her forehead and around her mouth. Even hidden under the multi-colored layers of frayed clothing, it was obvious her body was more bone than flesh. I tried to see past her bloodshot eyes and the scabs under her raw nose. "I'm sorry, but I ..."

"It's Janelle." She spread the fingers of one hand, showing off an ink-stained palm. "I used to go with Stewie. He played lead guitar in Trash." She cleared her throat and spat on the sidewalk. "Goddamn loser."

Trash. Billy's band.

This was Janelle? How could ten years have done so much damage? Gone was the ultra-short hairdo, the sparkle lashes and heavy black eyeliner. I didn't want to stare, but thought I saw a couple twigs caught amongst the tangled blond strands. She looked like a hard-ridden sixty-seven instead of twenty-seven. "Janelle. Hi." I opened my mouth to ask how it was going, but the shopping cart filled with empties plus her filth-encrusted clothing already gave me the answer. "Stewie. Wow, I haven't thought about him in a while. Are you guys still together?"

"Hell no. He split on me. Without even a goddamn goodbye. Stole my Walkman when he took off. Real prince. How about you? You in touch with Billy?"

Sweat ran down my spine. Was Janelle's question a trick? Though I had finally dredged up blurry images of Stewie driving the van from San Francisco to Mill Valley the night of the Orwell Massacre, I always came up empty where Janelle was concerned. For all I knew, Stewie and Janelle both came with us to the murder house. Or Billy could've had Stewie drop us off somewhere else. I had zero clue. I flashed on the blank look my neighbor Mrs. Stegman gave when I ran up to her the morning before I left for Mill Valley. Was this the sort of mental scavenger hunt she went through every day?

Billy was never identified as one of the Orwell Massacre victims – at least not in the news. For a while I thought maybe the cops couldn't identify him without his head. But then reality hit home: Billy had been arrested for both drunk and disorderly and shoplifting. His fingerprints were on file. That realization had been followed by a gut-twisting idea: Did Billy still have his hands when I saw him? Or were they cut off, too? Part of me had tried to recall his body sprawled on the floor, but a part of me refused. Had his name been withheld by the police or was he buried in a John Doe grave?

Ten years later, I didn't hold out much hope of Billy's murder getting solved. But that didn't mean I was going to share the fact that Billy was dead. Not even with Janelle – someone I once hung out with daily.

I took a deep breath. "Haven't talked to him in years."

"Yeah, he kind of dropped off the map. Screwed over Stewie big time – taking off like he did before a couple important gigs. I remember Stewie was pissed as hell about that. Goddamn loser."

"I pretty much lost touch with everyone after I moved away."

Janelle tilted her head up, the look in her bloodshot eyes sharp. "You took off around the same time as Billy. I always thought you guys ran off together."

A chill settled across my shoulders as I scrambled for a credible lie. "He left, too? I didn't know. But no way we would've gone anywhere together. Not after the fight we had. You know how that goes. One minute it's all good and the next you're no longer talking." The hunger seemed to leave her eyes. Had I only imagined that flicker of interest?

"Damn. Things change, huh? You guys were tight." Janelle scratched at a raw patch on her bony left wrist. "Sure you can't spare any dough?"

"Sorry." I patted my pockets again. "I don't have anything on me right now."

"Not even a cigarette?"

I shook my head. "I quit. Long time ago."

Janelle's eyes narrowed as they traced my body. "How 'bout the watch?"

It took me a moment to realize what she meant. "Sure." I undid the clasp of my Timex. The thing wasn't worth ten bucks, but if Janelle wanted it, giving it to her was the least I could do. She pushed herself to her feet, then slipped the watch inside a greasy-looking paper bag near the top of her shopping cart. "Here." I pulled off my sweatshirt jacket. "Why don't you take this, too?" My charity seemed far too meager and I couldn't meet Janelle's eyes. "Great seeing you, but I got to get going. You take care, okay?"

"Sure."

Out of the corner of my eye, I saw Janelle resettle herself on the sidewalk. Yet, as I walked away, I swore I heard the rattle of her shopping cart. The sound continued in my ears even after I put four blocks between us.

Ramona. I hadn't been called that in a decade. Not since the night of the Orwell Massacre. Billy gave me the name because I was a huge Ramones fan. And he introduced me to everyone that way.

"Ramona." The name felt like dust upon my tongue. I shook my head and sped up. Janelle looked like a seedling with heart rot. Nothing could save a plant once that kind of decay settled in. Seeing her was like getting a glimpse at the spiral my life could have taken if I hadn't got scared into reaching for something better.

With 'might have beens' nipping at my heels, I started to jog. Once I rounded the corner and was no longer in Janelle's possible line of sight, I poured it on to a full-out run, pounding my way along Corte Madera. These were the streets I used to run after I went out for track in junior high – before we moved midway through the semester. When we settled in our newer, bigger house in our more upscale neighborhood, I refused to join my new school's team. But I kept on running. It always felt good to push hard, to feel my legs and heart pumping.

Addiction. The word tumbled around my brain in time with my feet hitting the concrete: A compulsive physiological and psychological need for a habit-forming substance.

Every addict was enslaved by his or her addiction – it didn't matter which master an addict chose. When I met Janelle in 1983, she was pretty and fragile-looking with fine bones, honey-toned skin and large gray eyes. We hung out because our boyfriends were in the same band. Though we didn't have much else in common, we still spent four or five nights a week together getting high and dancing. We waited through rehearsals and sound system checks and the interminable discussions about the band's direction. We shared a lot of time and became more than acquaintances.

But the more time I spent with Janelle, the less I liked Stewie. The guy screwed around with the girls who threw themselves at him before, during and after each set. Hell, everybody knew that. Everybody except Janelle.

One night, a few weeks before I woke up to the nightmare of the Orwell Massacre, Janelle and I stood in the restroom of a ratty little club in San Francisco – one of the many basement gigs Trash played. I waited in the center of the grubby bathroom for the next open toilet stall. At the rust and dirt-stained sink, Janelle snorted a line. Coke was one of the things I wouldn't do. The high grabbed you too damn fast and hard. But I had smoked half a joint and had a couple beers and felt brave. I stared at her in the mirror. "Why do you put up with him?"

Janelle rubbed water on her nose and inhaled. She cocked her head and studied her reflection. Then she turned to look at me. "Put up with who?"

"Stewie."

"What d'you mean? Stewie's great. The best." She fumbled through her huge canvas purse and pulled out a compact. Turning back to the mirror, she began dabbing at the redness around her nostrils. She leaned forward for a better look then tossed her compact back into her bag. She chewed her lower lip, pulled out her vial of coke and prepared another line.

Stewie was the least of Janelle's problems. Stewie was hooked on nailing everyone in sight, while Janelle was busy racking up an expensive coke habit.

Watching Janelle that night hadn't cured my own self-destructive behaviors. At best, her example slowed my drug intake for one or two nights. I wasn't ready to break my own chains. But when I did reach that point, I remembered the look on Janelle's face: Stewie remained an abstraction, only the coke mattered. And I didn't want to end up like her.

I ran back to Miller then turned south. The cool air felt good, chilling my sweat-soaked back. If my father was alive and saw the way I lived today, I wasn't sure whether or not he'd be impressed with the changes I had made. A smart and shrewd man, he would've seen through the early transformations. Those first few years when I moved to L.A., I kept my nose clean, afraid of what might happen if I got in trouble. Scared if I did anything to draw a cop's attention, or worse – got arrested – my fingerprints would link me to the Orwell Massacre. But, maybe Dad would've figured out that, over time, more than fear had changed my life.

After five more blocks, I slowed, walking the last two back to The Deuce. My jeans were on the new side and a still bit stiff; not the best thing to wear for a run. But tomorrow I'd be home and back in my regular running gear. I stretched my arms above my head as I neared my car. The run had stopped me from dwelling on Janelle and might have beens and settled me down some. Though I remained edgy about seeing my mother, I also felt stronger, more able to face her.

Nine

When my mother answered the door, the smell of lilies and roses drifted from the house. Dressed in a pair of tailored gray slacks and a white silk blouse, she looked ready for a visit to the club rather than a day of sorting out Dad's belongings. A shallow V formed between her well-plucked brows. Was she irritated that I had shown up or by some non-me-related snafu? "Hi, Mom." The forehead crease furrowed into a trench.

"Miranda." She placed both hands on her hips. "I was expecting Mrs. Beekman from the church auxiliary."

"Oh. Um, I promised Gwen I'd come by to help you guys go through Dad's things." My mother showed great self-control when she winced but didn't sigh at my use of 'mom' and 'dad' within minutes of each other.

"Well, that explains your ensemble." Now Mom sighed. "Dear Gwen. The poor woman needs to feel needed. Always trying to help. Even when no help is required." Mom shook her head. "She called this morning, going a mile a minute about her plans to come by, but I told her I would be fine on my own. Your father was well-organized. There's very little that needs to be done.

"But since you're here, you might as well come in." She took a step back and waved me in. "Trevor and I have set some things out for you in the study."

Who was Trevor? I followed her into the foyer without asking for clarification. The entryway overflowed with floral displays from Dad's service. "These are gorgeous." A huge bouquet of roses sat atop the sideboard. Next to them was a mixed arrangement of white and pale violet gladiolus. I ran my index finger along one of the sturdy emerald stems.

"Don't mind those. Mrs. Beekman should be by soon to pick them up."

"Why?"

"Why what?" The edge to Mom's voice sounded sharp enough to hack through the forest of flowers with one swipe.

"Why's Mrs. Beekman picking up Dad's flowers?"

Mom huffed then placed her hands on her slim hips. "If you're going to act unreasonable, get all worked up because I'm not saving your father's flowers..."

At the standard accusation that I was 'getting worked up' about something, my face grew hot. "I'm not getting-." I broke off then took a deep breath. "I'm asking. That's all.

Why's someone from the church picking up the flowers?"

"They'll redistribute them. To the sick or needy." Mom straightened her shoulders then continued through the hall to the study. I shook my head, but wasn't surprised. In our various homes, tidiness had always trumped sentiment.

The study smelled of lemon oil but, other than the low-angled light of the morning sun, the room didn't look much different from the previous day. The only new additions were two file boxes atop Dad's desk. I glanced at them then turned back to my mother. "What do you need me to do?"

Mom made a 'shooing' sort of wave at the boxes. "Your father put those aside for you several years ago. I'd forgotten all about them. But, as I said, he was a very organized man and he'd informed Lloyd Jenson about them. After you left yesterday, Lloyd reminded me. Trevor brought them down from the attic this morning."

Dad put them aside for me several years ago? A chill spread from my fingertips to my palms. I wrapped my arms across my chest. "So, you want me to go through them or something?"

"I want you to remove them. Sort through them at home or back at the Inn. I don't want you rummaging through them here, getting dust all over everything."

"Oh. Right. Sure." But I wasn't sure. Something about those boxes made the skin at the base of my neck prickle. "If you do need any help around here, I can stay." After getting back to the Cozy 8 the night before, I had abandoned the idea of digging into my past. My one drive to the murder house had been bad enough. I'd find some way to make things work with Rob. Lots of couples didn't share everything. And, it wasn't like Mom was going to invite us for a visit. Rob wouldn't find out I'd lied about my name.

"No. I'm fine."

In spite of her tailored ensemble, 'fine' didn't describe how she looked. Always one to shield herself from the sun, her pallor wasn't unusual, but now her skin was ashen and a tremor ran along her jaw. "OK." Something in my mother's expression made me reconsider heading home. I had scheduled a late checkout for today, planning to hit the road by sunset, but the Cozy 8 wasn't so jammed that I couldn't move back my departure. "If you change your mind later, let me know. I'm here until tomorrow."

"You're staying another day?"

"Yeah." No way would she want to hear the reason for my change of heart. If she thought I was worried about her, she'd go on the attack. Mom hated being the focus of sympathy. Or pity. Weakness was one of the many things she abhorred. Which explained her behavior yesterday. Duh. I wrapped a curl around my finger and pulled. "A lot of time's passed since I was here. And who knows when I'll make it back again. I figure

I'll do a little exploring, get to know the place again."

"I see." She adjusted the shade on the floor lamp centered between the Eames chairs. "Of course, I appreciate your offer. But I can't imagine needing more help than I have already."

No matter how fragile she felt, I didn't think she'd ever ask for my help. Still, I couldn't cut and run. No matter how much I wanted to. I'd stay one more day. If I didn't hear from Mom, I'd suck it up and spend the time prodding old memories. "Right." I hefted the first box. Heavy. Much heavier than I anticipated. I set it down then hoisted the box again, this time wedging it against my stomach. "I'll be right back for the other one."

By the time I stowed the container inside the Celica's trunk, a man dressed in black trousers, white starched shirt and charcoal-colored vest stood at my elbow, holding the second box. Bald on top, his remaining rust-brown hair was buzz-cut short. Broad across the chest, he had three or four inches on me. The box seemed feather-light in his hands. "Are you Trevor?"

He frowned. "That's correct." Trevor deposited the box then strode back to the open front door.

"Thank you."

He nodded then closed the front door.

Once I got settled in the driver's seat, I closed my eyes and took several deep breaths. The few times I tried to explain to someone the strained relationship I had with my mother, I failed to capture what was 'off' about it. My father was the one who kicked me out and excommunicated me from my family. People understood how that could complicate my feelings. But Mom was trickier territory. I couldn't explain why my memories of her were tangled with dread. She didn't yell, she didn't hit. She didn't embarrass me in public. But she also didn't seem to want me around.

The urge to floor it rippled through me; to put some distance between me and the house. But the last thing I needed was to get pulled over. I forced myself to drive with caution along the winding residential street. But, each time I peeked at the speedometer, I discovered I needed to ease off the gas again.

By the time I parked in the motel lot, the sun had burned through the morning overcast. I breathed in the scent of soil beginning to bake. Bird song came from the roadside trees. A beautiful day. But I still felt like shit.

When I carried the first box up to my room, the smell of mothballs accompanied me. My tightening leg muscles complained with each step up the wooden stairs. Once I had set the second box on the bed, I stepped back and started chewing my lower lip. What in the world could be inside them? I postponed the moment of truth by calling the front desk to let them know I'd be staying one more night. Then I stared at the sealed containers. My pulse raced. Why did these boxes scare me? What could be so awful about their contents?

I flipped through the dangling keys and keepsakes hanging on my key chain until I located the Swiss army knife. Not a big blade, but sharp, it slid through the yellowed packing tape, cutting a line across both box tops. I stuffed the keychain inside my front pocket and debated which box to explore first. The lighter one probably held less, but less what? I pulled up the flaps. My mouth dropped open. Tears pricked my eyes.

My Ramones cassettes sat side-by-side in a lidless shoebox. They were all there: *Rocket to Russia, Road to Ruin, End of the Century, Pleasant Dreams, Subterranean Jungle* and *Too Tough to Die.* In the face of my father's rage when he banished me, I had run from the house with nothing but what I wore. All my beloved music left behind. I wiped tears from my face then picked up the tapes one by one and examined them.

Holding the plastic casings reminded me of the day Billy and I waited in line to buy tickets to a Ramones concert in San Francisco. A damp, biting chill had surrounded us, turning our thin jackets soggy. But we didn't budge from our spot in line. When the show date arrived, the two of us had pogoed like dervishes while we screamed, "Lobotomy, lobotomy," echoing the band as they chanted out the chorus of *Teenage Lobotomy.* I covered my mouth as I thought about all the nights I hung out after hours in the back of Bianca's Pizza Parlor. Me, Billy and the other band members getting stoned while sorting stems and seeds from pot leaves on large pizza trays. And Billy pushing the button for every Ramones song on the jukebox because they were my favorites. Even when at my lowest, bopping my head to one of my Ramones' tapes had always made me smile, echoing the joy I felt in moving fast.

After I replaced the cassettes in the shoebox, I turned my attention to the remaining contents. Inside a folded brown paper bag I found my *Rock 'n' Roll High School* T-shirt. I clutched the faded fabric to my chest and closed my eyes. I couldn't believe Dad saved these treasured things. For me.

Anxiety cast aside, I pulled up the flaps of the second box. My photo album. I hoisted it out. The large binder with its fake leather cover made me smile. I sat cross-legged on the bed and flipped through the plastic sleeves. There I stood next to Becky Feldman – my best friend from kindergarten through second grade. Both of us our wide grins showing off missing front teeth. And me with Sheila Witkow – best friends for half of third grade. Then Marty Miller – we palled around until my family moved at the start of fourth grade. There were also several shots of me with Hannah Beth Chang in our track shorts and gym shirts. My eyes misted as I turned paged after page. School photos, from a time when I still dressed up and smiled for the camera. A web of lost memories tugged at me.

The final photograph took my breath away. Billy's face looked out at me. I had forgotten how beautiful his smile was. He didn't smile often, but when he did, my knees always went weak. The day we took this picture, I had talked Billy into climbing into the photo booth with me. He kept the pictures of the two of us and I kept the third one – the one where I ducked down to get a photo of him alone. Not two hours after taking this, we had a horrible fight. That was the day I learned Billy did more than sell weed to his friends. Coked up and hyper, Janelle let it slip that Billy dealt coke and heroin. Afraid about what could happen to him, I had confronted him. His face had turned stony and the light in his eyes shut down. He told me I couldn't understand. Not a poor little rich girl like me.

Rich. Right. What a laugh. Dad had cut off my allowance months earlier. I still had a place to call home, but not much more than that.

I traced the frozen image of his bleached-blond hair, from its dark roots to ivory tips. I wished Billy had gotten a better, longer life. Heaviness settled in my chest. I flipped through the remaining pages, to make sure no photos got stuck in out of order. The rest of the plastic sleeves sat empty, waiting for pictures I never got to take, let alone save.

The sole item remaining inside the box was a large manila envelope. The gum sealing the it was brittle and the flap came up without tearing. An old semi-gloss Photostat sat inside. My birth certificate. When I petitioned to change my name, I had to get a copy from the Hall of Records. I couldn't imagine why Dad saved this for me. Didn't he know I could get a copy by contacting the County?

Then I saw it. My breath came so fast and loud I couldn't feel my heartbeat. This certificate was different than the copy I had at home. In the block where my father's name should have been, it read "Unknown."

Ten

Without planning a destination, I wound up at The Deuce. This time when I walked inside, I spied an open barstool and climbed up. The man to my right puffed on a stogie, the smoke mixing in a familiar way with the smell of spilled beer and strawberry margarita mix. The bartender, a short man with thinning brown hair, looked in a foul temper. That suited me. I didn't feel in the mood for chit-chat. He raised his bushy eyebrows rather than verbalizing his "Whaddywant" and I said, "Vodka tonic. With a twist."

A group of men in their late twenties and early thirties, all dressed in matching blue and white baseball T-shirts, whooped their way into the bar and took over two tables on the far side of the pool table. The bartender banged my drink in front of me, but didn't spill a drop. I squeezed the slice of lemon dry then dropped it into the glass. After swirling the contents with the red plastic stick, I closed my eyes and took a long swig. The clean tart scent of the lemon sharpened the edges of the chilled vodka.

The man we buried yesterday would always be my father. After all, he raised me. But he wanted me to know he wasn't my biological father. Why? Did he feel he owed me that bit of truth? If so, why not tell me while he was alive?

I rolled the side of my glass against my forehead, the beads of condensation leaving a broad, cool trail. The baseball team yelled again and I glanced at them. They seemed ripe with happiness, clubbing each other on the back as they drained their mugs of beer. I gazed from face to face and wondered what sort of man fathered me. Tall, short, fat, thin? Near sighted, far sighted? Blond or brunette? Did he have a strong jaw, like the man pouring himself a mug of beer? Or was he fair skinned and freckled like the redhead next to him? Did he even know I existed? I turned back to the bar and sighed. Maybe he knew about me but didn't care. He could even be one of the men in my parents' circle. Someone I met as a child.

I took another sip. The 'unknown' under the heading of 'father' was a lie. No way my buttoned-down mom had multiple sex partners. It was hard enough to imagine her having sex, let alone cheating on Dad. But she had. And she knew who got her pregnant.

When I was growing up, my parents never made a big deal about their wedding anniversary. No fancy dinners or special gifts. Maybe I was the reason.

In an odd way, it felt like things were clicking into place. Maybe biology – or my father's resentment of it – had caused the distance between us. Maybe he'd kept me at arm's length because he didn't think of me as his. But when did he find out? Did he always know – or did my parentage come as a nasty little surprise somewhere along the way? Maybe the fact that I wasn't his made it easier for him to kick me out and disown me.

But he was the one who had saved and boxed all of those mementos for me.

My mother might not be willing – or able – to answer questions about Dad's feelings. But she was able – though most likely unwilling – to tell me the name of my birth father. I took another healthy gulp of chilled vodka and thunked the glass back onto the bar. I couldn't remember a single instance in my life when I convinced Mom to change her mind about anything. I doubted my track record would improve over something as big as this.

My face grew warm. I stared at the mirror hanging on the wall behind the bar. My face looked flushed. Two empty glasses sat near my elbow. Oops. I pushed away my third vodka tonic. That warm fuzzy feeling was a definite sign to stop drinking and go back to the motel. I left enough cash to cover my drinks and the tip, then climbed into my Celica and stared at the passing cars. Shy of

4:30 on a Sunday afternoon, the traffic would grow snarled in another hour when the weekend travelers started their journey home. But, even so, a lot more cars moved along this stretch of road than when I was little. So much had changed and continued to change.

I considered calling a cab for the ride back to the motel, but felt sober enough to make the short drive. After all, I no more than tasted the third drink. Two blocks into my journey, the sight of a black and white Mill Valley Police car in my rearview mirror set my palms to sweating. The police car pulled into the right lane then turned on its lights and siren and passed me. I watched it zip off toward the 101 Freeway and breathed easier. Maybe it would've been smarter to take a cab.

Caught at a red light, my thoughts turned back to my father. Why not tell me the truth when he was alive? Did he want to escape the potential fallout? Or was his motive something more basic? When the light turned green, I switched on my turn signal and changed course, heading toward Mom's.

The sun cast an amber light on the bay laurels and Douglas fir. At the next stop sign, I rolled down my window and inhaled the Christmassy aroma, then turned my attention to the narrow roadways leading to my former home. I swallowed hard. The vodka seemed to be turning to acid inside my stomach. Or maybe it was my insides turning at the idea of tackling my mother about the birth certificate. Confronting her didn't seem like the brightest idea. But it seemed far worse to leave Mill Valley without asking who my birth father was.

I parked out front then trotted up the steps and pounded on the door. After a brief wait, it swung open. But instead of facing my mother, Trevor stood on the other side. "Trevor. Hi. I'm here to see my mom."

He stood in the center of the doorway, discouraging any forward movement on my part. "Is she expecting you?"

"No."

His mouth twitched in a small frown before he spoke. "I'll see if she's available." The door shut in my face.

No longer wondering how I'd broach the topic of my birth father, I marshaled my arguments for getting inside the house. After several minutes, the door opened three inches. Trevor peered out through the narrow gap. "I'm sorry, but your mother isn't receiving visitors."

The door started to close again. Face burning, I rammed my shoulder against the wood. The heavy door and Trevor gave a couple inches. I shoved again. Harder. Apparently not expecting such an uncivilized assault, Trevor lost his footing. He scrambled backward and I barreled through the opening. Once he had his feet under him again he straightened his cuffs and tie.

"Perhaps you didn't understand."

"No, I understood fine. But I'm not a 'visitor.' I'm her daughter. And I need to see her. Right now. It's important."

"I'm afraid your mother's indisposed."

"Tough."

Trevor appeared too well-bred to try to grab or tackle me, but he proved much more agile than I'd guessed. After several abortive attempts to gain the hall as he used his body to block my way, I slipped around him. Feeling ridiculous, I dashed up the stairs with Trevor on my heels. I ran down the upstairs hall and slammed through the door to the master bedroom.

A large, high-ceilinged room, the late afternoon sun set the picture window overlooking the backyard aglow. A day bed sat perpendicular to the window and Mom sprawled against its peach cushions, an array of magazines splayed beside her and on the floor below. A half empty bottle of vodka stood on the nearby mahogany table, the glass beside it drained. Mom turned toward the door, rosy-checked and slack-mouthed. Her gaze skidded past me to Trevor then returned to the view outside.

I gaped at Trevor who stood behind me panting, beads of sweat pocking his forehead. "She's drunk."

"As I said, your mother is indisposed."

"Potato, potahto. How long has this been going on?"

Trevor rested his hands on his hips, his breathing still labored. "How long has what been going on?"

"Please. I'm not an idiot." I closed my eyes, took a deep breath then glared at Trevor. "Does she get 'indisposed' like this very often?"

He shifted his weight from foot to foot, looking past me at my mother.

"Jesus. I'm not going to the society column or the Junior League with your answer. Tell me."

I pulled into the motel parking lot a few minutes shy of 6:00 p.m. Business had picked up at the Cozy 8 since I checked in on Friday. Several clusters of bag-laden travelers walked toward the office. After waiting for the drivers of a blue Volvo and an old Cadillac to work out who had the right of way, I snagged one of the few remaining empty slots. Though I had spent most of the afternoon sitting around, I felt grubby and drained as I climbed out of the car. The fact that my mother drank herself into a stupor every night sat like a stone in my stomach. According to Trevor, for several years Dad had pretended not to see the problem, but after Mom was ticketed for driving drunk three years ago, he hired someone to shepherd her. Trevor was the second person to hold the job.

If someone had asked, before today, I would've described Mom as a social drinker. On the drive back to my motel I had scoured my memory, but came up with no moments of seeing her sloppy-drunk, let alone hammered. At the numerous adult gatherings my parents hosted, my appearances were scheduled for the early hours and I was excused before anyone had a chance to overindulge. Of course once I hit my teens, I wasn't at home much to see what my parents got up to in the evenings. On the nights I was stuck at home, I saw my mother more as a wall to get around than as someone to observe and understand.

Maybe Dad's death triggered her current binge, but, since this had been going on for years, that wasn't the whole story. Mom had always seemed a bit like a birch branch in autumn – thin, unprotected, ready to snap under pressure. Maybe Dad never forgave her for having me. Or maybe she couldn't forgive herself.

I tucked my car keys into the front pocket of my jeans then followed two teenaged boys up the stairs. My leg muscles felt tight and sore from my morning's impulsive run, but it was a good kind of sore. A hot shower would loosen my quads and, hopefully, wash away the deeper ache I nursed in my gut.

Inside my motel room, I turned on the shower and pulled off my shirt, then reached in to test the water's temperature. A quick rap sounded on the room's door. I jumped, splashing water on my front. "Smooth." I grabbed a towel, dried off my stomach and the front of my jeans. Damp-dry, I pulled on my T-shirt again. "Give me a minute," I called out. Who knew I was here? I had already told the front desk I'd be staying another day. Maybe the clerk got the dates messed up. Or maybe they forgot to change the towels?

I pulled the door open halfway. The giant elf from The Deuce stood in the corridor. Dressed with a bit more style than he had been while on drink duty, but definitely the same guy. No way there were two of him. I opened my mouth to speak, but no sound came out.

"Surprise," he said. He gave an unfriendly grin then shoved the door. The knob hit my hip and I stumbled back. I understood how Trevor must've felt when I did the same thing to him earlier. The Elf pushed his way inside the room and closed the door behind him.

I regained my balance and found my voice. "What the hell do you think you're doing?"

"Coming in for a wee chat. Who's in the shower?" He grabbed my left elbow and hauled me into the bathroom as if I weighed no more than a stack of cocktail napkins. He yanked aside the curtain and glared at the empty shower stall.

I tried to wrench my arm free. "Let go."

He continued to grip my elbow as he turned off the water. Then he released me. "You're one stone cold bitch."

The words were said with a warm Irish lilt, but they still felt like a slap. "Get out. Now."

"Not yet." He moved to my left and leaned his hip against the bathroom counter. "You know, I'm not used to this bollocks. When I give a girl a wee bit of charm, I'm used to getting an invite to her room. I don't usually need to sneak around and follow her to her hotel to find out where she's staying."

I took a step back, turned and ran. I made it out of the bathroom before the elf grabbed my ponytail and gave it a rough enough yank to stop me. Then he used my own hair to reel me in. After he let go, he stepped between me and the door. I blinked back tears. I wasn't going to show this asshole weakness.

"Quite the chase you led me on last night. Lost you when that eejit driving the station wagon cut me off. Missed the damn signal. Liked to give him a hard kick in the arse. Mad chase that was. And by all rights, you should've invited me to your motel before you left the bar. I was all kinds of charming." He took two steps forward, looming over me and filling the narrow gap between us. "Made sure to look you deep in the eyes, called you 'Miss' with a knowing twinkle in my eye. Brushed your hand each time I handed you your drink. Poured the drinks with a very generous hand, I did. You can tell me, you frigid or something?"

"Get out." I backed away again.

"No."

My mouth dropped open. "Get out or I'll scream."

"Right." He smiled and crossed his arms over his chest, looking for all the world like he was enjoying himself. "Like you're the sort who'd make a fuss and risk the cops coming out. I know a thing or two. And one of the things I know is: You don't want the cops anywhere near you." He shook back his hair and smiled. "Not much of a bluff, but I'll give you points for trying."

A ripple of fear ran up my spine.

"Here's how things stand. I got a job to do here and I take pride in my work. There's a gent who's very keen to see you. Well, calling him a 'gent' isn't the best description of the fellow. Let's say you got an old friend who's quite keen to see you. Wants me to bring you back to meet with him."

The thought of getting dragged off to God-knew-where by this crazy giant twisted my intestines. "I'm not going anyplace with you." I took another step back.

"Well, that's where you're wrong. The only question is: What technique I should be using to persuade you? I could give you a thrashing. That usually convinces a body. But the way I see it, all I need to do is give you a good clatter on the nose or the cheek bone." He cocked his head. "You do have yourself some nice cheek bones there. Be a shame if they got turned to pudding. Disfiguring, you know?" He pulled what looked like a leather-covered sap from his back pocket. "With this extra wee bit of weight in my fist, it won't take much work to break your nose. Bit more effort to crack a cheekbone, but not too much. But I've found that breaking the nose gets to most women."

He took a step closer. "In my opinion, it doesn't pay to punch a gal in the stomach. Or the kidneys. Like I might a fellow. Or even to break an arm or leg. Sure enough any of those things will hurt like hell, but they won't get a gal to do what you want her to. Though you gals aren't as strong, you all can be a hell of a lot tougher about pain. Think it has to do with having the babies. But, if you mess with a gal's looks, and then threaten to mess them up more, most will do pretty much anything you tell them to."

I kept edging toward the bedside table and my purse. My mind scrambled to identify anything in the room I could use as a weapon.

"You think I don't see what you're doing? Stop your backing away. Right now."

I retreated another step.

The Elf moved fast. I turned and lunged for the lamp on the nightstand. Before I got my hands on it, he caught me and put me in a chokehold. Blood pounded in my ears as he tightened his grip and pulled me against his chest. The smell of sweat and Brut aftershave filled my nostrils as I gasped for air. "So tell me." His hot breath tickled my right ear and cheek, "You going to be a good girl. Or am I going to have to teach you a lesson or two?"

Eleven

"No lesson needed." My voice came out a whisper.

"Good girl. That's what I like to hear." After what felt like an eternity, he let go of my neck and grabbed my arm. "Now move your arse." He quick-walked me to the door as I rubbed my throat and sucked in mouthfuls of air. After opening the door a crack and peering outside he glared at me. "Don't get any clever ideas. Because I will make you very, very sorry if you do. You walk down the stairs and into the parking lot. We hold hands the whole way. When we get to the car, you climb in. No muss, no fuss. And don't be thinking that, because we're outside, I won't thrash you if you start making trouble. People will think we're one more couple having it out in public. And after the runaround trying to follow you last night, I'm in no mood for any shit. You believe me?"

I looked into his poison-green eyes and nodded. "Yes." The story Gwen Hardesty told me flashed through my head and my mouth sagged open. "You were the guy at the Inn. The one who punched the desk clerk. You went looking for me there, didn't you?"

"Helluva romp that was."

"But how- Why?"

"I asked a few friends of your ma's where her precious babe might be staying. People in this town are a right helpful bunch. At least they are if you're as charming as me. Now, do what I tell you or I start breaking bones." He touched my right cheek, his fingertips like sandpaper on my skin.

I jerked back.

"Starting with that one. You got it?"

"Got it."

"Move it then." He crushed my left hand in his right then dragged me out the door and onto the landing.

We hustled down the staircase, me struggling to match his long stride. I scanned the parking lot for someone, anyone who might be able to help. But the lot which had teemed with life and movement a short while earlier now looked empty. The Elf yanked me across the black asphalt, coming to a stop behind a white van. He pulled his keys from his pants pocket.

I stared at the van. I had seen *Silence of the Lambs*. And like any other sensible woman in America, there was no way in hell I was going to climb inside the back of a white van. In a moment of terror-fueled adrenalin, I remembered the Swiss army knife on the key chain in my front pocket. Not a big blade, but it still counted as a weapon.

While the Elf worked the lock to the van's back door, I slid my hand into my pocket and opened the knife. With his attention divided between me and the van, I doubted I'd get a better opportunity to act. I pulled out the knife.

Between our height difference, his speed, and the fact that I telegraphed my intentions, what followed felt inevitable. Though everything happened within the space of less than a minute, each move we made seemed crisp and sure, like a tango we'd rehearsed until every step worked.

He pivoted, pulling me to him, his right hand on my left shoulder. I swung the knife upward as he turned and the gap between us closed. With him so near, I wouldn't have the momentum I needed to plunge the blade deep into his flesh. Heart thudding, I threw my whole arm into the thrust. The small knife ripped through his thin cotton trousers as he pulled me toward him. Then came the sickening plunge of the blade sinking into flesh and a sound like slicing a cantaloupe. The Elf's grip on my shoulder tightened and his eyes widened. For a moment, I thought my effort was for nothing.

The high-pitched scream that came from his mouth made the hair on my arms ripple to attention. He let go, but before he doubled over, I saw my Swiss Army knife sticking out of his groin. I thought I might vomit, but then my sense of self-preservation kicked in again. I turned and ran.

My legs felt sluggish as I raced out of the parking lot. I wished I hadn't drunk those two vodka tonics earlier. The booze in my system was slowing me down. I stared at the busy main road and turned right, running toward downtown. To make things worse, the Elf had wheels while I was stuck with leg power. I needed every edge I could get. From running track and field, I knew looking over my shoulder was a mistake, so I resisted the urge. Even with a knife sticking out of his balls – or maybe because of it – the Elf wasn't going to stop until he caught me again. And he'd be damn mad when he did. I didn't want to find out what kind of payback he thought I deserved.

Near the rotary, I stopped to catch my breath. Hands on my knees, I scanned the street behind. Shit. A white van raced my way. Either the Elf had an amazing pain threshold or I had grazed rather than stabbed his balls. Three blocks away, the van was coming fast.

Up ahead, the sidewalk was full of strolling people out enjoying a balmy Sunday evening, gazing at the windows of the upscale stores lining the sidewalk. I jogged forward, hoping to lose myself in the crowd. Once I threaded my way among the pedestrians, I checked the road behind me again. A flash of white in the distance sent my heart thundering. I turned and rammed a woman loaded with bags from one of the boutiques. I kept going and didn't call out an apology, saving all my wind for my escape. People cursed and yelled as I ran between couples, cut off others and bulled my way along the block. I charged up the first cross street I came to then raced between cars to an alleyway. From there I ran north, taking occasional quick stops to rest and look back. My mouth was dry and my body weak. I sucked down air. I couldn't keep this up very long.

Shit. The white van again. Or was it some other white van besides the Elf's? I raced along the next street, then turned onto a side road and cut back south. An alley opened on the opposite side of the street. At a break in the traffic I ran across the open lanes.

Inside the narrow passageway, I leaned against the wall, my lungs desperate for air. I glanced behind me. A dead end, not an alley. The sunlight didn't reach the far end, leaving that portion in darkness. A Dumpster sat in the shadows, a few yards back. The closer I got to the rusty trash container, the greater the stench of rotting food and urine grew. Breathing through my mouth, I tucked myself behind the bin and I stared out at the street beyond.

I figured my nose would adjust to the foul smells. But instead my scent receptors seemed to sharpen. The odor of vomit, spoiled cabbage and broccoli mixed with a smell that reminded me of when the dreaded red tides hit the beaches. Maybe dead fish. And iodine. I hoped the van passed by soon so I could get out and run the other way.

A sharp scraping sound set my nerves sizzling. In a place like this, with all the discarded food, my likely companion was a rat rooting through the trash. But one that made this much noise had to be big. Even jumbo-sized. Shit. I closed my eyes and held my breath, as if that could fool a rodent used to locating food through its sense of smell.

Something scraped across the concrete a few feet from me. I stared at the corridor's dark terminus. A dim form separated from the deeper gloom. Not a rat. The silhouette of a man. Even through the shadows I saw he held something that looked like a baseball bat. The figure raised the bat and spoke. "What the hell do you want?"

The high-pitched voice sounded incongruous with the man's threatening posture. "Nothing." My voice came out a whisper. I swallowed and tried again. "Nothing."

"We're not sharing. Get lost."

"Shut up, Richie," a woman said.

The man's face remained obscured by shadow. A second figure appeared beside him, equally masked by the darkness. As my eyes adjusted to the dim light, I thought I saw a third figure huddled behind them near the dead end. I pressed against the cold metal of the Dumpster. "I don't want anything. I'm just here waiting."

"Yeah right." The high-pitched voice spoke again. "Next train'll come along in a few minutes. I don't know what Marco told you, but we only got enough for us."

Whatever the people in the alley had, I didn't want. "Fine. Like I said, I'm just waiting."

"Well, wait some other goddamn place."

"I'll leave as soon as I can." I glanced across the top of the Dumpster at the street, but didn't see the white van pass by.

The woman spoke again. "Who you hiding from, Ramona?"

Twelve

"What? How..." The voice in the dark set my pulse on fire as my heart tried to jackhammer through my ribcage. One shadowy figure moved from the huddle at the alley's end, emerging from the blackness. My pulse ratcheted back to normal as I realized who'd used that name. "Janelle. It's you." I took a raspy breath. "Didn't know who was back there. Look, I don't mean... I mean, I'm not trying to crowd you guys. I just need a minute or two here."

"Sure." She turned and spoke to the others. "I know her. She's okay."

"I don't care if she's your goddamn long lost sister. We ain't sharing."

Janelle turned to me and shrugged. "Pipeline's been dry a while. Everybody's on edge. We only got enough to get the three of us right."

"No problem." I wondered what drug the three planned to inject, snort or smoke, but knew better than to ask.

"Who you hiding from?"

Good question. I peered toward the alley's mouth before I answered. Still no sign of the white van. "Not sure. I mean, I'll recognize him when I see him. But I'm hoping I won't see him." If I spotted the Elf, I'd at least know which direction not to go in order to stay hidden. But seeing him drive by wouldn't help me figure out whose orders he was following. Or what the man he worked for wanted.

"Funny."

I turned to face Janelle. "What's funny?"

"You. Here. Hiding in this alley with me and the boys. You looked so full of yourself this morning. So confident. Like you got the world by the balls. Looking down at me. Giving me the coat off your back. Now look at you. That's what's funny. The wheel never stops turning."

Janelle's generosity about letting me share her alleyway didn't feel friendly any more. My heartbeat sped again as I wondered what she knew. "What do you mean by that?"

"By what?"

"The wheel never stops turning. You think I'm due for some payback or something?"

"Isn't everybody?"

The high-pitched man's voice cut through our tense silence. "It's your turn and we ain't waiting."

"See you around." Janelle smirked then turned and walked back to the dark end of the alley.

"The hell with this." I edged around the Dumpster to the alley's opening and peered up and down the street. There was no sign of the white van. My heart thumped a wild beat as I joined the shoppers on the sidewalk, keeping my head down while I focused on keeping my pace nonchalant and blending in. Out of the corner of my eye, I checked the cars as they drove by. A quick flash of white sent my pulse into overdrive, but the vehicle was a VW Rabbit.

Why had the Elf tried to grab me? He said an 'old friend' wanted to see me. But I didn't have any old friends. Did that mean Janelle was right? That some karmic wheel was still turning? Was this connected to the Orwell Massacre? But how? If there was anyone around who knew I was inside that charnel house all those years ago, they didn't know my real name. They couldn't. The only person from that time period who knew my real name was dead. As far as I knew, no one could identify me as one of the people who'd been at the murder house.

Except the killer.

A fire hydrant blocked my path. I cut in front of a woman with a baby carriage and tried to match the pace of the closest pedestrian. What was going on? What could the Elf want from me?

When I first encountered him at The Deuce after Dad's funeral, the Elf gave me his name: Sean. Okay, I knew the guy's name. And he was Irish. But how did that help?

What proof did I have that anything he told me was the truth? I had come back to Mill Valley hoping to find out what happened on that long ago night, but that wasn't possible with a crazy man on my trail. Bottom line, if the Elf had really been sent to bring me to someone, the reason didn't matter. It was time to get out of Mill Valley.

But how? My car keys were on my key ring – along with my Swiss Army knife. And the last time I saw the key ring, it was dangling from the Elf's balls. I doubted he'd be willing to hand it over to me.

I checked my wrist and remembered I gave my watch to Janelle early that morning – though it felt like days ago. I glanced up. Wispy clouds striated the sky. My best guess put the time at seven o'clock. That meant dark would settle over the streets in another hour, followed by the cold and damp two to three hours later. My belongings remained in the motel room and though I had my room key in my pocket, if I were the Elf, that's where I'd wait. I had no money, no charge card, no ATM card and no ID. If I managed to get out to my mother's house, I doubted Trevor would crack the door to loan me bus fare, let alone let me inside again.

If I figured out a way to get into my motel room without alerting the Elf, I could grab my wallet then call a locksmith to get me inside my car. Of course, a locksmith working on my car in the motel parking lot would draw the attention of anyone watching out for me.

Maybe the best choice was to get some money and haul ass out of town. I'd lose a few of my things, but that held more appeal than another run in with the Elf. My throat still ached from the chokehold he put on me earlier. The car would stay safe in the motel lot and I could come back for it in a few weeks. I hated the thought of leaving my Celica behind, but could get by without it for that long.

If the Elf was really working for some mystery guy who wanted to talk to me, why involve the Elf at all? It wasn't like I was an inaccessible mucky-muck surrounded by security. Maybe the Elf's whole story was a lie. For all I knew, the guy liked to filet his dates and use them for lunch meat. Another chill ran up my spine. The Elf told me he knew I wouldn't call the Mill Valley cops. True. But how did he know that?

The main streets through downtown didn't provide enough shelter. I ran along Parkwood and through the alley behind the quiet homes and yards backing onto the street. The smell of rose, sage and jasmine reminded me of my garden at home and pulled at my heart. I wished I had never come back to Mill Valley.

Few homes fronted the street I charged down, which gave the block an illusion of privacy and made me feel like I had a bit of breathing room. Still, running remained a temporary solution, not an answer. I needed some kind of plan. But I had no idea what shape that plan should take.

When the road neared one of the town's commercial sections, I doubled back into the quiet residential area along Laurelwood. Fearful the Elf might be tracking me without my noticing, I scanned the empty street. Once I felt sure I was alone, I cut through the exterior corridor of one of the offices that backed onto the street, then trotted down the open flight of stairs. It ended in the parking lot of a small strip mall on one of Mill Valley's busier streets. Pedestrians meandered along the sidewalk. I scanned passersby. At least the Elf's unusual height would make him easy to spot if he came after me on foot. Though, if I'd hurt him as much as I suspected, he probably wasn't walking.

A police siren keened. My pulse raced and I retreated into the shadowed doorway of a nearby shop. The black and white sped by. Nothing to do with me, but since the morning I discovered the Orwell Massacre, a siren's wail always shot a tremor of fear along my spine. I took a deep breath and resumed walking.

Besides my mom and Trevor, the only other person I still knew in town was Janelle. Not much help there. But, what about Mom's friend Gwen? She seemed like a soft touch. Of course I didn't know her phone number or where she lived, and, even if I did, I didn't have a dime for a call. I stopped in the middle of the sidewalk and rubbed my aching temples. While I stood like a stone in the river of foot traffic someone bumped into me. Heart lurching, I whipped around and glared at a frail-looking gentleman balancing behind me with the aid of his cane.

"Excuse me. My brakes aren't what they once were." He gave me a weak smile.

"No problem." Unclenching my fist, I moved under the awning of a dress shop. The old man running into me had set my senses on high alert. I watched him hobble on. By the time he had struggled all the way to the end of the block, my breathing had returned to normal. "I'm losing it." A tingle spread along my right hand. "No. No way."

A woman walked by holding a young child by the hand. She gave me an alarmed look and pulled the boy away from me. Standing on the street talking to myself wasn't going to help me blend in. But it was still better than the idea that had just bloomed. There was one easy way to get some money. Very easy. The old man had sparked the thought glowing inside my brain. "No." I shook my head.

Though I hadn't lifted a wallet in ten years, my hesitation didn't come from the fear that I couldn't still do it. Some things you never lost the sense for. Or the love of. This remained one of them. But I didn't want to slide back down that road. I didn't want to be that person again. I didn't want to become Ramona.

Ramona, the person Billy Bang helped set free.

Rob once told me that how two people met could set the tone for their entire relationship. He and I had met over a coiled rattlesnake. My then-boyfriend, James, and I were hiking in the Santa Monica Mountains, working our way up a well-trod trail. Coming from the opposite direction was Rob – not that I knew his name yet. When the chi-chi-chi rattling started, James ducked back, effectively putting me between him and the snake. Two paces away, Rob rushed forward, grabbed the snake behind its jaws and hurled the thing into the chaparral. Needless to say, that was the last date I went on with James. Rob and I started going out a week later. And he was right, that meeting did shape our relationship. I saw Rob as smart, fast-acting and courageous – the kind of guy I wanted to have around.

When I met Billy Bang, I was fifteen. Unhappy, friendless, and still called Miranda. The first time I saw him, I was standing in Lytton Square. Billy nodded at me then started walking in my direction. He smiled and I smiled back. "So, is that your thing?" he had said.

Baffled why he had crossed the square to talk to me, I said, "Is what my thing?"

"Boosting wallets." Billy grinned again then shook a cigarette from a hard pack of Marlboros. He held one out and I took it. He pulled a lighter from his front pocket, lit my cigarette and then tended to his own. "What's your name?"

He was dressed in faded black jeans, a skin-tight sleeveless T-shirt with a gaping tear that showed off a good three inches of his chest. With his bleached blond hair – complete with dark roots – Billy looked like no one I knew. He was good-looking and I got the feeling he knew it. He came across cocksure and seemed impressed rather than horrified by what he had seen. But I wasn't sure about telling him my name. Or admitting what I had done. Not yet.

"What do you mean, boosting wallets? I don't know what you're talking about. I'm waiting for the bus." I pointed at the bus stop sign as if it could corroborate my story.

"You may be waiting for a bus, but you also sure as hell took that guy's wallet. I saw you. You bumped the old guy and tucked his wallet into the pocket of your jacket." Billy smiled again and my heart did a flip-flop. "You want to make a bet about it?"

Though I didn't want to get in trouble, I also didn't want him to walk away. I chewed my lower lip before I answered. "What kind of bet?"

"If I reach in your pocket and don't find the guy's wallet, I'll give you ten bucks. But if I do find it, you have to give me something."

"I don't have to prove anything to you."

"Maybe not." Billy rubbed the dark stubble along his jaw and raised his eyes skyward, making a big show of putting his brain to work. "Maybe not. Would you feel different if I yelled for the cops right now?"

"You wouldn't." He didn't look like the kind of guy who would do something like that. But my palms still started to sweat.

Billy shrugged and took a drag from his cigarette. "How can you be so sure? We just met. You should know by now people aren't always what they seem. Like you, for instance. Look at yourself. I'll bet you another ten bucks that you don't go to Catholic school. But here you are, dressed in a plaid skirt, white blouse and dark jacket. Very innocent. Very school girl. I'm betting it's not by accident. And I'm betting that it's a load of horseshit."

He took another drag then squinted at me through the smoke. "Even if I decide not to tell the cops about the wallet in your pocket, maybe I'll still tell them about the two in your knapsack." When my mouth dropped open again, Billy smiled. "Yep, saw you bump the pregnant chick and the rich lady. What can I say, I'm an observant guy."

After chewing my lip for another thirty seconds I agreed to his bet. "OK, but I'm not letting you fish around in my pocket out here. Right in the middle of downtown and all."

Billy jerked his head. "Come on. You ever been to Bianca's?"

"The pizza place?"

"Uh-huh."

Billy started strolling in the direction of the pizzeria and I fell into step beside him. It never entered my head to take off and try to outrun him. He wasn't someone I wanted to ditch. "Yeah, I stopped in once." Truth was I had never been inside the place. Without someone I could call a friend, hanging out there alone seemed sad. And my parents would never dine at a dive like Bianca's.

"I know the manager. He's cool." Billy turned and smiled at me. I hoped my weak knees would support me the whole way to our destination. "You'll like him."

We skirted another pedestrian and as I drew beside Billy again, I eyed him from under my lashes. He was a good five inches taller than me, my forehead even with his jaw. Although I had dated a few boys, I never went out with anyone who was more than a year older. I tried to guess Billy's age. Twenty? He didn't look like a kid. He didn't walk like one either. I wiped my sweaty palms along the sides of my wool skirt as I eyed his rear end. He had a great butt.

We stepped inside Bianca's Pizzeria. The aroma of garlic and tomato sauce filled the entry way. I hoped the responding growl from my stomach wasn't audible to Billy. After my eyes adjusted to the dim interior, I saw jocks and stoners were settled in separate areas of the restaurant. Billy nodded to a few people in the stoner section and led me toward the rear of the room. As we passed the jukebox, I glanced at the visible list of tunes. The Ramones' *Beat on the Brat* was C102. I nodded in approval.

After we settled into a tall-backed booth, Billy spoke again. "Come on. Give it." He held out his hand.

I pulled the wallet from my jacket then handed it over. "OK, you got me. I took the old guy's wallet. You win the bet." My cigarette had died out. I pushed it into the dented metal ashtray in the center of the table. "You said I'd have to give you something if you were right. So what do I have to give you? You want the money?"

Billy pulled open the billfold and tossed four twenties and two fives onto the table, then shook his head. "Nice haul. But no. I don't want your money. All I want's a kiss."

Thirteen

I stared at Billy.

A tall, skinny man with a prominent Adam's apple and a bad case of acne stopped by the table, breaking the moment. "Hey man. What can I get you?" Dressed as he was in a Grateful Dead T-shirt and jeans, his hair pulled back in a ponytail, the dress code for the staff at Bianca's was definitely casual.

Billy bumped fists with him. "Bug, good to see you." He cocked an eyebrow at me. "You like pepperoni?"

"Sure." I picked up the one-page menu from the table and handed it to Bug.

"Pepperoni and olives." Billy looked back at me. "You okay with the olives?"

My mind felt mushy, still processing the fact that Billy wanted to kiss me. "Sure."

Bug didn't bother writing the order on his pad. "Man, you never order nothing different. You got to challenge me sometime. Ask me to put together something outrageous for you."

Billy smiled and shook his head. "Another time."

"Yeah, right. You want something wet with that?"

"Yeah. Thanks." The man slouched away and Billy smiled at me. "Bug's the manager. And head cook. He lets me eat here for free."

"Wow, a free meal. That's decent."

"But even free, it's better if you stick with something simple. You let the Bug get creative and there's no telling what kind of stuff he's gonna mix together. I once saw him give a guy a pizza topped with meatballs, pineapple, hot peppers and chocolate sauce."

"So, cautious is good." I resisted the impulse to ask why Billy called the man Bug. I hoped it had nothing to do with the state of the restaurant's kitchen.

"Yeah, he's a great guy. So, how 'bout you? You destined for greatness, too? That lift you did looked pretty damn impressive. The old guy never even reacted. He had like zero clue what happened."

I shrugged. "I get by."

"Where'd you learn to do it?"

"*Harry in Your Pocket.* The movie? That's what got me started."

"I'm gonna need more details than that." Billy leaned his elbows on the table.

"When I was thirteen, I caught the movie on TV." I shrugged. "It looked like fun. So I tried it at home – the way they did in the movie. Put one of my dad's jackets on a hanger with a bell dangling from it. Turned out I was pretty good. When I got to where I could lift the wallet without ringing the bell..."

"What?"

"I took my show on the road. So to speak."

"You were thirteen and scoring a couple bills a week?"

I did a quick survey of the nearby booths. They all remained empty, but I leaned closer to Billy anyway. "Sounds dumb, but I didn't do it for the money. In the beginning."

"Keep going."

"My first real-life try was at a school dance. I did great. Scored eight wallets." I shrugged. "But I gave them all back, each time pretending I'd found the wallet. I made sure to spread my efforts around the auditorium so it wouldn't look suspicious. Then I started going to football games at the high school and doing the same thing. But, after a few games, that got boring. So I came downtown." I lowered my voice. "I tracked the shoppers, looking for easy targets. And I kept playing Good Samaritan. I always gave back what I took."

Billy gave me a half-smile. "You didn't give back any of the money you scored today."

"Yeah." I cleared my throat. "Right before last Thanksgiving, I went downtown to do my thing. There were lots of shoppers out, but most looked way too stressed for me to take a chance. Then I saw this man in an expensive-looking suit staring at the display in the window of the shoe store. I pretended like I didn't see him, bumped into him, said I was sorry and walked on. I waited in front of the fabric shop planning to follow him and do my 'find and return' routine. But the guy was like molasses. I swear it took him ten minutes to walk from one store to the next. I tried to stay focused on the bolts of fabric, but the closer he got to me, the slower he moved. I was sure he knew I took his wallet. By the time he came up behind me, I was holding my breath."

"What happened?"

"He grabbed my ass. I couldn't believe it. He was an adult. And you know what he said?"

Billy shook his head.

"'One free feel deserves another.' Then the creep smirked at me and strutted off."

"And he had no idea you took his wallet?"

"Nope. And no way was I going to give it back after that. But I was freaked. I ran inside the grocery store. The one off Lytton Square?"

"Uh-huh. And?"

"I was practically running as I headed to the bathroom at the back. Almost knocked over a stack of cans at the end of one aisle." Billy's half-smile made me want him to ask for a kiss again. I looked back down at the table top. "When I opened the wallet, I found four hundred dollars." I didn't mention I almost peed myself when I saw all that green.

Good thing I was already inside a stall. "After that, knowing I could get money whenever I needed... It was pretty hard to resist, you know?"

Bug reappeared with two red-tinted glasses and placed them on the table. "Pizza'll be out in about fifteen minutes."

"Great. Thanks, man." Billy and Bug fist bumped again.

"Thanks," I echoed. Nervous about sharing my biggest secret and unsure what to say next, I picked up the plastic glass. Before I brought it all the way to my mouth, I could smell the beer. I looked at Billy in silent question.

"Yep. Told you he's cool."

"Wow." I swigged a mouthful. "Very cool." Lots of places in town served underage girls, but not usually during the day. I stared at Billy, wondering what to say or do next. *Give Me Shock Treatment* came on the juke box. My feet and head started moving with the beat.

"You like this song?" Billy said.

"Love it. Love them."

"Come on." He held out his hand.

"Come on what?"

"Let's dance. You're already dancing in your seat."

I surveyed the restaurant. People were eating pizza, drinking sodas. "Nobody else is dancing."

"That ain't the point. You like this song, right?"

"Yeah."

"You like dancing to this song?"

"Yeah."

"You feel like dancing to it now?"

"Yeah."

"Then who gives a damn what anybody else is doing?"

My mouth hung open. Billy was right.

He pulled me out of my seat and started to dance. I felt self-conscious and scanned the faces of the other diners. Then I looked at Billy. He smiled at me and moved with the beat, making his own world. I wanted to slip inside that world. To follow his lead and be someone who didn't care what other people thought. Be someone who danced when I felt like it. To be the person Billy wanted for a dance partner.

I started to move. Billy nodded at me. We both sang along as the chorus came around. After we danced through that song, Billy crossed the room and dropped several quarters into the machine. I called out a request for C102 and we danced through *Beat on the Brat,* followed by *Teenage Lobotomy, Sheena is a Punk Rocker, I Want to be Sedated,* and *Blitzkrieg Bop.*

By the time *Commando* came on, I was short of breath. We collapsed into our booth. I felt weightless and free, maybe for the first time in my life. I smiled my happiness at Billy. "The Ramones rule."

"They get the job done. You do, too. You're a good dancer."

"Thanks. You're not bad yourself." I cooled off with several gulps of beer and plucked my sweat-dampened blouse away from my chest.

"You like to dance, you should come see my band. We got a gig down in the city tonight. Tomorrow night, too. Should be wild."

"Huh. Sounds like fun." I wouldn't be able to go on a school night. But with some planning, I could weave a story good enough to pass Mom's inspection and get out on Friday night. "I can catch you guys tomorrow. What do you play?"

"Me or the band?"

"You. Your instrument. Or do you sing?"

"Lead guitar." Billy smiled again. "Sing some, too. But Stewie sings lead."

"And your music?"

"Punk. Is there any other kind?"

"Not for me. Where you playing?"

"The Empty Pitcher. You can ride with me and the band." His smile broadened. "If you want."

The smell of pepperoni, tomato sauce and cheese made my mouth water. Not as much as Billy's smile, but still... I pulled my attention from his face.

Bug settled the pizza tray between us on the table. He rested one fist on his skinny hip, pointing his other hand at Billy. "So, you going to introduce me to your lady friend or what?"

"Sure, man." Billy winked at me. My face

grew warm. I still hadn't told him my name. He grinned then said, "Bug, meet Ramona. I'm betting she's gonna become a real familiar face around here from now on. And, I gotta tell you, I ain't lost a single bet today."

"Damn, you're one lucky sonofabitch."

"Got that right."

I smiled at Bug. I didn't think Billy would lose this bet either. "Nice to meet you, Bug. Thanks for the food. And drink."

"Any friend of Billy's..." Bug shrugged. "Let me know if you need anything else." He nodded twice and then slouched back to the kitchen.

Billy lifted a slice of pizza, using his fingers to free it from the clinging strands of cheese. "So, C102. You knew the number of the song you wanted me to play. You come here a lot? 'Cause I do and I ain't seen you here before."

I shrugged. "No."

"But you knew the jukebox number for *Beat on the Brat*?"

I shrugged again. "I noticed it when we walked by. You know, when we came in."

"What are you, one of those speed readers?"

Around most boys, I hid my smarts. And I had never told any boy before about how I spent my afternoons picking pockets. But Billy wasn't a boy. I had the feeling he wouldn't be put off by my brain. "Um, kind of. I got this memory thing. With things I read."

"What do you mean?"

"Like the menu? Bet I can tell you the price of any item on it."

"You mean, I ask you to give me a price for anything, and you'll know what it is?"

"Uh-huh."

"So? Maybe you're just a good guesser."

"OK. How about this? I've got a book inside there." I pointed at my knapsack. "Pull it out."

Billy put down his slice, wiped his hand on a napkin then reached for my bag. He fished around for a moment then held up the paperback.

I leaned back against the padded booth. "Open it."

"What page?"

"Whatever page you want."

Billy flipped through the slim volume, stopping about two-thirds of the way in. "OK, what now?"

"You tell me the page number and I'll tell you what it says."

"You're messing with me."

For once I wasn't nervous about letting someone see this part of me. I smiled and said, "Go on."

"OK. So, what's on page 178?"

I closed my eyes and collected the image then began reciting, "'The back of Bobbie Faye's house looked dark.'" I continued on for two more lines before opening my eyes. "Want me go to on?"

Billy shook his head then riffled toward the front of the book. "Page thirty-nine?"

"OK." I recalled the page. "'He shut the car door and waited for the lock to click. Images jumbled through his brain. He took a deep breath, struggling for calm.'"

Billy set the book on the table and traced his index finger along the title. "You memorized the whole book?"

"No. I mean, yeah. But no. I don't mean to memorize things. Like, I don't study the words, repeat them back and stuff. I just remember."

"Damn. That's gotta come in handy in school. For tests and stuff."

"Yeah. But only if you do the assigned reading."

Billy laughed. "Too true." He pushed the book aside then smiled at me. "So, Ramona, how long you been a fan of the band?"

Billy named me. Billy accepted me. I became Ramona and, for the first time in my life, my name resonated, said something about me.

We used a little of the cash I lifted that day to buy a tape of the Ramones' latest album, *Subterranean Jungle,* then Billy parked me at the bus stop near where we had met while he took the rest of the money and scored some dope and downers. I got home late and looped, but my dad was still at the office and Mom didn't seem to notice my bunny-red eyes.

I told her an elaborate tale about a schoolmate having a sleepover the next night. She seemed pleased with the lie that I had made a friend and didn't look close at the holes in my story. That Friday, I went to the gig with Billy and never looked back. He introduced me to his world, a place of swirling color, vibrating beats, new clubs, new drugs, and an ever-changing cast of people who liked me. He called me amazing. Said I was special. He gave me what I needed: Someone who loved me the way I was.

He gave me so much, it seemed the least I could do was keep lifting wallets and contribute the cash I got toward his rent.

Fourteen

The cry of another siren pulled me back to the present. A fire engine parted the traffic like a big red carving knife. Along with all the pedestrians out enjoying the summer evening, I turned and stared after it. Black smoke rose in the distance. From the location of the rising plume, the fire had to be near Lytton Square. My stomach knotted. I told myself the blaze had nothing to do with the Elf, nothing to do with me. But my gut continued to argue. I started jogging toward the billowing column.

One block shy of the square, I slowed to a walk. A group of gawkers rimmed the brick-walled area. A tall, freckle-spattered teenager broke away from the crowd and rolled toward me on his skateboard. I flagged him down. "Hey, what happened?" I pointed toward the smoke.

The kid flipped his board on end. "Car fire. The thing's toast. And I heard some dude whacked the windshield to pieces and smashed in the hood with a pipe before torching it. A guy I know saw the whole thing. He ran into the Food Mart and told them to call the cops. But by the time he got anybody to come outside and check it out, the dude was gone. And the car was in flames. Whole thing went up like a goddamn torch. I missed seeing the full show, but saw most the fire. Way cool. Never seen nothing like that before. They pretty much got it out now. But the car's thrashed."

"Thanks." Weak-kneed, I continued on toward the square and edged between two onlookers. If I hadn't already guessed what was there, I never would have recognized it: My beautiful red Celica had been turned into a scorched metal mess. Dead center in the square, the car smoldered. A team of firefighters hosed the interior with a blast of water. My best guess: When the Elf failed to find me on the street, he went back to the Cozy 8, used my key and drove my car to the square – the most noticeable spot in downtown Mill Valley. The Elf wanted to make a statement.

If what the kid said was true and the Elf wailed on my car with a pipe before he set it on fire, I had either not hurt him enough to slow him down or hurt him enough to make him crazy. I really didn't want to find out which.

Three years. That's how long it took me to pay off that car. My most prized possession was now a fried pile of scrap. For the first time since the Elf grabbed me, I felt something besides fear. Fury warmed every inch of my skin. To get my insurance company to pay up, I'd need a police report. But the thought of talking to the cops turned my stomach. It was way too risky. In spite of ten years living clean, my fingerprints had to be on file somewhere. Though I doubted they printed the victims when they made a complaint, going to the cops landed way outside my comfort zone. But damn it, my Celica was ruined.

I couldn't walk away.

But there was one good thing. The steaming mess in Lytton Square opened a path for my next move. I doubted the Elf was lingering anywhere near the square. The danger of someone identifying him as the asshole who destroyed my car was too high. I didn't think he'd wait for me at the Cozy 8 either after his fit of arson. In spite of his confident words earlier, there was no way he could be sure I wouldn't call the cops after his assault on my car. If I wanted to retrieve my wallet and make my escape from Mill Valley, this was my chance.

I'd deal with the cops later. Maybe.

The smoke flattened and spread. My eyes started to water. The bitter scent of burned gasoline drifted from the square and I covered my nose. With a last look at my car, I turned away and began walking. By the time I reached The Deuce, the air was clear enough to breathe normally. I jogged the rest of the way. When I reached the motel parking lot, I wiped the sweat from my forehead and watched for signs of the Elf. Everything looked quiet. I crossed the blacktop, wishing I had a stick of gum to ease the dryness in my mouth. Though my assumption that the Elf was long gone seemed reasonable, my nerves still felt raw.

The stairway I wanted anchored the far end of an outer corridor. I kept half my attention on the parking lot as I trotted to the bottom step. There was still no sign of the Elf. But, as I crept upward, each squeak from the wooden treads made my heart lurch. When I reached the landing, I resisted the impulse to flatten myself against the wall.

Two doors away from my room, I stopped and peered over the railing. No one was down in the parking lot searching for me. No one near the Elf's size was acting suspicious or paying me any mind. I took a deep breath then hurried to my door and plunged the key card into the lock. The green light clicked on, I turned the knob and thrust the door open wide. For several heartbeats, I stood outside and stared into the room.

I didn't see anyone inside the L-shaped room. But someone could hide in the bathroom or on the other end of the L near the bed. I considered calling out 'room service,' to see if anyone showed themselves. But if the Elf was lurking, he wouldn't be thrown off by a lame trick like that. I exhaled then tiptoed inside. With a jerk, I flipped on the bathroom light. The small room appeared unoccupied. I tore open the curtain shielding the tub and shower. Empty. With another deep breath I walked farther inside, past the corner, where the room opened up. No Elf. I wiped my sweaty palms along the sides of my jeans.

The room stood empty now, but for how long? I dashed around the bed and grabbed my purse. I hesitated before I picked my overnight bag. The bag wouldn't weigh me down that much and the extra layers would come in handy. The two boxes my father saved for me still sat on the bed. I wasn't going to lose their contents again. From my luggage, I pulled out the dress and shoes I wore to the funeral and tossed them to the floor before stuffing the photo album, Ramones cassettes and the envelope with the birth certificate into the bag. Heavier than I wanted, but I needed to keep these things near.

A piece of paper lay on the floor inside the threshold. My legs failed me as I read the message. On my knees on the thin carpet, I stared at the tight, angled script re-reading the Elf's words: Don't be stupid, Ramona. Stay put. If you run, we'll find you.

No way would I stay 'put.' Not after that giant freak tried to strangle me. I hustled down the stairs to the parking lot. Away from the building, I breathed a little easier. With a last glance at the empty space where I had parked my car a few hours earlier, I scurried from the motel lot. I needed to figure out my next step. Now that I had gathered the belongings I cared about, should I ignore the Elf's message and run?

The guy knew who I was. He knew I was both Miranda and Ramona. That meant he knew about my past. What I had done. Who I used to be. If I ran now, I couldn't return to my life in L.A. That meant starting over. Again. A sick feeling swept through me.

Running meant losing Rob. "No." As much as I wanted the Elf out of my life, I didn't want to throw away what Rob and I had. Besides, if I did run again, the Elf would be on my tail. And I was tired of running.

But why was the Elf after me? What the hell did he want?

Out on the main street I slowed to a walk. When I reached Throckmorton, I turned, working my way along the tree-lined street, the gradual incline forcing a low-level complaint from my legs. My destination, Old Mill Park, wasn't much farther. As a teenager, I had found the park and the grove surrounding it claustrophobic, but the spot was dark and quiet. Private. Near the park, tall redwoods flanked the sidewalk, their deep shade cooling the summer evening. I stepped into the green-gray shadows. Under the shelter of trees, the ground became spongy, the decomposed pine needles muffling my tread. The sun would set in another forty minutes, but for now light stained the visible patches of sky the color of weak tea.

With the breeze came the scent of cedar and moss. I walked the dirt path to the children's play area and leaned against one of the swing set's support poles. My heart no longer thumped with a wild insistence. I closed my eyes and listened to my surroundings. Tree branches stirred and water rambled down in the gorge. Something rustled in the nearby duff – possibly a raccoon or a squirrel – foraging for its supper.

I knew these surroundings. That was my strength. I didn't know much about the Elf, but I doubted he knew the terrain like I did. I headed for the old gravity car that sat in the park. A remnant of the region's first thrill ride – though I never heard it billed that way – it had sat in the park for as long as I could remember. For more than thirty years, gravity cars had barreled down Mount Tamalpais, zipping around the twists and turns, giving revelers from the mountaintop tavern a breath-taking hour-long ride. The open-air cars ran with a single 'gravity man' on board to control their downward rush. As a teen, I used to sit in this pensioned-off car and wonder what would have happened if the gravity man fainted, had a heart attack, or showed up drunk to work. The gravity system lacked modern day redundancy. Something I also lacked. I needed a place to stay the night, but I also needed a plan and a back-up plan. I rubbed my hands together as I assessed my situation: I had zip, zero and zilch in the way of resources.

When the Elf burst into my room two hours earlier, he had said a man wanted to talk to me. Who could possibly want to talk to me this bad? Did this tie in with the Orwell Massacre? Or with some long-forgotten wallet I stole a decade before? The latter seemed unlikely in the extreme; I voted with the Massacre. The sole benefit of having something so heinous in your past was it made all other infractions of the rules pale in comparison. I couldn't think of anything else in my life that cried out more for payback.

My thoughts circled back to the first hours after I slipped out of that blood-drenched house, running away from danger. Running away from Billy's corpse and the five other victims.

On the morning that still haunted my dreams, I had scurried along the street, head pointed at the sidewalk to cut the risk of someone seeing my face and remembering me. The cold weather acted as my ally. People remained sheltered indoors while the temperature dropped to an unheard of twenty-eight degrees.

On foot it took me two hours to find a bus stop. After a gut-knotting wait, I caught a bus to the Mill Valley depot. Inside the station, I bought a one-way ticket to San Francisco. I settled on the far end of an empty bench, keeping my distance from the other waiting passengers. The station wasn't large, but still the heating system didn't meet the demands of the weather. Travelers huddled together, each within a cocoon of coat and scarf. I felt grateful for the cold, it gave a plausible reason for the way I was trembling.

When the bus arrived, I rode into the city. By the time I reached 8th and Folsom, it was almost 10 p.m. I disembarked then waited for another bus. When I got off the connecting ride, I walked the five remaining blocks to Billy's room. He lived in a residence hotel where most the guests rented by the week—if they could afford it – though a few tenants rented by the hour. I climbed the seven flights of stairs and unlocked the door.

The room always smelled like stale coffee and boiled cabbage, though neither Billy nor I cooked anything there. But a lot of illegal hot plates operated in the units around and below ours. The place was Spartan – from a combination of choice and finances. Billy made some money with the band, and by dealing pot and pills to his friends and a few club types. I contributed by lifting wallets. I thought we did okay. But now, without Billy there, the room looked ugly and tattered.

A mattress on the floor served as our bed with a faded quilt below and a second torn quilt to cover us. I collapsed on the mattress and curled into a ball. There I sobbed for Billy. I cried for the dead little boy back at the house and for his family. I also cried for myself.

Exhausted from my tears, I dropped into a nightmare-twisted sleep, waking when the upstairs tenant stomped across the floor in his heavy work boots. Wan sunlight breached the uncovered windows. I rubbed my eyes, feeling dead inside. I couldn't go home. Dad had made that clear when he kicked me out the previous year. I couldn't stay at Billy's either. Once the police found the bodies and identified him, they'd bring their investigation here.

The image of Billy's bloody neck stump brought up bile and I vomited on the comforter. I hunched on all fours and retched until nothing more came out. In the bathroom, I rinsed my mouth then washed my face. I stared at the hollow-eyed girl in the fly-specked mirror. My hair had grown since I last dyed it and two wavy inches of auburn root showed above the purple. My skin looked pasty and pale, the flesh on my face hard against the bone. When had I eaten my last meal? When had I last gone out in the sunshine?

Billy was gone. I didn't know who killed him or the other people. Or why. But I didn't think the cops would believe me if I told them my story. Hell, I didn't think my own parents would believe me. I didn't want to wind up in prison. If I wanted to avoid arrest, I needed to get lost. Fast.

In the main room, I edged along the north wall until I spied the small notch between the scarred wood floor and the baseboard. I hooked my index finger into the v-shaped slot and tugged. A foot-long section of floorboard separated from the others and I pulled out the metal coffee tin where Billy hid our cash. Even though it was partly my money, I felt guilty. Billy insisted he be the one who added or removed the money from our stash. I had never touched the large canister before. I always handed over the money I scored and he'd pocket a portion then tuck the rest inside the can. But Billy wasn't going to care now if I helped myself. He didn't need the money any more. With a ragged breath I ripped off the plastic lid and peered inside. Several rubber banded rolls of bills filled the can. I dumped them onto the bed. A torn photograph was lodged at the bottom of the container. After tossing the two glossy halves of the photo onto the bed, I unbound the cash.

Though good at math, I counted the money three times to make sure I got the figure right: Eight thousand four hundred forty dollars. Inside the coffee can we kept under the floorboards. Billy and I lived hand-to-mouth. Where did he get that much cash? And when?

I rocked back on my heels and rubbed my arms, feeling chilled inside the stuffy room. A year ago, Janelle told me Billy dealt coke and heroin. I hadn't wanted to believe her. But, afraid for his safety, I'd confronted him. He had admitted to dealing more than dope and downers, and we fought. But, in the end,

Billy promised to stop. And I had believed him.

But the tens, twenties and fifties stacked in piles on the mattress meant Billy had lied. Where else could he have gotten this much cash except by peddling coke and heroin? His pot and pill business didn't bring in this kind of money.

Numb, I walked into the bathroom and pulled out my own vial of pills. I pried off the cap then dumped the remaining tablets and capsules into the toilet and flushed. Billy had never been big on buying household supplies and didn't own a pair of scissors, but he kept a razor in the rust-stained medicine cabinet. I retrieved it, opened the top and took out the double-edged blade. I stared at my reflection again, then started cutting.

When I had hacked off all my hair above the purple dye line, only tight auburn curls remained. I dusted the itchy trimmings off my neck then gave my reflection a nod. If I didn't want to go to prison, Ramona needed to disappear.

In a corner behind a pile of empty Chinese food cartons, I found Billy's black and navy knapsack. I pawed through the pile of jeans and T-shirts on the brick and board shelves, stuffing the few clothes I owned inside the pack. I changed into my only turtleneck and a pullover sweater then pulled on my leather-look jacket. After I shoved the cash back inside the coffee can, I grabbed the torn photo halves from the mattress where I had dropped them. The picture showed Billy and another man. The man must have moved when the picture was snapped, blurring his face. But I recognized the setting: The two stood in front of a local movie house. When Billy and I'd get back from one of his gigs too wired to sleep, we often walked there for the late-late show. The marquee behind them advertised *Amadeus*. Billy wore the black leather jacket I bought him for his last birthday. The other man's arm seemed to weigh heavy on Billy's shoulders and Billy looked pissed. I tucked the torn photo inside the can, resealed it then scanned the room. My heart hitched at the sight of Johnny Lydon sneering from a poster. Billy loved the Sex Pistols.

I fought back tears, gave the room a final look, then jammed the coffee can inside Billy's knapsack and slung it over my shoulder. On the walk to the bus stop, I said goodbye to Billy and to everything I knew. And to everything I had been.

I caught a bus to the train station, then a train to Los Angeles. Without a firm plan, I decided to ride toward the ocean. From Union Station, I took a westbound bus and wound up in Santa Monica. Billy's money helped cushion the first few months of getting settled. But I never stopped thinking of it as blood money. In my head, the money and the drugs and Billy's murder remained tangled. Once I found a job, I put the remaining cash in the bank and didn't touch it. Not even when I bought my Celica.

My arm hit something hard. I sat up, surprised I had managed to doze. Memories of leaving San Francisco ten years ago had merged into my usual nightmare about the Orwell Massacre. I woke as I always did, the image of Billy's body-less head accusing me of deserting him fresh in my mind.

Night had settled over Old Mill Park. The chitter and squeals coming from above told me bats were readying to leave their roosts for a night's hunting. I stood and shook out the kinks in my legs and back as I tried to shake the image of Billy. Since arriving in Mill Valley, I hadn't slept much. My catnap in the gravity car left me feeling more worn and tired than before. I needed someplace safe where I could close my eyes. Then, when my head felt clear, I'd figure out what to do next. On the plus side, the belongings I retrieved from the Cozy 8 included my ATM card and a little bit of cash. On the negative: Mill Valley was hardly a hotbed of banking and I hadn't noticed any ATMs during my mad dash through downtown. To make matters worse, the motel selection in Mill Valley was slim. If the Elf was true to his word and kept looking for me, it wouldn't be tough for him to find me if I checked in somewhere new.

But I did know a safe place: Secure, well-guarded. And off-limits. The old saying

'Beggars can't be choosers' sprang to mind. The big question was, would Trevor let me in? I decided to find a pay phone, call a cab and find out.

Fifteen

The cabby let me out under the porte cochere. Cricket chirps came from the curtain of shrubs bordering the front yard. Harbingers of good fortune, I hoped their refrain would boost my own luck quotient. Trevor wasn't likely to let me in without an argument. I needed all the help I could get. I wished I felt more alert, more able to marshal my thoughts.

Though not yet 10 p.m., the porch light was off. Two lights burned inside – one upstairs and one down. I rapped on the front door then leaned against the frame and waited. After a few minutes the door cracked open. Beneath a rust-colored eyebrow, I recognized the frowning Cyclopsian eye peering from the gap. Edginess leaned on me and my words came out sounding snotty. "Hey Trev. Long time no see." The one visible eye narrowed to a slit. He showed great restraint and didn't slam the door in answer to my flippant greeting.

"What do you want?"

"I really need a place to stay."

Trevor snorted.

"Look, I know I kind of crossed the line with you today. But someone torched my car this afternoon. While it was parked in the lot by Lytton Square."

"That was your car? I heard about it. Your mother's friend Gwen Hardesty called. She saw it on the news." The door opened a fraction. "According to Gwen, the report said they didn't know who the car belonged to."

I resisted the impulse to close my eyes and massage my temples. "Well, I'm telling you, it belonged to me." He arched a solo brow, but I had no intention of explaining my situation. Still I had to give him something. "With my car destroyed like that, I don't feel safe staying in a hotel. I promise I won't bother my mom. I just need a place to sleep."

The door opened another inch. "What did the police say?"

My face grew warm and I felt grateful for the surrounding dark. Trevor didn't strike me as the type who'd understand my failure to file a police report. I shrugged. "They didn't seem to have any leads."

"How about you?"

"How about me what?"

"Your mother talks to me. Quite a bit. About a wide range of things. On occasion she talks about you. About the sort of people you chose to associate with when you lived here. The grief you caused her. It wouldn't come as a surprise to me, if you knew who'd done this. You strike me as the type of girl who makes enemies."

Jesus. "Look, Trevor, I'm sorry if I embarrassed you earlier. Or ruffled your feathers. Or whatever you call it. But I needed to talk with my mom. It wasn't a conversation that could wait." Though in the end, the talk about my birth certificate didn't happen. "But I won't bother her this time. Give me a solid eight, nine hours to rest my eyes and I'm back out of here. Please."

The frown on Trevor's face deepened as he opened the door. "You can stay in the blue room. But I'm letting you in because you're Marion's daughter. And she'd want you to be safe."

While I never thought my mother would want me to be unsafe, I doubted she spent much time or energy worrying about me. But I didn't share those doubts with Trevor. I hurried across the threshold.

Though still dressed in a starched white shirt and creased suit trousers, Trevor looked in 'after hours' mode, no longer wearing his necktie, vest or cufflinks. Did his idea of relaxation involve anything more frenzied than memorizing the works of Shakespeare or practicing his diction? Trevor stared at me as if reading my thoughts, a deep V carving a path between his eyes. He continued to watch me over his wide shoulder as he led me through the foyer and up the stairs. "You listen to me, young lady. I don't care if you are Marion's daughter. I swear I'll padlock you inside your room if you try to bother her. Your mother is in a fragile state right now. She doesn't need you dumping your shit in her lap."

"Fine." I hustled up the stairs after him. I couldn't believe Trevor had uttered the word 'shit.'

He pointed me toward the first door on the right side of the hall. "You'll stay here. You know where the bathroom is?" I nodded. "I'll be down the hall. Listening. Don't put a toe out of line, hear me? Your mother may tolerate your nonsense, but not me. I won't put up with your crap."

Shit and crap. From a dignified soul like Trevor. I had certainly made an impression on him. Not a good one, but an impression nonetheless. "Got it." I turned the knob and pushed open the door to 'the blue room.'

The rush of memory threatened to overwhelm me as I stood on the threshold to my old bedroom. In my mind's eye, I saw tangled sheets, ripe with sex and sweat. And Billy.

Billy's hands. Billy's lips. Billy's smile.

"Good night." Trevor's acerbic tone brought me back to the moment.

"Goodnight," I echoed. "And, thanks." I closed the door behind me then leaned against it. Through the thick wood, I heard Trevor snort again. Apparently we weren't going to become fast friends.

The room was indeed blue. Gone was the sunburst of color I had favored as a teen. The bed was now draped in a royal blue coverlet edged with lace, the wood wainscoting painted sky blue, and the walls above papered with white woven fabric featuring a dainty floral print. The carpet had been removed and the oak floor below gleamed. I climbed onto the bed. The mattress didn't give off its remembered squeak. I wondered if my father burned the old one. The one where he caught me and Billy screwing.

Billy wasn't someone Dad would have liked even under the best of circumstances. But things might have been different if Billy wasn't already suspect number one in the disappearance of Dad's diamond cufflinks. After that incident, Dad had called me into his office, face grim.

He'd stood behind his desk, arms crossed, his blond hair gleaming in the light of the nearby floor lamp. Still in his work clothes of dark slacks and gray striped shirt, he'd loosened his tie and draped his jacket over one of the Eames chairs. He remained calm while he told me how he'd discovered his cufflinks were gone when he dressed for work that morning. But then the volume of his voice rose and his face turned red. "Your mother told me you had that boy over here yesterday. The one I told you to steer clear of. If you want that hooligan to stay out of jail, I suggest you call him and get him to bring my cufflinks back. I'm happy to press charges if that's what it takes to get him out of your life.

"When he brings the cufflinks back, he

will deal with me or your mother. You are not to see him. Ever. Let alone allow him to set one foot inside this house again. Understood?"

Catching me in bed with anyone would have sent Dad's blood pressure into the red zone, but when he saw it was Billy, he'd kicked me out of the house and told me not to come back.

For the first time in a decade, I slept without nightmares. Maybe that was due to my lack of sleep since I'd learned about my father's death. Or maybe the memories of the happy, sweaty hours I'd spent in this room with Billy warded off my usual terrors. Instead of blood and a headless body, I awoke with the fading image of an empty station where I sat on a hard wooden bench waiting for a train. But not any station I recognized, just some netherworld depot where my mother's voice played over and over through the loud speakers, chiding me for bringing along the wrong things. I had gazed at the riot of suitcases surrounding me, and wondered how – with so much baggage – I didn't have what I needed. That was the lone night phantom I recalled. I stretched and sighed. I hadn't woken up feeling this rested in years.

The clock on the bedside table read 9:17 a.m. Amazing. Trevor hadn't wrenched me out of bed at the eight-hour mark. Maybe he tried, but couldn't rouse me. I sat with my legs dangling down the side of the bed. This was definitely a new mattress and bed frame. In years past, my feet had touched the floor.

Since I had slept in my T-shirt, I checked the closet for something more modest to don before I trundled to the bathroom. Inside I found padded hangers, but no clothes. Oh well. I grabbed clean underwear and a fresh T-shirt from my bag, and picked my jeans off the chair. I peered into the hall but saw no sign of Trevor and scooted down the passageway.

After showering, I stared at my reflection above the pedestal sink. I looked nothing like the sixteen-year-old girl my father excommunicated from his family. The purple and black hair, ghost pale skin, the hollow eyes and face – were all gone. But more than the externals had shifted. My expression held a look of purpose I hadn't possessed as a teen. Though my father had never picked up or returned any of my calls, if we'd bumped into one another sometime in the last few years, I bet he would've recognized the changes in me.

Rested and scrubbed, I felt more capable of tackling my problem. Though I didn't want to face the Elf again, I also didn't want to cut and run. To give up Rob. Or my identity. Not again. I'd been running for too long already. And for all that running, I hadn't escaped. Not from what haunted me. Now I had the Elf

– and whoever he worked for – to contend with. He wanted something from me and I didn't know what.

Why come after me now? The Elf could've scared Mom any time over the last ten years and gotten my phone number and address. Maybe he hadn't dared make that kind of move while Dad was alive. Still, he could've broken into the house and snatched their address book. What had changed to make me important now? No easy answer popped to mind.

Refusing to run was fine, but I needed more. Because wandering around blind could bring me face-to-face with the Elf again. I needed to know what he wanted and who he worked for. But, if I was going to snoop around, I'd need a car.

Halfway along the hall on my return to 'the blue room,' Mom's door squeaked opened. I gazed over my shoulder. Looking weak and wan, she leaned in the doorway. The emptiness in her expression chilled me. I couldn't tell if she was drunk, drugged or was having a stroke.

"You okay? Mom?"

She stared, eyes unfocused.

I hurried to her side and took her arm. Her skin felt cold and limp under my touch. "Let me help you back to bed." Where was Trevor when you needed him? I wrapped my arm around her narrow frame and supported her for the short walk back to bed. Her shoulder blades pressed into the flesh of my arm. She had gone on from trim to bony. The sour scent of alcohol sweat rose from her skin, overlaid with a fresh breath of vodka. When I settled her against the pillows, she ran her index finger along my cheekbone.

"Miranda?"

"Yeah, Mom. It's me, Miranda."

"Are you in trouble?" Her arm flopped onto the coverlet.

The words came out slurred, but I understood what she said. The chill moved from my chest to my spine. "Why do you think that?"

"Aren't you always in trouble?"

I felt a smile spread. Her expectation that I had screwed up felt familiar. Right now, familiar was reassuring. "Maybe so. You feeling sick? Should I get Trevor?"

"What the hell are you doing?" Trevor charged into the room and shoved me aside. He hovered over my mother's recumbent form, scanning her face and her arms as I got my feet back under me. I assumed he was looking for signs of daughter-inflicted damage. With the back of his hand he brushed Mom's fair hair off her forehead. "Mrs. Burgess, are you all right?"

"Trevor." Mom frowned at him. "Where were you? I needed you. You weren't here." She sounded more like a petulant child than a woman on the cusp of fifty, but Trevor seemed not to notice.

"I'm so sorry, Mrs. Burgess. What do you need?"

Her head turned toward me. She squinted, as if trying to figure out who all was in the room. She swiveled her head back to Trevor. "I'm out of tea."

The overemphasis she placed on the last word told me it wasn't tea she ran out of. It also settled my diagnosis: not ill, drunk

"Right away, madam." Trevor glared at me. "If you'll come with me. I think you've troubled your mother enough for now."

"Oh, let her stay. We can chat while you get my tea. It's better than waiting alone."

Trevor gave me serious stink eye, but didn't argue. He strode to the far side of the room then picked up the ladder back chair. As a child, I had tried to climb it and still bore a small scar underneath my chin from where the chair and I toppled against a sharp-cornered chiffonier. Trevor frowned at me, but set the chair alongside the bed.

"Thank you."

Voice too low for my mother to hear, he spoke into my ear. "If you upset her, I'll toss you out the front door."

I didn't respond as I sat on the hard seat. Trevor offering this chair wasn't random; he didn't want me to get too comfortable here. After he left the room, I waited until I heard the creak of his weight on the stairs. The fourth step remained the noisy one. My mother stared at the ceiling. Her lips moved, but no sound came out. "Mom?"

"Yes?" She turned her head and her eyes widened in surprise. "Miranda, what're you doing here?"

My stomach sank to the ground floor. "Visiting. How're you feeling?"

"Fine. Fine." She tugged at the shoulder of her nightgown.

"Uh, Mom, I came by yesterday to talk but you weren't feeling well."

"Oh?"

"If you feel like talking now, I have a couple questions for you." This was definitely dirty pool – broaching the topic of my birth father while Mom was blotto. Especially because the price of entry yesterday was my promise not to bother her. But this might wind up my one shot at getting the information. "Dad left me a copy of my birth certificate." My voice sounded loud in my ears and my palms grew clammy. "The original one." Mom turned away to stare at the open doorway. "The thing is, it lists my father as unknown. Dad wasn't my father. And he wanted me to know that."

I leaned forward and placed my hand on Mom's shoulder. "Who was my father?"

Sixteen

Mom swiveled back to stare at me, a small frown creasing her forehead. I pulled my hand away.

"Oh Miranda. You haven't changed at all."

Of course, what she said was, "You havzn't shanged 't'all." But the remark still stung. What right did she have to talk down to me? I wanted to yell, but kept my voice low. "Excuse me?"

"You know what I mean."

"No. I don't. Explain."

She sighed and gave her head a wobble, which I guessed she meant as a pity-filled shake. "You always rolled around in the muck. With the most appalling people. The things I wanted for you... Would it have killed you to bring home a decent boyfriend? Wear decent clothes... Come to your father's work parties – without making a fuss? You never liked the plans I made for you. Nothing I tried was right. The deportment classes. The cotillion. All a waste of time. You always wanted to play in the gutter."

A headache sprouted behind my right eye. I rubbed my forehead as if my fingers could stop its progress. "If there's something seamy here, it's from your life, not mine. I'm trying to find out who my father is."

"You know who your father is. Was." She wiped the sheet across her eyes, smearing mascara onto her cheek and the blue silk. "Let the man rest in peace. He was better than you. Better than me." Mom bunched the sheet and blanket in her hands then stared at the cloth bouquet. When she spoke again, her voice was a whisper. "I don't know why you want to put me through this."

Heavy damask curtains sheltered the room from the sun and the small bedside lamp cast an amber halo that touched the far side of her face. The hard wood chair groaned as I leaned forward. "I'm sorry I've upset you. The timing sucks, I know. But, let's face it, I haven't gotten an invite home in over ten years. So, I'm thinking my opportunities for talking to you face-to-face are kind of limited." I took a deep breath. "Look, Dad left me a copy of my birth certificate and his name's not on it. He wouldn't have done that if he didn't want me to know he wasn't my father."

"Why must you badger me?" Mom covered her eyes with a limp hand. "My husband just died."

A lump formed in my throat. I swallowed hard. "Don't get me wrong, Dad will always be my dad. He's the one who raised me. The one..." I blinked away tears. "I'm not looking for a new dad. I just want to know who my birth father is. If I could do it without bothering you, I would."

Mom uncovered her eyes then turned to stare at me. "Oh, Miranda. Why don't you go? If you're so determined to make things unpleasant, I think you should leave."

I stared at the deep hollows under her eyes. She looked unmoored. How bad did I want an answer? My stomach churned like I had swallowed boiling acid. If I backed down now, I might never get his name. And, unless I was willing to fight dirty, Mom wasn't going to tell me a thing. I took a deep breath and once again failed to make it to the high ground. "Sure, Mom. Since you're too tired to talk, I'll pop down to the kitchen and tell Trevor you want to rest. That you don't need your tea."

She tried to prop herself up and failed. After staring at me for close to thirty seconds, she let loose a shuddering breath. I thought she might start crying. But I knew she understood my threat: If she didn't talk, I planned to head Trevor off at the pass with her 'tea.' Her voice was small and slurred as she spoke; I had to lean closer to understand her through all the sliding consonants. "You've no idea what it was like then. Girls didn't have children out of wedlock. Not nice girls. Not girls who wanted to marry well. An abortion out of the question. Proper girls didn't get abortions. Not in 1966."

"OK. So that explains why you had me, but not how."

Mom waved away that remark with a careless hand. "Your father was a wonderful man. You've no idea. That he still wanted me... Even after... Del tried to overlook the shame I brought on him... Into his home and family. Because of my behavior... My..." She wiped the back of her hand across her eyes.

"Your father rescued me. There's no other word for what he did. Since then, it's been my responsibility to hold myself to the highest possible standards. To thank him. That was the very least I could do for your father." Mom toyed with the satin ribbon edging her blanket. "He'd always admired me. Back then, I was the belle of the ball." She sighed. "Del and I dated once or twice. But I had my eye on another boy. He came from a much better family."

I knew in mom-speak that 'much better family' meant a lot more money.

The sound of Trevor mounting the stairs meant my time on this topic was almost over. In a soft voice I pressed, "But who's my father?"

Mom had also heard her helper's heavy tread. "Trevor?" Her tone sounded querulous. I hoped she wouldn't rat me out when Trevor arrived with the booze.

"I'm here, Mrs. Burgess." Trevor glided through the door then rounded the bed and settled a large silver tray, complete with china teapot and a matching dainty cup, on the small table to my right. He circled back around the bed to straighten the covers. I reached out and touched the ceramic belly of the pot: cold as river water. My guess was right – no hot tea steamed inside, the pot was there to camouflage her vodka.

Trevor smoothed the bedspread then helped Mom sit up and fluffed her pillow. When he got her resettled, he stared at my hand on the teapot then glared. "Mrs. Burgess, Miranda has to leave now. She's driving back to Los Angeles, you know."

"Oh?" My mother's gaze remained fixed on the tea pot.

"Yes. She told me she could only stay a couple minutes."

I met his glare with a smile. "Pushing me out the door? I'm shocked, Trevor. That's not up to your usual polite standards. I'll be on my way in a minute. Mom was about to answer a question for me." I picked up the teapot, cradling it in my lap. "You got an answer for me, Mom?"

"Miranda." Mom once again struggled to sit up. When she spoke, her voice sounded surprisingly strong. "Give me my teapot."

"Not until you give me a name."

Trevor swiftly rearranged the pillows so Mom could recline against them. "Here you go Mrs. Burgess. Is that better?"

"Thank you." She patted his cheek.

Ick. Was something going on between the two of them? We buried Dad two days ago.

Did Trevor call her by her first name when they were alone or call her Mrs. Burgess – or worse, Madam? – as she caressed more than his cheek? I shuddered. "Look, Mom, I want a name. I'm not asking for the how and the why. Only the who."

"Trevor, please escort my daughter out of the house." She smiled at him and clasped her hands in front of her chest.

I thought I might puke.

Trevor nodded then stared at me. "You've got until I walk around the bed. Then I'm taking that tea pot and leading you down the stairs by your ear."

I looked from Trevor to my mother. "Mom. Please. I already know it's not Dad. So, what do you think will happen if you tell me?"

She turned again to look at me. "You'll make trouble. Like you always do."

Trevor rounded the foot of the bed. I stood, still holding the teapot. "Fine. I'm out of here. I don't need a personal escort." I glanced at Trevor's frown and, once again, swerved away from the high road. I turned and hurled the china teapot at the wall. It smacked the wallpaper and broke into three large pieces, the contents splashing both the wall and carpet. The astringent smell of alcohol filled the air as I backed away from the mess. When I looked at Trevor his face was mottled red.

"I'll escort your daughter out now, Mrs. Burgess," he said through clenched teeth, "then bring you a fresh pot of tea."

I winced when he gripped my shoulder. He wrenched my arm then led me out of the room. I gave a backward glance at my mother. She smiled at me, the light of triumph in her eyes. I wouldn't be getting an invite to come back anytime soon. Trevor released me at the door to the blue room, and scrutinized every move as I gathered my few belongings. Once back in the hall, he gripped my arm again then dragged me down the staircase.

"You can let go now, Trev. I'm leaving."

"Bet your ass you are."

"Cab," I said when we reached the bottom of the stairs.

"What?"

"I need to call a cab."

"How is that my problem?"

"If I don't get to call a cab, I'll sit on your front porch all day. You want that?"

"No wonder your mother doesn't want anything to do with you." He pulled me across the entryway to the study door.

I resisted the urge to ask him if she actually said that. It was one thing to suspect your mother felt that way, but another to find out she had discussed the matter at length with her butler-cum-possible-lover. Trevor pushed me toward my father's desk then waited, arms crossed over his barrel chest. From memory, I dialed the cab company's number, while I searched for the phone book. It sat in the bottom right hand drawer, same as always. I leafed through the thin pages.

Before I reached the listings for car rental firms, Trevor held out his hand in front of me, palm up.

I looked down and realized I had picked up Dad's gold Cross pen. I handed it over. "You want to check my pockets for ashtrays and towels, too?" I said.

"Don't tempt me."

I didn't need the pen. Once I found a suitable listing, I made a mental note of the address and returned the book to its place in the desk drawer. As soon as I completed my call to the cab company, Trevor once more grabbed my upper arm and led me back across the entryway to the front door. His shove propelled me out onto the porch.

As he started to shut the door, I said, "You know, Trev. I am sorry." The door stopped midway to closing. Trevor frowned at me through the opening. "I thought that teapot would make a much bigger mess. I should've thrown it at the window." No surprise he slammed the door in my face.

Pulse racing, I sat and waited under the porte cochere for my cab. My hopes of shoring up my relationship with Mom were in ruins. I yanked at a curl. Why couldn't I keep my mouth shut and get along with her?

The driver dropped me in front of Roger's Rentals. The place looked pretty much like what I expected; I had selected the listing for its advertised bargain basement prices, not its ambiance. Located near the 101 Freeway, it consisted of a low-slung bungalow attached to a small parking lot. Both the bungalow and lot looked like they had seen better times, though probably not in the last decade. Beige chunks of stucco had fallen off the building leaving bare patches, as if some form of industrial leprosy attacked the structure. The asphalt lot had chasm-like cracks. Roger had seen better days as well – at least I hoped they'd been better. The comb over he sported had broken free and long greasy strands drooped down the back of his head rather than across his bald pate. He looked like he had outgrown his gabardine trousers at some point in the distant past, the brown pant legs showing off a good two inches of white sock between the cuff and his tennis shoes. A large asterisk of sweat darkened the back of his blue polo shirt.

Roger pointed at the small green hatchback, the closest of the five cars on the lot. "Over here, we got a 1972 Ford Pinto. You're looking at a 1.6-liter engine with seventy-five horsepower. Gets great gas mileage and's got plenty of storage space in the back. Real easy to park. Lots of my customers appreciate that feature."

From the dents and dings in all the vehicles, I wondered how these customers showed that appreciation; it sure wasn't by carefully parking any of Roger's cars.

"Now, the next car's a real beaut." He led me to the boxy maroon vehicle beside the Pinto. "A genuine classic. The 1986 Cadillac Seville. Costs a bit more to rent and a bit more to tank up, but you get yourself a roomier ride. If you're carrying passengers, this is the way to go." He ran a thick hand along the scratched trunk top. "Now, I know what you're thinking." He wagged a finger at me.

Doubtful. But I held my tongue.

"Styling's a bit bland, but it's a real sweet ride."

When I didn't respond, he led me to the next car. The sun had broken through the usual morning fog and was warming my shoulders. I paused to enjoy the sensation. After Trevor had slammed the door on me at Mom's, a chill crept inside me that I hadn't yet shook.

"Then you got your Festiva. You look like a Festiva gal. Am I right?"

I pulled myself together and focused where Roger was pointing.

"This baby's a 1989, got a 1.3-liter, four-cylinder engine. Fuel injected. Gets great gas mileage. Not to mention the paint job. That's a custom job. You don't normally see this color."

"I imagine not." The piss-yellow hatchback looked like some type of noxious garden pest and the fuzzy gold cover encasing the steering wheel looked like a dying crop circle.

"No siree. Very special that is. Now, the hatch don't open, so if you plan on carrying a lot of stuff, you got to put your cargo in through the back seat."

"What about the other two?" I pointed toward the Volkswagen Golf and the Chevy Nova parked a few yards away.

Roger squinted at the remaining cars then gave a hearty sounding laugh. "Those are out of rotation right now."

I raised an eyebrow, but Roger didn't elaborate. I suspected 'rotation' acted as Roger-speak for a car that ran.

I chose the Festiva. Even with its cracked vinyl seats and a scent that reminded me of a dentist's office, it looked like the best option. The car would get good gas mileage and not explode if I got rear ended. Plus the price fit my budget.

The first part of my plan – find affordable transportation – was complete. But part two – locate the Elf – promised to be more of a challenge. I had to find him without giving the Elf a chance to take control of the situation. This time I'd be the one who got to pick the time and place we made contact. Since our first encounter took place at The Deuce, that seemed as good a place as any to begin   my   search.

When I entered, it took a moment for my eyes to adjust to the dim interior. The narrow-shouldered bartender from my previous visit stood behind the bar. I settled on an open stool then waited for him to make his way to me. Besides me, there were eight other patrons drinking their lunches. The click of pool balls ricocheting mixed with a Huey Lewis song playing in the background. In our previous encounter, the bartender hadn't come across as the friendliest guy in the world, but maybe he'd be willing to answer questions for a paying customer.

He stopped opposite me and raised his bushy eyebrows, his cheerful parrot-patterned shirt at odds with his grumpy expression.

"Diet Coke," I said.

He walked away without acknowledging my order. When the bartender came back, he plunked a frosty glass in front of me, managing to not spill a drop in spite of his apparent carelessness. He started to turn away.

"Wait." Not quite the way I had envisioned things going. He faced me and raised his eyebrows again. "How much do I owe you?"

"Two fifty."

"Here." I handed him a twenty. "Keep the change."

He eyed the bill then returned his gaze to me. "Gee. I can retire now."

Off to a great start. "Anyone ever tell you you're a charming devil?"

"All the time. Now whaddya want?"

The jig was up. "The $17.50 tip gave me away?"

"Yeah." He crossed his arms over his pigeon chest.

"I'm looking for someone. Tall guy named Sean? Irish accent. He was here Saturday night. Served me my drinks."

"Look, if the guy took something of yours or you got a bone to pick with him, that's nothing to do with me or the bar."

"I'm not... It's not like that. When is he scheduled to work again?"

"He don't work here."

"He quit?"

"Nah, he never worked here."

"But he brought me my drinks."

The bartender shrugged.

"Wait a minute." I leaned forward, pulse racing. "You said he never worked here. You know who I'm talking about."

He looked away, toward the far end of the bar. "Never said I knew the guy."

"Yeah, you did. If you didn't know him, you would've said something like, 'No one matching that description's ever worked here.' But you spoke like you know the guy. So, if he doesn't work here, why'd he serve me my drinks the other night?"

The bartender frowned but didn't answer.

"Fine. You the owner here?"

"Nah."

"Didn't think so. I'm going to contact the owner, tell him you let some guy deliver drinks to my table and the guy slipped something in one of them. And that I plan to sue." The bartender's Adam's apple bobbed as he gulped. "Or, you can tell me the guy's name, why he was here, and where he works. Do that and I go away."

"Bitch."

"When necessary."

The bartender shook his head then made a quick circuit of the room with his hard stare. He took a step forward and dropped his gaze. "I don't know the guy's last name. But I do know he's connected. And violent. He came into the place right after you. Gave me fifty bucks to let him be your waiter. When a guy like that asks nice, you always say 'yes.'"

"Who's he work for?"

The bartender's eyes searched the room again before he spoke. "The guy... Dammit." He rubbed the back of his head before continuing. "The guy he works for runs all the drugs in the area. I shouldn't be telling you this."

"I won't tell anyone."

"You do, it's your funeral. You don't wanna mess with this guy. Trust me on that. He's..." The bartender scanned the room one more time then sighed. "The guy he works for, his name's Will Williamson. But, everyone calls him Billy."

My pulse drummed inside my ears.

Billy.

Seventeen

Ten years ago the story of the Orwell Massacre loomed huge, getting coverage even in Hollywood-centric L.A. At the time, I didn't have the stomach to read the stories in full. But each day I scanned the papers for the Orwell Massacre, avoiding the pictures looming large above the fold, skipping the gory details and skimming for anything that could identify me. I looked for the words 'unknown young woman' or worse, my actual name. And I hunted for news about Billy. Had his body been identified? Did his father know he had lost his remaining son? In all my timid searches, I never saw anything about him in print – no mention of Billy Bang or his real name: William Williamson.

Huddled in the Festiva, clutching the steering wheel's fuzzy cover, I breathed through my mouth to avoid the 'eau de sweat sock' coming from the upholstery as the day warmed. I didn't need anything else twisting at my gut while my head whirled with possibilities. Billy faked his death? The Elf had claimed he was following someone's orders. That he wanted to take me to see a man. The bartender at The Deuce said the Elf worked for a man named Will Williamson.

Who went by the name Billy. No matter how many times and ways I tried to rearrange these scraps, I kept winding up with the same result.

Ten years ago, I thought I found Billy's decapitated body. For ten years his body-less head haunted my nightmares. Was it all a lie? Was he alive?

But why pretend to die?

Maybe Billy had gotten into trouble dealing drugs and had to disappear? That would explain the thousands of dollars I found tucked inside the coffee can in our room. But if he was forced to go underground, why not take me with him?

The teenage me couldn't have come up with a credible answer to that question. But the twenty-seven-year-old me could: Though I had loved Billy with all my heart, he hadn't loved me back. Fifteen and stupid when I met him, and sixteen and stupid when I moved in with him. I lifted wallets, gave him the money I scored, and was his lover. All in all, not a bad deal for a part-time musician and small-time drug dealer.

Oh God. Did the money I stole give him the scratch he needed to buy his way up the drug ladder? Give him the means of getting in over his head?

Back in high school, my Creative Writing teacher used to tell us to focus on what we knew. I knew Billy was inside the house with me on the night of the murders. That much was certain. If he wasn't dead, that meant he either killed those people or was complicit in the murders. Or abducted by aliens – and I didn't believe in aliens. My stomach knotted tighter at the thought, but Billy had to be involved. How else had that dead body ended up wearing his clothes? Did Billy cut off the poor man's head and hands? Did he shoot and stab the women I found, including the one whose stomach had been cut open? Did he knife the little boy, too? Leave him bleeding to death in his Spiderman jammies?

I wrapped my arms across my chest and rocked back and forth in the saggy bucket seat.

The first couple Novembers after the murders, around the anniversary of their discovery, newspapers and TV stations had dredged up the past and replayed the gory details of the killings. At least I always assumed they gave the gory details. But I didn't know for sure since I had avoided them all – the same way I avoided all true crime stories. Despite the fact that I woke up inside the murder house, there remained a lot I didn't know about what happened. That I didn't want to know.

But now, I needed to remove my blinders.

The closest parking spot I could find to the Mill Valley Library was three blocks away on a residential street. The sun's rays cut between pine branches, but the air temperature in the shadows still held an edge. I rooted in my bag and grabbed a long-sleeve flannel shirt. My hand grazed the manila envelope holding my birth certificate. I pulled out the stiff packet and stared. A mix of anger and sadness churned and I wondered if the 'unknown' printed under 'Father' was the sole answer I'd get.

Though I possessed no crystal ball for predicting my mother's behavior, I felt pretty sure I wasn't going to get any more chances to talk to her about my parentage – or any other topic – for a long time. I turned the envelope upside down and shook out the birth certificate. Was I probing this wound to delay learning more about the killings? Probably. I needed to shunt the father question to the backburner. But I hung on to the sheet, staring at the gray typeface. In time, Mom might come around. Or maybe, once I sorted through this situation with the Elf, I could dig a little, discover who Mom's friends were twenty-seven years ago. Someone besides her might have the answer. Though I couldn't assume my birth father knew about me, Mom must've had a confidante. Or maybe someone in her circle figured out about the pregnancy. I returned the certificate to the envelope then noticed a small square of note paper in my lap.

The paper felt brittle. When I unfolded it, small chips crumbled free from the worn crease. Inside, my father's precise penmanship covered the page.

Miranda,

I've revised my last will and testament. As much as I hate planning for a time when I won't be here among the living, I must have everything organized for your mother's sake. When you read this note, you'll have already learned of my decision to limit your inheritance. I think you'll understand my motives. But I want you to know that I'm impressed with the changes you've made in your life. I suspect you'll resent me, but I hired a private investigator to check up on you. He was able to track you down from the return address on the cards you sent — in spite of you changing your last name. I can't deny that your shedding my last name hurt. But, considering everything between us, I know I have no right to lodge a complaint.

From what I understand, you're living the type of life that would make any parent proud. However, as you know, I'm a cautious man and I worry that you might revert to your earlier problematic behavior. To that end, I have counseled your mother to leave you whatever sum she feels you capable of handling when she passes on. Of course, if she has predeceased me and you are reading this letter, that means I have found your behavior wanting and haven't seen fit to revise my will.

I want you to know that I have considered the pros and cons of giving you the enclosed document. Difficult though you may find the information, I still believe you are entitled to it. Your mother doesn't agree. I regret that I can't give you the full story, as I don't have all the answers. For many years, I assumed you were the result of a liaison with the man who was your mother's beau before we married. I think I can, with a strong sense of fair play, say that Drew was a selfish spoiled boy. Your mother needed a man who could provide for her. Though his family's wealth was substantial, his character wasn't. It didn't surprise me that he left her in such an unfortunate condition. Because of my assumptions, for many years my regard for him was more reduced than he deserved, much to my later regret. Over time, circumstances occurred which made me question this assumption, then a chance comment by your mother forced me realize I had been wrong about Drew.

Your mother was quite inebriated when she told me it was no wonder she'd preferred making love to Hamilton when she was young. She passed out shortly after making that statement and refused to say more the next day – in spite of my best efforts. You know how stubborn your mother can be. Over the years, she has remained adamant in her refusal to talk about this topic. I tried to make delicate inquiries among her friends. I even hired a private investigator (the one I later used to check on you), but never found a Hamilton in her life.

I should have anticipated the tendencies you exhibited as a teenager, since your mother's drinking was already an issue between us. Yet I failed to do so. I suspect your mother's beauty blinded me to the nature of her problem – as well as to the fact that her tendencies might be passed on. Or maybe it was my own upbringing that hampered my ability to fully perceive the situation. In some ways I led a sheltered life, my parents were teetotalers in a world where only men drank hard alcohol. Had we raised you now, I would have handled things in a different way. But when you were growing up, admitting your family had a problem – admitting this problem to the world – carried a heavy stigma. Nowadays I would place you and your mother both into counseling or a rehab center. I suspect that today, rehab is seen as a status symbol. But I failed you in my parenting and only saw you as wild and irresponsible.

I trust your mother – if she's still alive – will give you the rest of the story of your parentage. I wish I could tell you who started you on your journey to life. But I hope you will always think of me as your father. Although we have had our differences and I haven't always

approved of how you lived your life, you
have always been and will always be my
daughter.
　　Love,
　　Dad

Tears coursed down my face. I used my
flannel shirt to wipe my runny nose. My
insides felt like they had gone around several
times in a blender. On liquefy. Dad had
learned about the changes I made in my life.
Through a private detective, but still, he
knew.

Yet he chose not to return my calls.

The letter was dated July 3, 1990. For
four years after writing those words, he
continued to refuse my attempts at contact. I
stared at the 'Love, Dad' and shook my head.
I would never understand the choices he
made, as he – had he known them all –
wouldn't have understood mine.

"I love you, too."

After staring with blurry eyes through the
windscreen for several minutes, I looked at
my father's letter again. At least Hamilton
wasn't a common name like Smith. But if my
dad's detective couldn't locate anyone by that
name, what were the odds I could? My father
had already tried and failed to find the man,
did I want to waste my efforts on what could
end up a futile search?

Yes. But now wasn't the time.

I sighed and climbed out of the car. My

birth father's identity could wait. The Elf, Billy Bang and the Orwell Massacre couldn't. Not anymore.

Eighteen

After the reference librarian told me they had upgraded from microfiche to microfilm two months earlier, she frowned and walked me to a computer carrel. "Progress." The statuesque woman sniffed as though the word itself gave off a suspect odor. "People trot the word out like it's a synonym for labor-saving. But whose labor? They never stop to think about all the work they're creating with their 'improvements.' First we had to requisition new storage cabinets. Spending money which could've been used for books. Then we had to remove the old materials from the collection and catalogue the new items. Not to mention shelving everything. It's not like changing the medium improves the quality of the information."

I gave a non-committal "Hmm" and watched her load the machine. She would look attractive, with her pale eyes and high cheekbones, if she took the time to bleach her Chaplin-esque moustache. Once she appeared confident I could handle the equipment, she gave a final frown then left me to my research.

Two hours later, I still stared at the small screen, scanning microfilmed articles about the Orwell Massacre. Taken one-by-one the stories remained heart-breaking. Read in sequence, they turned my stomach.

Back in November, 1984 – before the Massacre – I had dropped out of school. My father had kicked me out six months earlier and Billy invited me to move in with him. With nothing more than the clothes on my back, I'd made myself at home in his one-room apartment in San Francisco. Though I didn't miss any of my classmates – or all the rules at school – I discovered I missed learning. To fill the void, I became a biweekly visitor to the local branch of the San Francisco public library, checking out as many books as they would lend me. While Billy hung out with his band or peddled pot and pills, I curled on our mattress and read. For hours on end, I wrapped myself in a cocoon of words, drinking in the various characters' lives and adventures while ignoring my own life story.

In November 1984, I read George Orwell's *1984*. With the year counting down to its conclusion, it seemed like a timely thing to do. After the murders, when the newspapers labeled the killings the Orwell Massacre, fear had pooled in the pit of my stomach. Had I left my library book in that blood-soaked house? Was that why the murders carried that name?

For ten years, I had no answer. But as I read the microfilmed news stories from the local paper, I found out.

Six found dead in brutal slaying

A day into the investigation of a brutal slaying in the sleepy town of Mill Valley, police have more questions than answers. Mill Valley Police say the bodies of five adults and one child were found in an upscale home outside the small town. Two of the victims were beheaded, the remaining four victims died from a combination of gunshot and stab wounds. No murder weapon has been found.

Once a quaint gathering spot for hippies, the peaceful town has been ripped apart by the horror in its midst. It is rumored that drugs may have been a factor in the murders. According to sources close to the investigation, the killings were committed sometime in the preceding week. Investigators are optimistic that the medical examiner will be able to narrow the time frame for this grisly crime. Three women, two men and one child were all found dead at the scene. The identities of the victims have been withheld pending notification of their next of kin.

Locals in this quiet community are shocked at the vicious nature of the slayings. "Who'd want to kill a little boy like that? Whoever did it, we're going to find the sicko," Officer George Willis said. "I've never seen nothing like that before. And I hope I never do again." A ten-year veteran of the police department, Officer Willis was first on the scene after a postal carrier on his route reported a suspicious odor coming from the house.

Novel plays key role in murders

George Orwell's novel, *1984*, may have been the inspiration behind the killings, according to a source who asked to remain anonymous. Slogans from the novel were scrawled across the walls in one of the rooms where the victims' bodies were discovered. Officials would not comment upon the meaning of the quotations found at the crime scene.

Published in 1949, the novel *1984* describes a nightmarish vision of the future, with the tentacles of government invading the lives of private citizens.

My skin tingled. I rubbed my face and stood. After taking several slow deep breaths I went to the card catalogue, opened one of the center drawers, and started riffling through the titles. When I found what I wanted, I noted the Dewey decimal numbers, then hurried to the bookshelves. I stared at the spines, reluctant to pull down the first volume. In the end, I selected three books on the Massacre and brought them to my carrel. In addition to the printed text, these chronicles of my past included photographs. The first glossy page I came to showed the three murdered adults I had found in the living room. In the grainy reproductions, their blood appeared black. The broken bodies of the victims looked like they had been caught in an oil slick. Next came photographs of the walls. Below a series of four photos, one caption noted the messages were written in the victims' blood. I didn't remember seeing any words scrawled on the wall. How had I not seen that? When I closed my eyes and tried to recall that awful morning, I only saw the bodies. Had shock at the sight of the bloody corpses blinded me to the rest of the room? I read the words scrawled on the wall and bile rose in my throat: 'Death to Big Brother,' 'Destroy Minitrue,' and 'Room 101 is Here.'

Though my memory for the written word was usually exact, seeing these photos jarred me. Unsure if I could trust my brain when it came to this subject, I made a beeline for the library's fiction section. Midway along the O's, I found the book. Not the spine-broken paperback I had carted to underground clubs and rehearsal spaces. A glossy oversized paperback version, the cover still crisp and clean. Back in '84, whenever I could get Billy to sit and listen, I had told him about the world Orwell created. About Minitrue. About Big Brother. About Room 101. I thumbed through the crisp pages, checking to see if I remembered the story with accuracy. I wondered if Billy had used what I told him about Orwell's masterpiece to set a false trail for the police. Or to make me look guilty.

My fingers felt like they had been dipped in ice water. I rested the book face up on an open length of shelf as I tried to rub away the chill. But the cold had seeped too deep inside to shake off.

For weeks after that dreadful morning, in addition to the nightmares, upset stomach and constant fear I lived with – I had worried about that other library book. I'd imagined its cracked and curling husk sealed away in an evidence bag in the Mill Valley Police Department, my fingerprints dotting every page. I still wondered if the book wound up there.

While walking back to my carrel, I skimmed pages. After I set the book on the work station's fake wood surface, I stared at the computer screen. "Jesus, Billy. Why?" A sigh came from the adjacent carrel. I leaned back. The gaunt man at the next cubby frowned at me. Right. The library was a no talking zone. Keeping my mouth shut was probably for the best – since a part of me wanted to start screaming and never stop.

I picked up one of the three true crime books from the stack, *Murder in Mill Valley,* and flipped back to the photos. With a shudder, I set the book aside and looked again at the decade-old newspaper article.

The reporter must have read the Cliff's Notes version of *1984*. He wasn't wrong about the story – in the broad strokes. But he didn't get the meat of the material. I thumbed through the novel as I reviewed the story line: Winston Smith gets tricked by an undercover member of the Thought Police and is lured into reading a treatise on the true nature of the totalitarian superstate where he lived. What he learns ends up drawing Smith to the ideals of The Brotherhood – a vast underground anti-party fellowship.

I closed my eyes to better picture the story's details. Along with the threat of arrest and torture, Big Brother controlled the populace with twenty-four hour-a-day surveillance. Throughout the bitter tale, war raged between ever-changing alliances of superstates. But the war wasn't fought with the goal of winning. The government knew no one would win and the purpose of battle was to keep people busy, use the fruits of their labor for the war machine, destroy any surplus industrial production, and prevent a rise in the standard of living. The superstates' collective goal was to keep the people economically suppressed. An impoverished, desperate people made for a malleable people.

When I first read the story, I was an impoverished person. Pretty damn malleable, too. Maybe that was why the story angered me. The worst part came when Smith received his punishment. Miniluv, the ministry which identified, monitored, arrested and tortured dissidents – both real and imagined – locked up Smith then used his own nightmare to torture him. Equal parts disturbed and fascinated by this twist, I hadn't been able to stop reading. When I reached the final page, I had closed my eyes and re-read the story from start to finish inside my head. I remembered how I stared at the water-stained ceiling of our room as I tried to imagine how it would feel to live in a world that waged war all the time while people scurried like cockroaches, hoping to escape the ever-present scrutiny of Big Brother. I tried to picture how I would cope with the deepest horror within the novel: Room 101, the torture chamber. When confronted by his own nightmare of having his face eaten by rats, Smith chose to save himself, pleading that his lover's face be gnawed off instead.

Stoned and sprawled on our mattress, I'd spent hours pondering whether I might do any better, always fearing I would act as weak as Smith.

In the end, Miniluv won. The torturers forced Smith to betray the one person he loved, breaking Smith's spirit. The book contained the stuff of nightmares often found in sci-fi. But in this case, the nightmare had spilled out from the well-thumbed pages of my paperback to become the Orwell Massacre.

Nineteen

After another twenty minutes reading microfilmed newspaper stories and looking at pictures of the dead, I needed a break. I walked to one of the armchairs placed in a semicircle around the library's large fireplace, but didn't sit. The artificially cozy atmosphere felt oppressive. I took a sip of water from the fountain, stretched and headed back to the carrel. Once seated, I tried to keep my attention on the screen, but I felt saturated with the story. The knots in my stomach tightened another notch. Even after reading dozens of articles, I still couldn't dredge up any new memories. The night remained a blank. I pushed my chair away from the computer. I couldn't face looking at another photo or reading another word about the murders.

Fresh air. That's what I needed. I turned off the screen, collected my materials then returned the microfilm to the front desk before grabbing my bag. Outside on the broad front patio of the library, the sky had darkened to night and a steady breeze rustled the needles of the surrounding redwoods. Somewhere in the tree canopy, an owl hooted. I breathed the dusty scent of olive trees and pine wafting by and wondered what to do next. The bench in front of the building was empty. I sat on the cool pearl granite to think.

Did I know anything about Billy? Anything he hadn't told me himself? Anything I could prove was true? He was a musician, true. He sold pills and pot for a living, also true. But I couldn't say much else about him with certainty. Before the Massacre, I spent most my time stoned, and all the time starry-eyed with love. I had trailed after Billy, no questions asked. The only times we argued were when I shared my worries about his safety dealing drugs. He must have seen me as an easy meal ticket. But when I dug in and started to give him a hard time about pushing coke and heroin, maybe he started to see me as millstone. Something he felt happy to unload.

My hands twitched and heat roared across my face – in spite of the cooling evening. I needed to move. I began walking down the hill, away from the rental car. Once I calmed a bit, I could trust myself behind the wheel. This wasn't the time to do something stupid. Or rather, something else stupid. I had already done enough foolish things in my life.

If Billy was the man looking for me, I wanted that meeting to take place.

My nails dug into my palms. I unclenched my fists and shook out my hands. I wanted to confront Billy, but wasn't about to trust his or the Elf's good intentions to make that happen. I needed to be the one in control. If Billy was behind the Orwell Massacre, he deserved payback. Payback for those six dead people. Payback for the years of nightmares I suffered on his behalf. Payback for the guilt, the grief. He wasn't going to get away with this.

The Elf remained the strongest lead to Billy. But he was dangerous. A whole flock of butterflies fluttered around the knots in my stomach each time I pictured the Elf. Okay, I was afraid. Good. Fear would keep me cautious. But I couldn't let fear drive me. There'd be no running away this time. No one would force me to abandon my new life. I wasn't going to change everything again for a man who never loved me. Billy got to ruin my life once – that was enough.

The first thing I needed to do was find the Elf and follow him, to trail him back to Billy. The Deuce was the one connection I had to him. I turned around and began striding up the hill. Ten minutes later, I reached my car and settled behind the fuzzy gold steering wheel. Warm from the walk, I unrolled the window. Billy was alive and probably a murderer. He'd left me in that house to wake and find those bodies. To find his 'body.' To feel haunted and guilt-ridden the rest of my life.

Or maybe I wasn't supposed to wake up. At least not before the bodies were found. I would've made a hell of a suspect.

The night air was already starting to whisk away my body heat – or maybe the chill was coming from inside me. I rummaged through my bag for another layer to pull on. My hand brushed the cool plastic case of one of the cassettes my father saved for me. Perception and memory – much of what I thought was true had ended up dead wrong. Just because I could recite entire passages from *1984* didn't mean I remembered the details of my life with the same accuracy. Life was too complex for that. In some ways I was like my neighbor, Mrs. Stegman, unaware of the crucial missing bits of my past. Did she constantly feel betrayed by her brain? Was every day a fight to fit together the pieces of a world she no longer recognized? I took a deep breath, snagged the sweatshirt from my bag then dragged it on over my head.

The car's starter grated when I turned the key. After giving the motor a rest, I gritted my teeth and tried again. With a phlegmy rattle, the engine turned over. Apparently the Festiva didn't like the cold night air. After I made a U-turn, I drove through the center of town. The lights inside the Mill Valley Inn glowed a soft gold, promising warmth and comfort to those who could afford it. But no place was safe. The Elf had managed to dent even the Inn's reputation.

At the intersection of Throckmorton and Miller I turned right, heading toward The Deuce. I found a space in the small parking lot a few yards down from the bar, then tried to get comfortable for a long wait. My plan remained amorphous. If the Elf showed up, I'd follow him when he left. A sad strategy. But, since I didn't have any other bright ideas at the moment, it seemed worth a try.

Time dragged. One hour inched its way to two. I shifted in the Festiva's saggy bucket seat, trying to keep my right leg from falling asleep. My strategy of sitting out here in the dark seemed sketchier with each passing moment. But having no backup plan at the ready, I stayed put. While I watched the cars zip along Miller, my thoughts drifted back to my father's letter. Though he at first suspected someone named Drew was my biological father, a single insult from Mom changed his mind. I wondered if more lay behind his change of heart. Because she preferred sex with the man Hamilton, did that really blow this Drew guy out of the running as a sperm donor? Who was Drew? Even if he didn't knock up my mom, he might possess some clue as to the identity of my birth father. Was Drew a first or a last name?

With a start, I jerked awake. Uh-oh. I rubbed my eyes then shook out my arms and legs. A stake out became more than pointless if I couldn't stay awake. Too dark to read the clock on the building across the way, I raised my left wrist to check the time and remembered I had given my watch to Janelle. It felt like it was close to 11 p.m. I yawned. Even if my vigil didn't work out, it wasn't like I had somewhere else to be.

To keep alert, I reviewed what I knew about the mystery of my parentage. Not the most inspiring activity, but the best I had. Drew wasn't a common name. But it rang a bell. Didn't I meet a friend of my parents by that name? When I was in high school. No, not a friend of theirs, a friend of Mom's. The guy had something to do with the San Francisco Opera. I pictured Dad talking about the guy and his support of the arts. Though as I remembered my father's voice, when he said 'the arts,' the T and A definitely sounded capitalized – and not in a good way. I closed my eyes and tried to picture the scene. My parents had just come home after an evening out in the city. Mom wore an ankle-length skirt that swished when she moved. Even at the end of the day, her hair blond hair fell ripple-free, gently curling under at chin level. Dad wore a tuxedo but had loosened his tie. He stood with his back to the empty fireplace. Mom poured a drink from the sideboard then sat on the settee a few feet away, her face rosy. At the time I assumed her face had been reddened from the chill night air, but now realized she was probably already well lubricated before drinking her glass of cognac. I had been out in the backyard getting high when I heard the car crunch up the drive and had scurried inside as the key sounded in the front door lock. Neither seemed to notice my red eyes nor the dope-scent clinging to my hair and clothes.

Frozen in the doorway to the study, I listened while Dad called Mom a sycophant. "You always do that, dear," he said, the 'dear' sounding like a stone hitting glass. "Kiss up to the people who have more money than we do. Not a very becoming trait. Quite unattractive really." Mom sucked down the contents of her glass, staring past Dad at the dark place where a fire should have crackled. "But you get worse with Drew. You can't seem to stop simpering when he's around, can you? Him and his patronage of The Arts. You made a spectacle of yourself tonight. Talking about the opera like you actually attend. Who were you kidding? I'm sure the man knows you can't tell an aria from an etude." At that point, still unnoticed, I rolled my eyes and stalked off, as uninterested in the lives of my parents as they acted about mine. I didn't know what, if anything, Mom had said in response.

Wasn't there a Drew Cross? Some sort of big wheel and behind-the-scenes influence in local politics. A stalwart supporter of the arts. The Cross family was one of San Francisco's oldest and wealthiest families. Landowners, developers, shipping magnates, at one time the Cross family had owned most of San Francisco and the surrounding countryside.

Could Drew Cross be the man Dad at one time pegged as my biological father?

I wished the library was still open so I could check Drew Cross's age to see if he and Mom were contemporaries, making him a possibility for her one-time love interest. While I chewed this idea, the door to The Deuce opened. The Elf exited.

Whoa. He must have arrived after I nodded off. I ducked, held my breath and peered through the arc of the steering wheel. He walked with a limp and appeared to hold himself with care. I assumed his balls still throbbed where I stabbed him.

Good. I liked the thought of pain making life hard for the Elf.

He stopped by a dark Carman Ghia and unlocked the driver's side door. Though the lighting in the lot was poor, I could see he had trouble lowering himself into the compact sports car. I assumed the Carman Ghia wasn't a good vehicle choice when your balls were on the mend. When the Elf cranked his engine, I did the same. Again the Festiva sputtered and I cursed it as a rusting piece of crap. On my third try, the engine turned over and I pulled out of the lot. By now, the Elf was well ahead of me on Miller Street. I floored it. If I lost him now, who knew how many days might pass before he returned to The Deuce? The Festiva's engine sounded sluggish, but worked its way up to forty-five miles per hour. With the majority of the evening traffic traveling at the posted

194 | P a g e

thirty mile per hour speed limit, the Elf hadn't made much headway and I was able to gain on his distinctive car. At Throckmorton, the Carman Ghia veered right then took a left onto Blithedale. Soon we climbed out of the basin and north into the empty land between the towns of Mill Valley and Corte Madera.

I chewed my lower lip as we moved away from the lights of civilization. Sweat from my palms dampened the fuzzy steering wheel cover and it started to feel like I was gripping a soggy cattail. I slowed and hung back farther. Following the Elf into the inky countryside didn't give me a good feeling. Granted, he didn't know I was behind him, but the idea still weirded me out. The road twisted deeper into the undeveloped hills. My gut tightened up again. No. He couldn't be going where I suspected. He wouldn't. There was no reason to go there. But at the familiar corner, the Elf turned left. With shaking hands, I turned, too. When his taillights disappeared around the next bend, I pulled over and cut the engine.

Oh God. I covered my mouth and stared at the dark incline of road. I hadn't bargained on coming back to the murder house in pursuit of the Elf and Billy. After my taxi ride here Saturday night, I thought I'd never return to this spot again. What the hell was the Elf up to?

The Festiva didn't have a dashboard clock, but I guessed the time as after midnight. Did I feel good about following a giant madman back to the scene of the Orwell Massacre? At this hour? And who ever really returned to the scene of the crime? Why had he come here of all places?

My thoughts scattered as bright headlights rounded the curve above. Blinded, I lifted my arm to shield my eyes. The headlights grew in size. The car was barreling straight at me. I cranked the key, but the Festiva only whined in response. Heart pounding, I tried again. The Festiva gave an anemic cough then died. I grabbed the latch of my seatbelt, but the mechanism wouldn't unfasten. I swore, gripped the wheel and closed my eyes against the coming impact.

The thundering jolt of metal ramming the Festiva's bumper rattled my teeth. My skull slammed against the head rest then bounced forward, my forehead smacking the steering wheel. I looked through tearing eyes at the furry gold cover, grateful it had softened the blow. The seatbelt latch stayed fastened, keeping me anchored in the bucket seat. My forehead sent a sharp message of pain to my brain. I reached up. My fingers touched hot stickiness. A coppery scent filled my nostrils. I stared at the bright red stain on my right hand. Shiny with blood, the skin of my hand felt heavy and thick. But head wounds bled a lot. The blood didn't necessarily mean anything. I did a quick inventory. Other than the sharp pain coming from my forehead, I was okay. Shaken up, but OK. I looked at the other vehicle now sitting perpendicular to mine.

What kind of maniac drove this fast on a dark winding road? The other car's engine still rumbled. Then the car began to back away. "No." I grabbed the door handle. No way this loser was going to take off without giving me his insurance information. The Festiva might be a piece of crap, but it was Roger's Rentals piece of crap. I wasn't taking the rap for this.

But the door wouldn't budge. My grip was clumsy and uncoordinated. I wasn't sure if the door wasn't working right or if it was me. I shook the handle anyway. No luck. I tried the seatbelt latch again. Still couldn't get that open either. My mouth felt dry. I looked at the other car. Ten yards away up the road, the vehicle stopped. My heartbeat ratcheted up another notch. I recognized the Elf's Carmen Ghia. "Oh no." I turned the key in the ignition. The now-familiar sputter sounded again. "Damn it." I said a small prayer then turned the key again. The engine coughed to life and the Festiva jolted forward. The Carmen Ghia started moving toward me. I floored the Festiva and jerked the wheel to the right, hoping to avoid another collision. The Festiva seemed to crawl as the distance between us narrowed.

Metal scraped metal, followed by another jolt. My bloody hands flew off the fur-covered steering wheel. When the car stopped spinning, it was facing downhill, but the motor still ran. I grabbed the wheel again and stomped on the accelerator, praying the engine held together long enough to get away from the Elf. And get me back to Mill Valley. Beyond that, I had desperation, not a plan. The motor skipped, but didn't die. I headed down the road, gas pedal pressed to the floor. One of the Festiva's headlights no longer worked and the other beam pointed cattywumpus toward the roadside, leaving the twisting route ahead buried in darkness. Something dripped into my eyes, blurring my vision. I wiped at my forehead and hoped the wetness was sweat not blood.

Headlights rounded a bend behind me in the distance. The Elf was on my tail. He didn't appear to be gaining on me. Maybe his car was damaged, too. I death-gripped the wheel around another sharp bend. Though I couldn't see much of the road, at least I knew the terrain. After the next turn, the road would straighten and I could give the car more gas. Not like that would do much good. Another quick peek into the rearview. The Elf was still behind me, but at least ten car-lengths back. A plume of sparks gushed from the right side of his vehicle, like his car was dragging something. I hoped it was a vital piece – like the engine.

After rounding the final bend, I slammed my foot on the gas and got the Festiva up to fifty miles per hour. The lights of downtown Mill Valley created a corona in the dark sky. If I could maintain the distance between me and the Elf, I had a chance of ditching him in the city. But did Mill Valley offer enough traffic to provide effective cover after midnight on a Monday night? Probably not. A lot had changed in the ten years since I left, but not that.

My arrival back in Mill Valley seemed much faster than the drive out to the murder house. Most of Mill Valley's streets meandered in closed circuits through the narrow tree-lined valley. The town's only other big through street – besides the one I was on – wasn't much better. Wider and a little less curvy, it still had a traffic circle to contend with. But it might be my best bet for getaway driving. But it was probably a prime route for the Elf, too. Under the sparse streetlights, I saw red handprints splotched the fleece steering wheel cover. Not wanting to give the Elf another opportunity to spill more of my blood, I turned off the Festiva's one functioning headlight then skidded around the next corner. After a short block, I cut right then took a quick left. The road behind me appeared dark, but I didn't slow. The Elf seemed crazy enough to drive without headlights, too. A scraping noise came from the Festiva's engine. The car wasn't long for this world. But I hoped like hell it held together until I lost the Elf.

The Festiva gave a throaty rattle then the engine plunged into silence. I cranked the steering wheel hard to the right and pumped the gas, hoping to get another couple miles out of the car. The Festiva didn't take the bait. I guided the car to an empty patch of curb where it rolled to a stop. I tried the engine again. Nothing. I had killed the Festiva. Or rather the Elf had. I hoped I could keep him from doing the same to me.

I checked the street in both directions. The car had stopped a few yards shy of Throckmorton. One of Mill Valley's main streets, Throckmorton bisected downtown and was one of the first major cross streets when you entered town. The Elf would come this way too. The door still wouldn't open, but I finally managed to get the seatbelt latch to release. I climbed across the passenger seat, leaving bloody handprints on the mustard-colored upholstery. My right leg got tangled in the strap of my bag and I kicked twice before getting free, knocking the bag's contents to the car floor. I scrambled out the other side, planted my feet on the curb and swayed. Leaning against the Festiva, it felt like a jackhammer was nearby chewing up the road, but the shaking came from me, not the street. My arms weren't doing much better than my legs. I held up both hands and watched them tremble before wrapping them across my chest.

Part of my brain screamed for me to pound on a nearby door and ask for help. But that meant cops and cops meant trouble. If I knew which way the Elf was heading, I could run in the opposite direction, find someplace safe to hide. Eyes wide, I stumbled along the dark sidewalk, watching for traffic on the cross street ahead. A dark car rumbled up Throckmorton, headlights off. I lurched into the trees edging the sidewalk and fell to my knees. Front right tire flat, the Carmen Ghia jounced up the hill on the wheel's rim. A metal piece dragged along the asphalt. It looked and sounded like the car's muffler was the source of the sparks I had spotted earlier. No question – this was the Elf. Mouth dry, I waited until he rounded the next bend then pushed up to my feet, broke into a jerky run and headed around the corner in the opposite direction. Once I settled into a rhythm, the comfort of running took over. I wasn't going to set any speed records, but the shakiness seemed to fade the longer I ran. When I reached Old Mill Park, I staggered across the rough ground to the wooded section farthest from the street. I hoped that once again my fifteen year advantage hiding out in Mill Valley would keep me safe.

Twenty

I crouched behind the gravity car. The sled-like shell made a solid shield. I peeked into the dense grove of trees separating the clearing from the street. Though built over a century before, the wooden car still felt sturdy. Maybe not surprising, considering it had been designed to survive an hour-long hurtle down the face of Mt. Tamalpais, making over two hundred turns on its way to the mountain's base.

My nerves jumped at the sound of a car engine grinding its way past the park. When the motor's growl grew distant, I let myself exhale. I straightened my complaining legs and stretched. Leaves crackled nearby. It sounded like something was pawing through the duff. Too small to be human. A raccoon? I hoped so. Just to be safe, I stepped up inside the gravity car.

In my haste to ditch the Festiva, I hadn't stopped to gather the contents of my overnight bag. If the street remained quiet for a few more minutes, that probably meant it was safe to make my way back to the car. Even if the damn engine still refused to start, I could at least get my stuff. But, if the Festiva was dead, that meant spending the night outdoors. This time of year, the daytime temps usually hit the mid-to high-seventies, but Mill Valley nights tended to lurk in the low-fifties. Not appealing, but still safer than staying at a hotel – at least after what the Elf did at the Inn. On the plus side, it wasn't the rainy season. If I did end up spending a night under the stars, I wanted all my extra layers. I could always sleep in the gravity car. The bench seats weren't cushy, but I'd be off the cold, hard ground.

While I waited for any sign that the Elf was still on my trail, my fingers grew numb. Grateful for my sweatshirt, I pulled the cuffs down over my hands then curled on the bench seat, tucking my knees inside the fleecy inner layer for more warmth. I pressed the ribbed sleeve cuff against the cut on my forehead to staunch the flow of blood. My whole body felt jarred and I was light-headed, but nothing seemed to be sprained or broken. The pain from the cut on my forehead remained minor. I could've gotten hurt much worse when the Elf rammed me. Good thing he was driving the Carmen Ghia and not that cavernous van.

The thick grove of trees blocked out the stars. The pine needles whispered in the wind. I stared up and remembered how much

I hated the feeling of being smothered by nature when I was a teen. Not that I didn't like trees and plants. I did – they ended up my stock in trade as an adult. But here in Mill Valley, nature seemed over the top. The trees blocked the sun, the clouds, the stars and the moon. When I grew up here, it felt like I was trapped in a stifling nature bubble.

A twig snapped. I froze and held my breath. A muffled crunch followed, the sound of pine needles giving under a stiff-soled shoe. This was no critter. I wasn't alone inside the grove. I pushed myself up and peeked over the seat back then spied a halo of light bobbing between the trunks, strafing the darkness beneath the sheltering trees. With my knees snarled inside my sweatshirt, it took me several panicky seconds to extract them. Once free, I slipped out of the car and crouched behind the wood frame, listening. Whoever held the flashlight was heading my way. I wanted the person to be someone besides the Elf, but couldn't think of a good reason for anybody else to be tromping through the trees at this hour.

I crawled toward the river, grateful for the cushiony layer of duff. The inky darkness gave cover, but also meant I needed to pick my path with care. The riverbed lay a good ten to twelve feet below the rest of the park and I didn't want to fall in. If I failed to find a place to hide before I reached the gorge, I could crawl over the edge onto the steep river bank. I bit back a cry as something sharp punctured my palm. After I pulled out a large thorn, I continued crawling toward the sound of churning water. Besides guiding me, the rushing river helped cover the sound of my movements. On the minus side, the water also masked any noise that might be coming from the Elf. I looked over my shoulder, saw the wavering light piercing the darkness to the north of my position. He was angling away from me. Good.

From the growing roar of the water, the brink had to be near. I kept low as I scurried on. My right hand missed the ground and I tipped forward. I jerked back on my haunches and caught my breath. Reaching out again, I felt the soft edge of the dropdown. Laying on my belly and hoping I didn't break my neck, I eased past the lip then dug my fingers and toes into the steep sides of the channel for purchase. With my body snugged against the bank and my eyes cresting the rim of land, I watched the Elf's beam. For a few more minutes, he continued searching to the north of my spot then the small circle of light turned. I ducked and began climbing down toward the moving water. On my next step, the soil crumbled and I slid. Dirt scraped my right cheek as my hands and feet scrabbled for a hold. Shy of the water, the riverbank softened again and I dug in hard, managing to stop my descent. I held my position, straining for any sound besides that of the water below.

This time of year, the waters ran swift,

but I wasn't worried about drowning if I fell in. My main concern remained the risk of an audible splash. If that didn't get the Elf's attention, then came the worry about hypothermia since snow melt fed the river. I molded my body to the shape of the gully, carved by the river during deep water season, and waited.

After what seemed like an hour, but probably lasted fifteen or twenty minutes, I forced trembling hands and feet to move again and scaled the steep incline. Shivering, I peeked over the edge, scouring the night-shrouded parkland for the Elf's flashlight. All remained dark. I hauled up onto flat land then stayed hunkered by the rim for several minutes. I breathed through my nose as my ears strained for any noise that shouldn't be there. Aside from the rushing river, the sole sound I heard was the rustle of pine boughs on the breeze. No sign of the Elf. My pulse slowed, but didn't return to normal. I crawled to the gravity car and climbed onto the bench seat. My teeth chattered. I tucked my knees and hands back inside my sweatshirt.

Even though the Elf had left Old Mill Park, that didn't mean he had abandoned his search. I wondered if he had found the Festiva. If he had, that would make a great place for the Elf to watch and wait for me. As cold as I was, hiding among the trees awhile longer before I tried to retrieve my belongings seemed like a good idea. I curled into a tight ball on the bench seat and tried to picture golden fingers of sunshine reaching out to warm me. The visualization exercise did nothing to thaw me; the night was definitely getting colder. I tried imagining Rob's strong arms circling me. My insides twisted. I hoped I hadn't ruined things with him before I left. If only I'd told him the truth the night he proposed.

No. It was better he didn't know. If I'd told him and it turned out he still wanted to marry me, Rob would've come to Mill Valley for Dad's funeral. And wound up in danger, too. I couldn't stand the thought of that. But, when I got out of this mess, I'd come clean and tell him about my past. I had to if I wanted any kind of future with him.

A shiver wracked my body. I gave up trying to imagine myself warm and stared ahead at the opposite side of the gravity car. Sheltering here seemed apt in a way. Back in the gravity car's heyday, no engines powered them. The combined force of the mountain's sharp slope plus the weight of the car and passengers pulled the vehicle to its final destination. It must have been an amazing feeling: speeding downward, the wind peppering your face. No fake rollercoaster safety there. A lone gravity man at the brake, ready to throw all his strength and weight against the lever if the car ran too hot or fast. In my teens, I could have used a gravity man to throw his weight against my destructive speed and slow me down. But, even if someone had been willing to try, I doubted they could have stopped me. Back then, I was too much of an adrenaline junkie, constantly searching for out-of-control situations to feed my need.

I rolled onto my right side, still shivering. Those early riders must have been cold, too. Maybe not this cold, but cold enough. My eyelids drooped and I jerked my head. I needed to stay awake, stay alert in case the Elf came back. The impenetrable darkness above combined with the wind-riffled sound of branches swaying, the hum like a distant lullaby. The pines in our backyard made that same sound when I was little. Which house was that? Right. The one we lived in the year I turned eight. I spent most of that summer playing games of Hide and Seek in the woods bordering the yard. Right about now I could use someone yelling "Olly olly oxen free." My eyes closed again.

When I awoke, sunlight pierced the canopy. Not a single nightmare had disturbed my slumber. My legs, arms, fingers and toes all tingled and felt cramped inside my sweatshirt. Uh-oh. The skin on my hands felt rough and strange. Did I damage my skin sleeping out in the chill night air? I pulled my hands and knees from their fleecy cocoon and examined my fingers. My stomach did a backflip. A mix of dirt and dried blood covered my palms. The sight stirred memories I didn't want to revisit. I probed my forehead and scalp and found a large tender spot above my hairline on the right. My neck muscles promised to ache for a few days, but there seemed to be no permanent damage from my run-in with the Elf.

Old Mill Park had a restroom by the small tot lot. From the angle of sunlight through the trees, I could tell it was early. The restrooms probably weren't yet unlocked. But, on the off-chance they were, I headed their way. Though I couldn't picture the Elf inconveniencing himself by lurking in the park all night, I used trees for cover as I made my way down to the tot lot, working out the kinks in my legs and arms as I went. At this hour, I seemed to be the park's only visitor. I tried the restroom door, sighing when it refused to budge. So much for a civilized attempt at clean-up. Maybe if I climbed down to the river, I could wash the dried gore from my hands.

I continued to pause periodically and listen for signs of the Elf as I crossed the confetti of pine needles on the grove's floor. The Old Mill rose above the wide waterway. I stopped at the precipice of the deep riverbed and stared. The last time I visited this stretch of river I'd been in my teens. Back then the mill had been a lot more skeletal. In the dappled morning light, the one hundred-year-old building looked surprisingly fresh and stable. I guessed that meant the Historical Society had finally raised enough money to restore the structure.

At the gully's edge I sat, peering down at the water flowing three yards below. I rolled over onto my belly then swung my legs over the edge. When the toe my right shoe finally landed in a solid foothold, I shifted my weight and started my descent. My fingers clutched at the heavy clay soil as I moved my left foot downward. About halfway to the river bottom, the soil's composition changed and it became tougher to dig in or gain any traction. One yard from the bottom, the soil gave way. I tumbled, swallowing a shriek. I scrabbled but my hands and feet found nothing but loose sand. With a splash, I landed on my butt in the river. I jumped up, gasping from the cold, knee deep in the water. My jeans were soaked, my top and sweatshirt wet, I stood there shivering like a pine bough in the wind. Perfect. At least I didn't hurt myself.

The icy water took away my breath as I washed my hands. Under the refurbished Old Mill, I scrubbed the dried blood from my skin until my flesh felt raw. I dabbed at the scabby mess at my hairline, wetting my hair and face in the process. Already drenched by the time I finished my clean-up, I walked in the current for several yards, until I reached the corrugated tunnel that passed under the park's one road. I climbed the narrow trail to the right side of the tunnel and up the riverbank. At the top, I wrung out my pant legs as best as I could then walked the road to the grove's edge. Behind a broad redwood, I stood shivering as I peeked at the sidewalk and street beyond. Cars streamed along the hill, locals getting an early start on their commute into the city for another tedious Tuesday. I didn't see a white van or a dented Carmen Ghia parked anywhere along the curb, nor any vehicles cruising the street in obvious search mode. After a deep breath, I thrust my way out of the grove and onto the sidewalk. I kept my pace fast while trying not to run. It was a long shot, but maybe after a night's rest the Festiva's engine would work again.

When I turned the corner onto Lovell, my teeth stopped chattering as my mouth dropped open. The Festiva sat on four puddles of rubber; someone had slashed the tires. I ran to the car and peered inside. The driver's side window was smashed, clusters of glass fragments littered the front seat and floor. My overnight was bag gone. My purse, birth certificate and Ramones tapes were gone. My father's letter – gone.

Everything Dad had left me was gone.

Heat came off me in waves, ending the fits of shivering which had racked me since my fall into the river. This was too much. First the Elf torched my car then he stole the remaining links to my father. No way was I going to leave town without those precious bits of my past. But how to find the Elf without him finding me first?

After giving myself a couple minutes to absorb my losses, I strode down Throckmorton. I needed money, dry clothes and wheels. But first I needed to get off this tree-shaded street and into some sunshine. If

I got warmed up, maybe I'd be able to organize my thoughts. Walking helped take some of the edge off my anger as well as warming my limbs. I began to take closer note of my surroundings. There were no other pedestrians out on the street. My wet clothes already made me stand out. I needed to find the cover of more people.

Halfway down the hill, a metallic flash of white set my heart racing. I turned to face the window of the closest shop, pretending to gaze at the children's clothes on display. The reflection of the vehicle in the glass showed a pickup truck. I waited for my pulse to return to normal then resumed walking. At the bottom of the hill, I crossed to Lytton Square. The remains of my Celica had been towed away, but the square's blackened brickwork testified to what had happened.

Because of the early hour, all the tables edging the square were still vacant. I picked one of the few getting some rays from the weak morning sun and settled on it to dry off. Located off to the side of the market, my spot provided a clear view of anyone approaching on foot. Plus there was no easy access for vehicles. I wound up on the awkward end of a few stares from approaching shoppers, my dripping hair an unusual sight in public – outside of poolside at the club. But most the early morning customers seemed too preoccupied with their grocery lists to pay me more than a passing glance. I raised my face to the sunshine. In another couple hours, the bone-chilling air would be a memory. Though I knew what I needed to do next, I didn't think dripping on anyone would help my plan. The river water had only drenched the bottom half of my T-shirt and sweatshirt. Both were still wet but would soon near the damp-dry stage. To speed the process, I draped my sweatshirt on top of the table. My jeans had gotten a more thorough soaking, but they were drying.

After sunning myself for forty-five minutes, my stomach began to growl. I turned to stare at the metal clock tower. Half past eight. The plaque at the base reminded me the clock had been presented to the City by the volunteer fire brigade in 1929. Amazingly, it still kept time. With each passing quarter hour, the number of shoppers seemed to increase. The market entrance was less than thirty feet away and a steady flow of people streamed in and out, but, thanks to the Elf, I had no money. I cursed him for stealing my wallet along with my other possessions. I appraised the passersby as I reviewed my situation. If the Elf was halfway decent at his job, he'd have gone back to Billy with my things from the Festiva in tow. Then he'd try to use what he stole as keys to figuring my next step. Though, from what I had seen of the Elf so far, he might have taken my belongings for spite. I tried not to think about the Ramones tapes Dad saved for me. Tried not to picture the Elf reading my father's letter and smirking at my birth certificate. I didn't want him to have that window into my psyche, didn't want him to have that kind of power. I'd try to take a page from my mother's book and turn a blind eye to that possibility.

But pretending would only get me so far. Without cash or credit cards, I couldn't buy food or shelter. And I wasn't prepared to spend another night in one of Mill Valley's parks. My stomach growled again as if to add an exclamation point to that thought. I ran my hands along my pants legs. Though not dry, I looked almost presentable. It was time to set aside my morals. Time to pick a target and pluck a wallet.

A matronly-looking woman stumped toward the market's entrance, her angry eyes a clue to the misery inside. But her inner demons weren't my concern. I shifted my gaze: Her brown pumps looked broken at the sides and the heels were worn. They also didn't match her blue purse and her dress looked sun-faded. Though not a science, clothes and shoes were usually a pretty good indicator for the amount of cash on hand. The woman entered the store. I scanned the field of incoming shoppers. Two teenage girls – free from school for the summer – sauntered toward the store. One clutched the other's arm while she guffawed. I didn't bother checking their shoes. Any money they displayed in their attire was their parents' and the contents of their wallets not worth the time or risk. A figure caught my eye.

Dressed in black trousers and a brilliant white shirt, the man appeared more formal than the other shoppers in their hiking boots and khakis. That type of upscale dressing was a good sign. His leather shoes, polished to a gentle gleam, were another heartening indicator. He looked like a good risk. I stood, grabbed my damp sweatshirt then eyed the man from beneath my lashes. With a start, I realized I was spying on Trevor. I averted my face but continued to watch. He strode into the Mill Valley Market. Was he there to stock up on booze for Mom?

One way to find out. I crossed the square to the store. Ten years had passed since I last stepped inside the market. Some minor remodeling had occurred, the walls were now a pale blush of pink instead of stark white, but, other than that, the store looked basically the same. The smell of oranges and baked bread greeted me. The warm yeasty scent made my stomach growl. The older woman standing to my left gave me a disapproving look. I scanned the bakery: half-a-dozen shoppers, but no Trevor. I hurried up and down aisles. When I reached the far end of the store, there he was, standing in the liquor section holding two bottles of vodka. Gotcha. If Mom ever let me inside the house again, I'd be sure to tell her she was kidding herself if she thought the stuff was odorless.

Engrossed in his study of the bottles, he didn't notice my approach. "Hey Trevor. How's it hanging?" My casual greeting was sure to irk him. The man really did bring out the worst in me.

He spun around and pointed a bottle of Stolichnaya at me. "You."

"Yeah, me."

"Are you proud of yourself? Your mother was upset for hours after you left."

I flashed on the tender way Mom had touched Trevor's face. "But you found a way to calm her again, didn't you?"

He ignored my innuendo. "It wasn't easy, believe me. I don't know how you live with yourself. The woman lost her husband."

Heat raced up my neck. "And I lost my father. Believe me, you don't have any special insight into our relationship."

Trevor shifted both bottles to the crook of his arm. "What do you want?"

"What?"

"Why are you here, haranguing me? I assume you want something. Money? Good luck. You won't be getting a chance to hit up your mother for a loan. She's given strict orders not to let you inside the house again."

His words landed like a slap, chipping my insides. But I still had a job to do. I took a deep breath then tapped his chest with my right index finger. "Tell me something, Trev. I deserve the truth. You sleeping with my mom? Or rather, were you sleeping with her while Dad was alive? Because from what I saw of your bedside manner, you two seemed pretty chummy."

"If you're implying I've behaved with any

impropriety as far as your mother is concerned-"

"I'm not implying. I'm asking. A man with a clear conscience would answer. Without sputtering all over Mom's vodka."

Trevor looked like he wanted to smack me with one of the bottles. He turned away and jammed them both back onto the shelf with a clang. Hands free, he spun and grabbed the neck of my T-shirt. "You listen up. If you spread lies about me in this town, I'll make you sorry. Understand?"

The smell of stale coffee bridged the gap between us. I pushed my hip against him and shoved.

Face red, Trevor held his position along with his grip on my shirt. "The fact that you're Marion's daughter only gets you so far. I won't let you muddy my name." He let go, thrusting me back.

Somehow, I managed to stay on my feet. "That means you're sleeping with her. Because in all that bluster, I never once heard you deny it." He lunged and I retreated. "Not to worry, Trev. I'm out of here. I won't come back. You've got my word."

Several shoppers huddled together about five feet away. Trevor noticed them and stepped back, straightening his shirt collar. "Your word means nothing to me."

"Good point." I gave him a quick salute and headed for the exit.

Mom didn't want to see me again. My stomach was knotting so bad I thought I might vomit. I also had no car or plan of action. But I did have one thing going for me: Trevor's wallet.

Twenty-one

I hustled down the street, putting distance between me and the grocery store where I had lifted Trevor's wallet. When he reached the cash register, Trevor would probably fumble around wondering if he had left his wallet in his car or back at the house. But once he checked the likeliest spots, the guy would start to explore other scenarios. One of the many details of my life that escaped discovery by my parents was my pick pocketing ability. Even without that kernel of knowledge, Trevor would suspect me. It might take him a little while to get there, but, disliking me as much as he did, he would leap to that conclusion sooner rather than later.

When I reached the Old Paseo, I stopped. Beneath the arch of the shadowy passage cutting through the city's center, I extracted Trevor's wallet from the pocket of my still-damp jeans. My trembling fingers fumbled and I dropped the billfold onto the concrete.

The jolt of adrenaline from my successful bump and pluck had set my pulse and heart racing. After picking up the wallet, I leaned against the cool plaster wall and took several deep breaths. Unlike when I was a teen, I felt no giddiness, no triumph. Instead my nerves jangled like a downed power line, still sparking and dangerous, but without purpose. Why had taking needless risks once felt so good?

The familiar scent of leather and money greeted me as I unfolded the calfskin wallet. Through the years, I had learned you could never tell how much money someone carried just by looking at them. You could improve your odds of a decent score, but there were no guarantees. Even so, Trevor surprised me. He had a hell of a lot more green on him than I would have guessed. The foil-wrapped condom tucked between two fifty dollar bills made me grimace. That was a speculative journey my brain refused to take. In addition to the rubber and the fifties, Trevor had a few ones, a twenty, two tens, a couple fives, and four crisp one hundred dollar bills. He was going to be good and pissed when he couldn't find his wallet.

Trevor's unexpected riches solved a couple of my problems. I could buy food and afford shelter for the night. It was a shame Bianca's was no longer in business. A slice of pepperoni and olive pizza would hit the spot. I shoved the bills into my front pockets, tucking the condom back into the billfold. In the past, I would have tossed the wallet. Though I disliked Trevor, I didn't want to put him through the chore of replacing all his cards and ID. I shoved the wallet into my back pocket, planning to buy an envelope at the stationery shop and mail it back to him. I couldn't make a claim of doing the right thing, but mailing Trevor the stuff I didn't need stood out as the most 'right' thing I could do.

After playing bumper cars with the Elf last night, the thought of driving alone through Mill Valley held no appeal. With Trevor's help, I could hire cabs for transportation. When I felt safer, I needed to contact the car rental agency and report what happened to the Festiva. Thank God I paid the extra few bucks for insurance. Roger's inventory looked like crap but I bet none of his customers had ever destroyed one of his vehicles before. Oh no. Roger would probably want a police report on the incident, something I wanted no part of. Maybe if I ignored the problem long enough, one of the homeowners along Lovell would call the cops about the vehicular eyesore left on their well-maintained street. Not the best way for him to learn about the car's damage. Roger would probably assume the damage was my fault and give the cops my name.

It might be smarter to call Roger after all. If he knew I was the victim, perhaps he could leave me out of things. But if he proved unwilling, I hoped the Mill Valley cops had more important crimes to investigate than hunting down a wayward rental car customer.

I emerged from the darkness of the Old Paseo, loitering in the entryway as my eyes readjusted to the morning sunshine. Dry clothes and food remained at the top of my list. Then I would figure out my next step. Lucky for me, one of the dozens of women's clothing stores that peppered downtown already stood open for business. When I entered, the middle-aged sales clerk stopped in the middle of straightening a stack of V-necked sweaters and frowned at me. I did my best to ignore her while I searched for blue jeans in my size. A pair in hand, I trotted to the dressing room. Billed as stone-washed, they felt smoother than any jeans I had worn before. Once my bottom half felt warm and dry, it seemed silly not to get a shirt, too. I left the jeans on and checked the store's supply of tops. There was a table of 'Dipsea 1994' sweatshirts marked fifty percent off. In a nostalgic nod to the long ago years when I thought I'd someday compete in Mill Valley's famous footrace, I retreated with one to the dressing room.

I checked my reflection. If I arranged my curls right, pulling them down in front, the scab and bruise on my forehead weren't too noticeable. I finger-combed the rest of my hair, taking out the worst of the tangles. When I considered the night I had been through, I didn't look too terrible. Still, I braced myself for another frown; the saleswoman out front wasn't grading on a curve the same way I was. After transferring Trevor's money and wallet from my old jeans to the pockets of my new ones, I walked to the cash register. The clerk rang up my purchases in silence, but I sensed she was using all her self-control to refrain from asking why, on a dry sunny day, I came into her pristine shop damp from head to toe. I borrowed a pair of scissors to cut the tags off my new clothes then gathered my wet belongings. The squishy feeling of still-soaked socks hit a discordant note with my newfound dryness. I paid for a pair of sweat socks then tugged them onto my cold damp feet. The wet sneakers took away some of the enjoyment, but the socks still gave a protective layer between me and the cold soggy.

Though my outside felt more comfortable, my growling stomach demanded food. I bought a sandwich and a Styrofoam cupful of tea at a small coffee shop. A sense of urgency overtook me when I sat to eat and I chomped my way through the turkey sandwich – aware of the taste of the meat and mustard, but not stopping to enjoy the flavors. In spite of knowing the hard part still lay ahead, I emerged from the eatery feeling much improved. Plus I now had a plan: to re-visit the scene of the Orwell Massacre.

The murder house must have been the Elf's destination last night when he spotted me tailing him and crashed his car into mine. But had he run into me as revenge for knifing him in the balls? Or was there something – or someone – at that house he didn't want me to see? That house was the last place where I saw Billy. My gut told me it sat at the center of things. When I took a cab out to the house after the reading of Dad's will, the driver told me no one lived there. But his description of the Orwell Massacre had been full of inaccuracies. Maybe he got it wrong when he said the place was empty. I needed to go back.

When I walked into the lobby of the Mill Valley Inn, my stomached fluttered. Though I had been dragged there many times by my parents for lunches and dinners with their visiting friends, I felt out of place. But with two of Trevor's hundreds, I could sleep here for a night. After going to the murder house, I would need a secure place to retreat. The Inn seemed the safest option. Since the Elf had already shown his face here and punched out a check-in clerk, I felt sure the staff would react immediately if he returned – unlike with the romance novel-reading desk clerk at the Cozy 8 Motel.

An oily-looking man in his thirties with a gold-toned badge that said 'Kyle' stood behind the Inn's check-in desk. Obviously not the clerk the Elf decked. He stared at me from beneath hooded lids, his façade of courtesy as thin as one of the bougainvillea petals in the floral arrangement centered on the marble counter. After he consulted his registration book, he gave a close-lipped smile. "Would you like a creek-side cabin? We have one left."

The creek-side cabins ranked as a big part of the Inn's attraction. But no way I wanted a room off on my own or to pay the high rent for one of those little slices of paradise. "No. I want the main building."

"Of course." His tone sounded smooth, but Kyle's expression told me he had already added up the cost of what I wore and found me wanting. He knew I didn't belong at the Inn.

The urge to hop on a bus or hire a cab and get out of Mill Valley grew. I had allowed myself to forget how imbedded the snobbery and stratification by tax bracket felt here. I longed for a place that welcomed all comers. A place like L.A. I tuned back in to the clerk in time to hear him say, "...at this hour."

"I'm sorry. What?"

Apparently unhappy I wasn't hanging on his every word, Kyle made no attempt to hide the stink eye. "I said – for the second time..." He made a half-assed attempt to cover his sharp tone with fake-looking smile. "We don't have any rooms available at this hour. Since you didn't call ahead and request an early check in. That's what most our guests do – who want a room this early. But we can get you in at three o'clock. That's the standard time."

With my free hand, I tugged on one of my

curls. If I had agreed to pay for a creek-side cabin, I bet the room would've been ready – with a mint on the pillow and a sachet in each drawer – by the time I finished filling out the registration form. What a jerk. I gave him my best fake smile in return then held up my damp sweatshirt, socks and jeans. "I assume I can check my luggage until the room's ready?"

"Of course, miss." From the look on Kyle's face, I thought he might excuse himself to fetch a pair of tongs to handle my belongings. But he straightened his spine and took my clothes, holding them at arms-length from his maroon jacket. "If you can wait for a moment, I'll deposit your luggage and give you a receipt."

"I'd appreciate that." I hoped my insincere smile matched his. I watched him trot into the back room and shook my head. I hadn't expected to get into a room at this hour. But there was no reason for the guy to act like such an ass. Oh well. As wonderful as it might feel to bury myself inside the safety and tradition of the Inn, Kyle reminded me that wasn't possible. The quick skedaddle option remained tempting, but I knew escape was a fantasy. Besides, my anger at Billy demanded action. I wanted to look him in the eye and tell him what I thought. Tell him what he had done to me for the last ten years.

But, if Billy's imagination worked at all, he knew what he had done. And, if he was the sicko I suspected, he had already enjoyed my nightmare for far too long. I needed to face him. To face my nightmare.

The cab driver swore as he rounded the corner, then swerved to avoid the broken glass and torn metal littering the site of last night's collision between my rental and the Elf's Carmen Ghia. Farther along the street, a large oil stain marked the spot where the Elf idled as he prepared for another assault on the Festiva. I hoped he had driven the car's oil tank dry and corkscrewed the engine.

"Stop here."

"Where? In the glass?" Unlike the cabby Saturday night, today's driver bordered on surly. His unshaven face frowned at me in the rearview mirror.

"No. A few more yards up. There." I pointed toward the empty curb paralleling the sweeping lawn fronting a vast colonial-style home. The cabby pulled over then told me the fare. I pulled Trevor's twenty from my pocket. I didn't like the idea of revisiting the Orwell Massacre site without means for a quick getaway. "How much more for you to wait for me?"

"How long you going to be?" He glared into the mirror.

I had no idea. I gave him the answer I hoped would keep him there. "About thirty minutes. Maybe less." A lot less, fingers crossed.

"Gimme two more of them twenties and I'll wait." For the first time since I climbed into the cab, he smiled, revealing a gold capped front tooth.

Two more twenties and I bet the guy would peel out, telling himself his day was off to one hell of a start. "How about this. I'll give you a ten." I offered another of Trevor's bills, then pulled two fifties from my front pocket and held them up in my other hand. "If you're still here when I come out, you get two pictures of Ulysses S. Grant. Easy money, right?"

The cabby's eyes narrowed and his smile vanished, but he nodded.

A good sign, but I felt no real confidence he would stay.

From where we sat at the curb, the murder house wasn't visible. Whoever lurked inside couldn't see the cab either. That worked for me both ways. I didn't want the driver to see me creeping around as I peeked in the windows. But I also didn't want anyone who might be inside that house to know I was here. My plan felt lame and foolish, but I climbed out of the cab anyway. I could do this, use the element of surprise to my advantage. Stay below the Elf's – and Billy's – radar.

The memory of my one time inside the house remained spotty and skewed, but I remembered the general layout. Both the front and back offered a lot of big windows, perfect for snooping on the home's occupants. With a dose of caution and a bit of luck, I'd sidle up to the house and see if Billy was now using the murder house as his center of operations.

I aimed for the look of someone out for a casual stroll and walked to the small rise where the road curved to the right. Once I'd rounded the bend, I saw the Spanish-style home of my nightmares. It sat at the center of a large expanse of greenery, sheltered by Douglas fir and redwood trees. The front door that starred in my sweat-drenched dreams loomed dark, a scabbed-over wound, warning me of pain to come. The blinded eyes of the home's shuttered windows presented an apt metaphor for the ugliness that once hid inside. But I told myself that a blind eye was a false eye. I now knew the source of the ugliness that had unfolded here. I didn't understand why things had happened the way they did, but I couldn't turn my back any longer. Or pretend I knew nothing useful.

This was the type of street where residents made no attempt to hide their wealth. Each home sat on an island of green, separate and unequal, the battle to outdo their neighbors in full swing. The plaster-fronted house that haunted me looked less opulent than the rest of the block. The current owner wasn't trying to stand out from the crowd. Interesting. Another plus of a wealthy neighborhood was a desire for privacy. Massive hedges separated each property offering helpful cover for my approach. Between the murder house and its neighbor, a line of flowering night-blooming jasmine fronted a tall column of coffeeberry bush. The lazy sweet scent from the petals clung to the dusty leaves like an invisible web. I stepped into the narrow defile between the shrub screens then edged my way up the gentle incline toward the house.

Through the tracery of spear-shaped leaves, I spied the arched entrance framing the doorway. Years ago I had leaned against the opposite side of that door and gathered my courage before sneaking out to the street. That same door had supported me as I heard the hum of feasting flies. The flies which led me to Billy's decapitated body. Or what I thought was his body. Who was the poor s.o.b. who died in his place?

A shudder rippled through me. I took a deep breath then resumed threading my way through the shrubs. Branches caught on my sweatshirt and curls, and scraped my hands as I wriggled deeper into the bush. All the windows along this side of the murder house were shuttered. Was this to stave off further vandalism or because the owner desired seclusion? I pushed through the hedge, closing in on the high wall shielding the backyard from the neighbors to the right. Ten years ago, I had sat on the other side of the wall, staring into the swimming pool's murky water, my brain trying to process what my eyes saw. The brick barrier stood at least seven feet tall. But with something to climb on, I could get a handhold on the top. I pushed farther through the bushes. My cheek stung, cut by a sharp branch tip. If this route turned out to be a bust, I would try the other side of the house.

The screen of jasmine ended at the wall, but the taller coffeeberry hedge continued along the neighbor's property. The trunk of the coffeeberry wasn't as thick as I would have liked, but it still looked sturdy enough to bear my weight. At least for a short while. I thrust my way through the mesh of thin limbs, branches poking my skin. I reached over my head and grabbed the trunk, putting my right foot on one of the few tough-looking lower branches, then hauled myself upward. The coffeeberry swayed with my weight, but both the trunk and branch held. I kept climbing. When my shoulders were even with the top of the wall, I shifted around to face it. A foot-wide gap separated me and the red brick. I clutched the trunk with my right hand and reached out with my left. The shrub swayed with me, making my task easier. I grabbed the rough edge and hooked my hand over the top. With a grunt, I jumped then hauled my chest on top of the wall. The shrub snapped away then lashed back and away again with a light whistling sound. Once I heaved my torso up, swinging a leg over was easy work. Flattened atop the wall, one leg dangling on either side, I stared at the property below.

No dog came charging. That was something. Dry leaves huddled against the base of the wall. The place looked deserted, but the yard's layout appeared the same as I remembered. The swimming pool was about ten feet from the wall where I perched, the surrounding concrete apron merging with the back porch and deck by the house. The water below looked dark, but this time, a carpet of pine needles floated there instead of a dead body. The grass needed a trim and numerous cracks traveled along the plaster finish of the house while mold stains marred the bottom two feet of the walls. If my gut was right and Billy lived here, it wasn't because he wanted to preserve the place.

Here in the backyard, the windows weren't masked by shutters. Good thing since I wanted to peek inside and see if the place looked lived in. But the poolside lounge chairs were gone. That would make climbing back over the wall tough. I wasn't about to climb down without some sort of exit strategy. Near the deck sat an empty wood crate. If I upended that and stood on it, I should be able to reach the top of the wall.

Something shiny crossed my peripheral vision. I looked out at the street. A car's bumper nosed into view, followed by a yellow hood and fender, cruising at about five miles per hour. My heart raced. If the cabdriver decided to park in front of the house, he could make real trouble for me. The rest of the car came into view. There was no cab company name or logo on the door. I gusted out a breath. The driver's head turned my way. For a moment, I thought he spotted me atop the wall. But then he returned his attention to the road and kept driving. The sudden urge to pee lessened when I realized the guy didn't look big enough to be the Elf.

After wiping damp palms on the back of my sweatshirt, I lowered myself into the backyard. I dropped the final few feet, the impact of my sneakers on concrete making only a small squish when I landed. I scurried around the pool's shallow end toward the house. When I reached the building, I flattened myself against it. My heart raced and sweat drenched my armpits. I froze and tried to slow my breathing. No cries of alarm sounded from inside. Weak-kneed, I took a deep breath then began inching along until I reached the first window.

At the embrasure, I faced the wall then leaned to my right until I could peer past the frame. "Shit." The window wasn't shuttered, but a heavy curtain masked the interior. While I felt safer knowing whoever was inside couldn't see me either, this wasn't going to help me spy on the occupants. Caution pushed me to my knees and I crawled past the cloaked opening. When I stood, I rubbed my hands along the sides of my jeans. Though I had worked hard to free myself from the person I was as a teen, I hadn't grasped how deep the changes ran. My old taste for risk-taking was gone for good. And right then I could have used a bit more of my youthful audacity.

Since it didn't look like Billy had spent any time remodeling the place, when I rounded the corner, I should find a door with a window in its top half. If that window was blocked, there was also a sliding glass door farther along. I continued forward. It seemed like five minutes passed before I worked up the nerve to peek around the corner. Small pine cones dotted the pavement and cracked brick steps led to a weathered backdoor. But there were no guards. No Elf. No Billy. I edged my way to the door, trying to avoid crossing any potential lines of sight from the window – should anyone lurk inside. When I reached the chipped door frame, I discovered a gauzy curtain covered the smudged glass.

I took a step forward and peered into the murky interior. Something solid on the other side of the glass blocked my view. A loud pop took my breath away. I jumped back, looking for the source of the noise. The back door screeched open.

From the open doorway, Trevor frowned at me.

Twenty-two

"Told you I saw her on top of the wall. You can't let your guard down with her for a second. She's a liar and a thief. " Trevor crossed his arms in front of his wide chest and gave a vindictive-looking nod.

My mouth dropped open. I stared first at him then at the Elf looming behind. "What the... Trevor? What're you...?" My thoughts wound around like a Mobius strip while I tried to make sense of what I saw. Trevor and the Elf were working together? How? Why?

The Elf smiled; my intestines twisted.

"Oh, I know all about our girl. Don't I?" The Elf raised and lowered his eyebrows at me, a la Groucho Marx. "Though I appreciate your kindness. Giving me the warning about her and all. More than a spot of trouble, she is. A hell of a lot more." The Elf tilted his head then winked at me. "Couldn't leave well enough alone. You had to play detective, didn't you?" With cat-like speed, he raised his right arm and clubbed Trevor on the side of the head.

I scurried backward as Trevor's face went slack. He collapsed to his knees with a dry crunch, eyes unfocused. I retreated another step, but remained wordless. Trevor keeled onto his side.

"Told you men were easier to hurt than women." The Elf tossed a leather sap from hand to hand then smiled at me again. "But since I've been looking forward to hurting you, I don't mind if it means a wee extra bit of work."

Trevor looked like a marionette whose strings had been sliced.

"Is he...?"

"He's alive. For now. A busy body, that one. If I was you, I wouldn't get too worked up about his welfare. You got a world of trouble of your own in front of you. Why the hell couldn't you run away? Wasn't me crashing into your car enough of a warning?"

Bile burned my throat. I took one more giant step back then swallowed hard. "You left me a note, telling me to stay."

"The note wasn't from me."

"Oh." I shook my head as if that would organize my thoughts. "So, first you tried to kidnap me then you tried to scare me off?"

"You getting smart with me?" A frown twisted the Elf's face. "Shit. You sure do know how to get under a person's skin." He pointed at Trevor. "Look at this poor sod. Follows you to the house without a thought to his personal safety. Comes to the front door, all full of himself. Says he's got to talk to the owner. Has a warning for us. The man wants me to know some girl's trying to break in. Says it's the same hellion who stole his wallet." The Elf flexed the fingers of his left hand. "I like that word, 'hellion.' Suits you. Anyway, fellow says he saw you climbing over the wall. So, I invite him to come in and check out the situation with me. He seemed right happy to oblige. Now look at him." The Elf nudged Trevor with the toe of his Doc Martens'. Trevor remained unresponsive. "Still and all, I guess I should be grateful for the warning." He drew back his leg and kicked Trevor in the ribs.

The unconscious man groaned.

The Elf tapped the leather sap against the side of his thigh. "I hate feeling grateful to anybody."

My face grew hot as my hands curled into fists. "Then we're going to get along fine."

"Yeah, no gratitude or love lost between you and me. Only cold, hard hatred. You don't know what kind of trouble you caused me." The Elf stepped around Trevor's inert body. "If I had my way, I'd kill you. Here. Now. You're one lucky bitch."

"Lucky," I repeated.

"That's right. Go ahead, flap your cakehole. Doesn't change a thing. You know why?" The Elf jerked his thumb toward the house then continued. "Because the man inside wants to see you. If he didn't, you'd be dead already. That's the only reason I'm not carving you up right now. Like you did me. But, do I look worried? Not a bit. The way I figure it, when the man's done chatting you up, you and me will get a chance to settle things. One on one."

His smile sent a chill through my bones.

He took another step closer. "One on one's more fun anyway. Just the way I like it. I'm looking forward to that."

I edged back another step.

The Elf gestured at the open door. "Get inside."

The dark doorway gaped like the entrance to a tomb. Without taking time to calculate the odds for success, I turned and ran for the wall. Too far a leap for me on the best of days, I hoped fear and adrenaline would give me a surge of power, one that enabled me to jump high enough to grab the top of the wall. Didn't little old ladies lift entire cars off their grown children with the help of adrenaline? Not a great plan, but better than following the Elf's order. Eight steps into my dash, a rocket went off inside my skull. Bright splashes of red, purple and yellow filled my vision.

Then darkness grabbed at me and sucked me down.

A hammer pounding inside my skull pushed me toward consciousness. But both my eyes refused the command to open. An angry balloon was trapped inside my brain, bumping against my gray matter, trying to fight its way out. The right side of my head felt ready to burst. I tried to touch the irate spot, but couldn't move either hand. Panic brought me up another notch from my dark, aching confusion. My spine and neck complained, too. I worked out why: I was slumped over. I managed to lift my torso into more of an upright position. Once again, I tried to open my eyes. This time, my left eye opened, but my right felt glued shut. Light stabbed at my one exposed pupil. I closed my lid then waited. On the next attempt I squinted through my lashes.

"Hey sleepy head. I was starting to think you weren't going to wake up at all. Thought maybe Sean killed you. He must've smacked the shit out of you. Even the old guy's already awake."

A familiar voice. Deep and rich like toffee. Not Billy's voice. Not the Elf's either. But someone I knew. Once upon a time. Again I tried to move my arms. My elbows had some freedom but my wrists felt pinned in place. The light no longer hurt my left eye, so I opened it wider. A pale round face floated before me like a stretched out man in the moon. I closed my eye again.

"Here," the voice said. I winced as he ran something wet and rough over my right eye, banging against the section of skull where the angry balloon was trapped. "Should be able to open that eye now."

Both eyes opened to slits, my lashes furring the edges of my narrow field of vision. I stared at the pale moon-faced man. Bald. Fat. Blood-drenched wash cloth in his hand. I closed my eyes again. "I think I'm going to hurl."

"Here." Something solid landed in my lap.

I squinted. Wastebasket.

"I got it covered. I'm not making the same mistake twice," the fat man said. "That old guy barfed on my shoes. My goddamn Florsheim's. The dumbshit."

Another surge of nausea. I fought the urge, found neutral ground.

Then my meal of turkey sandwich and tea rose up and landed in the hard plastic can balanced upon my thighs. When I got down to dry heaves, the moon-face man wiped my mouth with the bloody wash cloth. The coppery scent turned my stomach, but my stomach had nothing left to reject. The light bulb inside my brain clicked on. The blood on the cloth was mine. I closed my eyes and tried to inventory the damage. My mind felt cluttered, like movers had brought in bulky pieces of cloth-draped furniture while the lights were out. I tried to work my way around the obstructions blocking my thoughts, but the confusion remained. "What happened? Was I in an accident?" From the glimpses I had gathered, this place didn't look like a hospital. But the moon-faced man had helped me. Not with a gentle hand, but still...

"Sean decked you. Used that nasty sap of his and bashed you one. You did a Humpty Dumpty when you fell. Hit the wall. Swear I heard your skull crack from here. You bled all over the place. That's why you're having trouble opening your peepers. Blood gummed your eyes shut. Probably looks worse than it is. But I bet it hurts like hell. Still, nothing a little Darvon won't cure. Or better yet, codeine. I seem to remember you liked the mellow styling of a handful of codeine. Right, Ramona?"

Fear buzz sawed through the cloaked objects in my brain. Sean. Sean was the Irish Elf. I was inside the murder house. The site of the Orwell Massacre. Billy's house. Trevor had to be the old man who upchucked on the moon-faced man's shirt. No, not his shirt. His shoes. Jesus. I needed to get out of here. Now.

I looked down. I couldn't move my arms because my wrists were duct taped to a chair. An Eames chair no less. The same Brazilian Rosewood veneer as the two in my dad's study. Billy's narcotics business must bring in a handsome profit if he bought collector-quality furniture to use as an anchor for his hostages. I could move my fingers and elbows a fraction, but no more than that. The silver bands of tape secured my forearms and wrists to the wood and leather armrests. The chair arm only extended about an inch past my taped wrists. Given enough time, perhaps I could wriggle one of my hands free.

The man dropped the bloody washcloth into the wastebasket then leaned in to retrieve the container from my lap. The smell of sour milk and popcorn rose from his skin. He waddled away with the reeking wastebasket. His Charlie Brown head floated over a huge body, his gait shambling and awkward. But his voice felt like a favorite tune. So familiar – like once we got to the chorus, I'd be able to hum along. But everything I saw remained an unknown melody.

Whoever the man was, I needed to get away. Away from this house. Away from Billy. So far, my welcome had left a lot to be desired; I didn't want to find out what more lay in store. If my brain would work, maybe I could come up with a plan of escape. I wished I still had my key chain with the Swiss army knife. Small, but it was sharp enough to cut through the tape quickly. But without some sort of blade, it would take a long time to rip it loose. If I could do it at all. Even if I managed to get free, I'd need to find some kind of weapon. I stared at my surroundings, but all the edges blurred. The fat man seemed clear enough – at least I thought I saw him clearly – maybe because of his size. But the smaller objects in my field of vision seemed to shudder and shift.

"So, how you been, Ramona? Man, you like dropped off the edge of the planet. Here one minute, then poof! Like some kind of magician's trick. Billy always said you had the smarts. But, damn. I mean, no one could get over the way you Houdinied. No trace. No clue. That ain't easy to do. Believe me, I know. And damn. We looked for you. Big time. But you were gone." The fat man shook his round head and repeated, "That ain't easy."

He retreated behind a wide desk. With a grunt, he lowered his bulk into a leather chair. He had to weigh well over 300 pounds. Again, I felt the visceral tug of an old melody line. But I couldn't name that tune. "Who are you?"

"Is that how you talk to old friends? If I gave a good goddamn, that probably would've hurt." Again, he shook his head. "Can't believe you forgot all your old friends."

Old friends? Even all those hours I hung out with Janelle had been a matter of convenience. This guy wasn't an old friend. Other than Billy, I didn't have any. And now I knew Billy wasn't my friend either. Who else did that leave?

The door creaked. I turned to look. A shooting pain rocketed through my temple. I closed my eyes and waited for the throb to subside. When the angry colors stopped dancing inside my eyelids, I opened them again.

The Elf walked toward me. "Told you she had a head like a goddamn rock. She's fine." He moved to the side, revealing the man behind him.

I thought I might hurl again.

Billy Bang was back from the grave.

Twenty-three

He moved with the cock-of-the-walk strut I knew so well. The half-smile on his face straightened my spine and sent my pulse into overdrive. His hair flopped forward in an oh-so-familiar way, but was now sandy-colored instead of bleached blond with dark roots. His eyes looked different, too. Harder. Much colder than I remembered. More wary.

The passage of time changed a person. I had proved that. But, first impressions aside, this wasn't Billy. Disappointment battled with confusion and fear. "Who are you?"

"I'm the man whose house you tried to break into. What's your story? Gonna tell me you snuck around the place hoping to steal the family silver? Or you gonna try the old 'I wanted to stop in and say Hi.' routine?" He stood in front of me, arms crossed over his broad chest. "I heard a lot about you and I'm betting you're smarter than that. Smart enough to play things straight with me. What's your story, Ramona? Out slumming?

Or, would you like it better if I call you Miranda?"

He gave a slow, wolfish smile then wagged his index finger at me. "What a piece of work you turned out to be. I still can't believe you gave Billy a fake name. That boy thought you loved him. What the hell kind of game were you playing with him?"

If Billy chose not to tell this goon about how I became Ramona, he sure as hell wasn't going to hear the story from me. "Who are you?" I repeated. "Where's Billy?"

"Oh, I'm sorry. Are you the one calling the shots here? Demanding personal appearances? Because from where I stand, you're the dipshit taped to a chair. My chair. In my house. So, you might want to dial down the attitude. Before I ask Sean to dial it down for you." The man shook his head. "Look at yourself. At your situation. Both are a genuine goddamn mess." He leaned against the desk and stretched out his long legs before crossing them at the ankles. "Sean and I go back a ways and the guy's known for his short fuse. But I gotta say, you dug your way into his bad side in no time. I've never seen him grow to hate a woman as quick as he did you. And that tells me something. Sean's never gonna win a Nobel Prize, but he knows people. Knows what fires them up. What drives them to keep going. His reaction to you makes me wonder. Makes me wonder what you were up to with Billy. Were you using him? Because, according to Billy, you two were 'in love.' But, reality check: You didn't give the poor sonofabitch your real name. Is that what love means to you, Ramona?"

The man glanced at his watch. "We got some time. Not a lot, but, I think I can spare a few minutes so you and me can get to know each other better." He turned to the Elf. "Cut the tape off her." The Elf opened his mouth, but the other man waved him silent. "Look at her. She's no threat to anybody."

The Elf unsheathed a wicked looking blade and crouched in front of me. A grin broadened his angular face. Sweat chilled my spine as he ran a callused fingertip along my forearm, the small hairs rippling at his touch. I tried to keep my hands from shaking.

The not-Billy-man spoke, his voice grinding through the brittle silence. "Cut the tape, Sean. You puncture her, you're gonna regret it."

The Elf did as ordered, his grin twisting into an angry mask as he ripped the duct tape first from my right wrist, then from my left.

Tears wet my eyes and I sucked in air. Small blood-pocked pores covered both my wrists. "Can I get some water?" If they were willing to unbind me, they might let me rinse the sour vomit taste from my mouth.

The man who looked so much like Billy nodded. "Stu, get Ramona a drink. Sure you want water? Billy told me whisky was your favorite."

I flexed my hands, trying to get the

circulation going. "Water."

The fat man lumbered out the door on the far side of the room.

"That's Stewie?"

"Yeah. Goes by Stu now. But that's him. He's changed a bit from his lead-singer-coke-snorting-bang-anything-that-moves days. But who hasn't, huh? Ten years is a helluva long time." The man spread his arms wide then shrugged. "I'm no shrink, but I'd say the man's got some kind of hole inside him that he just can't fill. Plus one hard core addictive personality. Food's his current drug of choice." He pointed at the Elf. "Take off."

The Elf sauntered toward the door Stu had exited through. At the threshold he turned, made a gun with his right hand and pointed at me. "Pow." He winked then left.

My stomach lurched. I feared I was going to need the wastebasket one more time. I took several slow breaths, waiting for the feeling to pass. I couldn't let myself become incapacitated. More than I was already. I would need my wits and all my strength to get out of here. I heard Stu's heavy footfall before I saw him. How could he have changed so much in ten years? His bone structure hidden under hillocks of fat, I couldn't find any landmarks of the handsome face I remembered. He handed me a tall glass, the ice clattering as I gripped it. "Thank you, Stu."

"You finished over there?" The not-Billy man gestured at the desk. I hadn't noticed before, but small stacks of paper covered the surface.

"Got about another hour's work," Stu said.

"We'll leave you to it. Come on, Ramona. Let's give Stu some quiet." The man grabbed my upper arm with force and confidence. The matte black handgun gripped in his right hand stifled any niggling impulse to run for it.

When I stood, it felt like I was walking across a wave-tossed deck. By the time we reached a gloomy sitting room, my sea legs had returned. Large windows punctuated one wall, each sealed from the sun by a pair of heavy wooden shutters. "How can you live like this? Lurking in the dark." The question slipped from between my lips without thought. The gatekeeper in my brain seemed to have shut down.

The man grinned and my heart clenched. His resemblance to Billy intensified when he smiled. "I never lurk. Never. Trust me."

How could he look so much like Billy but not be him? "Who are you?"

He nodded at an overstuffed armchair and said, "Sit."

A command, not an invitation. I sat.

"Haven't figured it out yet? With that big brain of yours?" He settled opposite me in a sleek-looking chrome and leather chair. "Gotta say, I'm a little disappointed. I'm Grady."

My jaw slackened as I stared. "Billy's

brother?"

"Yep."

"But you're dead..." My grip on the tumbler tightened.

"There's a lot of that going around in my family."

"But, Billy told me..." I pictured Billy's face as he recounted how Grady died. "He told me you were killed in Viet Nam. In the war." I closed my eyes and saw it all in detail, Billy's handsome face twisted in anger. "He told me." I looked again at Grady. "I believed him. I even cried."

"That's what weak people do. Or so I hear." Grady ruffled his sandy hair with his free hand. "But, hey, if it makes you feel any better, when Billy told you that, he believed it. I didn't hook-up with my little brother until early 1984."

"Oh." I studied Grady's face. Where Billy's sculpted cheeks gave him a raw beauty, Grady's made him look predatory. "So, he didn't lie to me right away. Great. That's special. I'm almost moved. When do I get to talk to this paragon of honesty?" I knew I should feel more frightened than angry, but my emotions seemed to be running free. Had the Elf caused some kind of brain trauma when he decked me?

Grady laughed. "Billy never told me you had a temper."

To shut myself up, I took a sip of water. "Yeah, well, I'm no longer altering my personality with chemicals. I've got a much wider range of emotions now than when Billy and I were together. And a helluva a lot more to feel pissed off about." Dammit. Why couldn't I stop talking?

"Hey, maybe you haven't heard: life's hard. But, while it's just you and me chewing the fat, there's something I've wanted to tell you for a long time." Gun still pointed at my midsection, he smiled again. "I want to thank you. I dug the book."

"What book?"

"*1984*. George Orwell's masterpiece." Grady leaned forward, his expression earnest.

A feeling of dislocation washed through me. I took another deep breath. "Okay."

"Yep. Billy introduced me to it."

Another surprise. "He did?" I remembered how Billy would sigh and roll his eyes whenever I recounted some bit from the story. "Really?"

"Yeah. He wasn't a big reader... Never had the patience. Well, you know that. But Billy dug the story line. He turned me on to it and I ripped through the book. Great plot. Lot of meat on that bone."

The wobble in my brain wasn't coming from my head injury alone. Billy's dead brother held a gun on me while talking about a favorite book. "Okay."

Grady leaned back in his chair and stared at me for about thirty seconds before giving a crooked smile. "Between you and me, you really didn't know he worked for me back then, did you?"

"No."

He nodded, a look of surprise dancing across his handsome face. "Good. I never could be sure about that. Billy said he hadn't told you. But where you're concerned, that boy's loyalties... Well, 'divided' is a good way to describe them. I always wondered if he told me the truth about that."

"Great. He told you the truth. He kind of glossed over a lot of the truth with me." I shook my head then regretted the action. A fresh round of throbbing started up followed by a wave of dizziness. I held my head still and waited until I felt able to continue. "So for the majority of time we were together, Billy worked for you?"

Grady shrugged. "I'll say it again: life's hard. If you haven't figured that out by now, I got a bit of advice for you: Get used to it. It never gets any better. No one's riding in on their white horse. And nobody gives a damn about anybody but themself." He stood then strode to a sideboard near the door we had entered through. "But, Billy only worked for me part of the time you two were together." He lifted a decanter, removed the crystal stopper, inhaled and nodded. He poured himself a generous serving, took a sip. "Anyway, like I started to say, before you lost focus there, *1984* impressed me." He strolled back to his chair. "The whole idea of superstates and Big Brother... Entire civilizations living under the eye – and the thumb – of government. Pretty amazing stuff.

I mean, think about Nixon and what he tried to do to the country. But, I gotta say, I dug the whole nightmare thing the most. How the guy's punishment was living his own nightmare. Very cool. Effective, you know."

"'Cool'?" I rubbed my face. Was this conversation real? "Um, not the word I'd use." I looked again at Grady, cataloguing the differences between his appearance and Billy's – at least Billy as he looked a decade ago. What if Billy had changed as much as Stu? Did I care? The man I once loved was gone. The Billy I would soon see was a stranger.

The leather of Grady's chair squeaked as he crossed his right ankle over his left knee, bringing my thoughts back to the moment. He appeared relaxed, as if he was enjoying chatting with me. The best of my limited options seemed to be keeping him talking. If he wanted to talk about *1984*, I could play along. I took another sip of water then cleared my throat. "Since you read the book, I imagine you've given some thought to your own worst nightmare. What it would be."

"Yeah, I have." Grady studied the contents of his glass before he continued. "I used to worry about dying somewhere alone in the jungle. Flesh rotting away, falling off my bones. No one knowing who I was. Now..." He shrugged. "Guess it's some Columbian trying to take over the business. But that's not a nightmare. That's more a day-to-day business risk. How about you?"

"What?"

"What's your worst nightmare?"

I couldn't wrap my head around this. Grady sounded like he actually wanted to hear my answer. I let my rage burn through as I said, "Waking up to find what I thought was your brother beheaded in this goddamn house."

He uncrossed his legs and leaned forward, a small smile lifting the corners of his mouth. "That screwed you up, didn't it?"

"Of course. Who wouldn't get messed up by something like that?"

He set his glass on the side table. "But, it gave you nightmares? Like for real?"

"Yes. Every night. Until a couple of days ago."

"What made things change?"

"Finding out your goddamn brother's alive. So, when do I get to see him?"

Grady shifted in his chair and tapped his knee with the gun. "You know, I told Billy not to bring you along that night. He should've come alone. But the little shit couldn't stand to spend a whole night away from you. Can you believe it? At his age? He should've known better. Still, he did try to keep you out of it."

I shook my head then regretted the action. Waves of pain sent the world spinning. When the twirling stopped, I looked again at Grady. "Right. Leaving me to wake up with all those dead bodies. That sure kept me out of it."

"Hey, I'm trying to explain. Like I said, he didn't know what was going down that night. Just that he was supposed to come alone." Grady picked up his glass, brought it to his lips but didn't sip. "When I got here, he told me he left you at home. Later on I clued in that you were upstairs. Billy finally admitted he slipped you a roofie, to make sure you missed the action. He thought that was just as good as not bringing you along. Stupid shit got that wrong."

"He drugged me?"

Grady arched an eyebrow. "Right. You treated your body like a temple back then. Don't act like pounding down drugs was a real 'no-no' for you."

"That's not the point. I chose what drugs I took. Billy slipping me something or giving me something but telling me it was something else... That's sick. No wonder my memory the next day wound up scrambled. I still have huge chunks missing from that night."

Grady shrugged. "You seemed to like it when you took it. At least that's what Billy said. I had him test marketing them. Back then roofies were big in Europe but hadn't hit the streets here yet. Of course, we didn't know all of the drug's properties. But it was a fun little number for a while – before the perverts got a hold of it."

"Wow. You're a real man of standards."

"You know, I'm still holding the damn gun. You might want to watch your attitude."

He had a point. I softened my tone. "Right. So, you convinced Billy to lie to me and got him peddling roofies, heroin, coke and pot for you back then. What does he do for you now?"

"Gives me peace of mind."

Grady wasn't going to tell me anything. I guessed that meant Billy would give me all the bad news about his life. I chewed my lower lip and stared at Grady. He looked so much like his brother. But, Billy without a heart. If you got past the fear-inducing quality to Grady's eyes, he looked good. Hard to believe he was forty-two. To look that good he probably didn't sample his own product. I wondered if Billy had managed to cut back on the drugs and alcohol. If those habits didn't kill you, they aged you.

I tried to catch Grady's deadfish eyes. "You're saying Billy didn't know you were alive before you – what? Came back from the dead and offered him a job?"

"Yeah." Grady gave a low chuckle. "That first visit gave him a bit of a shock. He thought he was hallucinating. It was pretty funny."

I began to shake my head, but feared another wave of pain from my skull. "I'll bet."

"Hey, forget about the shock. Billy was thrilled to have his big brother back."

Grady probably got that right. Hero worship had filled Billy's voice whenever he talked about his brother. But I wished Billy had chosen to share Grady's resurrection with me back when he reappeared. "And you took all that happiness and converted it into loyalty. Got yourself a new employee in the family business."

"Hey, I helped him. The guy was living in a flophouse. Hookers in the next room renting beds by the hour. How do you think I felt, knowing my little brother lived in a goddamn bonafide rat hole. You were there. You know what the place was like. I made it possible for him to earn some real money and get out of that dump. Of course the stupid douche refused to move. Believe me, I busted his hump about that. I think Billy was too scared to tell you he could afford a better place. Scared you'd want to know how he could pay for the upgrade."

I took another sip of water. "When can I see him?"

"Thought you were all pissed off at him. You getting a warm fuzzy feeling for him again? Or you want to see him so you can ream him out?"

"I don't know."

"An honest answer. I don't get many of those, you know?" He sighed. "Look, Billy didn't get into the business to make me happy. He needed the dough. And I didn't pick this life. It picked me. Think about it. I get sucked up by the government a few days after my eighteenth birthday. I mean, it's nineteen-seventy and everyone knows the war's winding down. Still I get my ass drafted. Shipped to Nam. I was screwed.

Knew I was gonna die in that goddamn jungle." Grady shook his head. "But when I got there, things weren't as godawful as I imagined. I mean, yeah, things were way screwed. Nobody knew what the hell was going on. Guys got blown up, lost feet, legs and crap like that. But if you got smart, greased the right wheels, you could avoid the messier situations."

Grady looked at me like he expected some type of comment. The pounding in my head had receded a bit, but a fresh wave of nausea rolled through. From the back of my mind a small voice whispered: If you want to live, keep this asshole talking. "Uh, I don't know a lot about that time. But Billy said our army guys got slaughtered."

"Billy's grasp of history wasn't real strong. But he got some parts right. Most the time it was a crapshoot who would survive. But, if you figured out who owned who, there were ways to improve your odds. Didn't hurt none when I made a few connections. You know, became the guy no one else wanted to see get blown up. Got myself a nice little business. Sweet times, you know? You could get it all – pot, heroin, hashish. Everything. At a good price. I ended up supplying a good percentage of the guys where I got stationed. Man, the money poured in." Grady stared off into the middle distance.

I knew I needed to speak. But instead, I focused on the gun. They way Grady held it, the weapon looked like a part of him. I sat straighter, wondering how far I'd get if I threw myself at his gun hand. No one but Trevor knew where I was and it sounded like he was out of commission. No one was coming to the rescue. I took a deep breath and looked at Billy's brother. "Billy told me when you went to Vietnam the war was close to over, but that most our guys got used as cannon fodder. If you were in the last wave, how'd you make it out?"

"First off I've gotta ask, did Billy actually use the term 'cannon fodder?'" Grady stared like he expected an answer.

"No. That's how I think about what he told me."

He nodded. "Makes sense. A lot of our guys got the Swiss cheese treatment. There was this kind of hopeless vibe hanging over the guys each time a new decision came from the brass. We kept hearing that within the year, the US would pull out. Most guys thought they'd die before that happened. Rumors of a full withdrawal had been flying around for a long time, but this time, it felt like the end was close. I wanted to get out with my ass in one piece. But I also didn't want the ride to end."

"Ride?" Was I a fool to think I would survive if I kept Grady talking until Billy showed his face? Was there a chance Billy would let me go?

"You couldn't understand. When you grow up with nothing and then you can get it all..." Grady looked at his empty glass and shook his head. "I wasn't gonna let it all slip away. I managed to hook up with a sergeant who was shipping stateside and the two of us expanded the business into the U.S. Those were some good times." He leaned forward. Both hands – including the one with the gun – dangled between his knees. "I was never big on school, never took any business classes. But, man, I so got it. The whole supply and demand thing. If you've got a product people want, they'll crawl over the next guy to give you their money. I'm a real champion of free enterprise." He stared at me as if he expected some reaction.

"Go capitalism?"

"Shit. This is so beyond your world. Spoiled rich kid like you. Crying yourself to sleep while daddy's money pays for your designer clothes and your fancy house in your million dollar neighborhood. When people work for it, they understand the value of a buck."

Anger boiled. Though it was foolish to take a verbal dig at him, I couldn't stop myself. "Right, you work for it. You slave in the fields harvesting your crops and then hauling them to market. You're like the backbone of America."

"Jesus, but you've got a mouth on you." Grady smiled.

He looked more like Billy than I could stand. I cast my gaze at the thick carpet between us. "So how'd you do it?"

"You mean, get out?"

"Yeah. With everyone else dying or coming back crippled, how'd you manage to come back dead, rich and alive?"

Grady chuckled, the sound reverberating like bone caught in a blender. "With the full troop pullout around the corner, I had to get gone. I wasn't ready to close up shop and get shipped back to the US with my unit, so I did the AWOL thing for a while. Didn't go very far, because I was still selling to my guys, but I stopped bunking with them. My friends kept telling me how the brass looked all over for me, but they couldn't have looked too hard. Still, faking my death seemed a more permanent solution to the problem. I have to admit, I got lucky there."

"Why do I think your good luck hinged on someone else's bad luck?"

Grady threw back his head and laughed. "Billy never told me how funny you are. Not many folks make me laugh. You're right about the good luck-bad luck thing. But it's not like I caused the bad luck for the guy or anything. That's just the way of the world."

He picked up his glass again, saw it was empty and slapped it back onto the table. "I was with a couple guys from my old platoon when we got ambushed by the Cong. We hit the dirt, returned fire. Everybody retreated to a better position while the guys called in for support. With back-up on its way, I needed to get my ass out of there. That's when I saw one of the guys was down. Shot in the head, half his face gone. A real mess. But I knew a once-in-a-lifetime chance when I saw it. While everybody else moved to better positions, I ripped off his tags and put mine around his neck." Grady smiled at me. My stomach dropped. "Flesh rots real fast in the jungle. I figured, once the guy got transported to the hospital, the medics would go by the tags. Then send his body and my tags home to my family. No one saw me make the switch and the Army wasn't gonna worry about checking his dental records."

"Somewhere out there, that man's family is waiting for a son who's never coming home."

"That's true of a lotta folks."

"Not that I don't appreciate the history lesson, but I still want to talk to Billy. I figure your story's supposed to soften me up or something. You come out first, tell me how poor Billy was only helping you out with the family business. How he didn't know about the plan to murder all those people here. How Billy had no idea that leaving me behind with the dead bodies might be a problem for me."

Grady laughed and once again my pulse raced. The laugh sounded so much like Billy's. "Yeah, pretty hard to explain away leaving you here. At least so Billy comes out sounding good. But I think I can do it. You know the point of the killings, right?"

I shrugged. "I assume it had something to do with drugs."

"Duh. The Orwell Massacre – don't you love that name?" Grady smiled again. "The

Orwell Massacre was about power. About strengthening my position. Some crappy little upstart was cutting into my business in a big way. Big enough to settle his family in this goddamn mansion. The bodies you found? His family. I took out his wife, his kid, his brother and his brother's wife, and his mother. And sent a message to any other greedy sonsofbitches not to horn in. I also wanted to use the killings to tie Billy closer to the business. He got a little soft on me back then, said he didn't feel right about pushing heroin. Said you didn't like it. You sure messed with that boy's head.

"Billy didn't know about the plan I had for him to fake his own death. But unless he broke free from his semi-normal life, he wasn't ever gonna be useful to me. Let's face it, Ramona, you were holding the guy back. I knew once I got him away from you, I could move him up the ladder. But you were one dead weight Billy didn't want to ditch. The guy should've been thrilled by the chance to take on more of my business and make a shitload more money. Instead the little shit tells me he wants out." Grady shook his head. "All because you didn't like him selling the hard stuff."

A candle-size glimmer of warmth flickered in my chest. Billy hadn't wanted to leave me. He'd talked about getting out of the drug trade. Even though Grady managed to change his mind, it gave me a small rush of pleasure knowing Billy had wanted to hang on to me. That he hadn't just been using me for sex and money. "How'd you talk him into it? Into leaving me. Into faking his own death?"

It was Grady's turn to shrug. "I didn't."

"You forced him to do it? How?"

Grady shook his head. "Billy always called you a smart cookie, but you're sure as hell not getting the point now."

"What point?"

"Billy wouldn't budge. Said he loved you. I told him I'd get him a hundred girls a helluva a lot prettier than you to bang his boney ass, but no, he only wanted you. Dumbshit loser. He told me he quit."

I stared at Grady, waiting for the punch line.

Grady raised his eyebrows and looked at me.

"But you changed his mind."

"Guess you could say that. If sawing off his head didn't change his mind, I don't know what else would."

Twenty-four

My pulse rocketed. Grady's mouth moved, but I only heard the whoosh of blood. The sound of life. My life, not Billy's. Billy's blood had pooled out behind him, below the spot where his head should have been, crusting as it dried on the floor of this miserable house. After all this, Billy was dead again. Killed by his own brother.

I jerked to my feet, staring at Billy's killer. My knees refused to lock and I crumpled back onto the chair.

"Guess you didn't get where the story was headed. Surprise." Grady wagged the gun at me. "If you're gonna puke again, speak up. I got a trash can right there." He gestured towards the sideboard. "I don't want to bring in cleaners to scrub your upchuck out of my good Persian rug. The thing cost a fortune. Your pal, the old guy, already spewed all over the guest room carpet."

"I'm not going to hurl." My voice sounded far away and my throat hurt. I wasn't sure I was telling Grady the truth, but didn't give a damn. I stared at him, waiting for the feeling to return to my limbs. How could I have thought – even for a minute – he looked like Billy?

"Yeah, well, if you think you are, tell me. You look kind of funny. You gonna pass out?"

"Right, I look funny. Try hysterical. How... How could you go on and on like that? Let me think that... Let me think Billy was alive? Let me get all angry with him? Oh God." I leaned forward, head in hands, and tried to find my breath.

"You're one of those, huh? Think you can't be pissed at a dead guy. The hell with that." Grady stood. "The way it works is this: A guy screws you over, get pissed. It don't matter if he's alive or dead. Well, that's not true. It's always better if the guy that screwed you over winds up dead."

I raised my head and glared at Billy's brother. The man was like honey fungus, blooming at the base of a tree, taking out the roots bit by bit, but always killing what he fed on. "Why?"

"So they can't come back at you. Thought that seemed pretty plain."

"No. Why'd you kill him? Why couldn't Billy just refuse to work for you? Why not let him walk away?"

"That was never gonna happen. Billy

knew my operation inside and out. My sources. All my connections here in the States."

"But... He worshipped you. He never would've turned you in."

"Maybe not right away. But things change. That wasn't a risk I could take." Grady shrugged then grinned. "Weird thing is, I didn't plan everything out. When Billy told me he quit, that was it for me. No way could I trust him after that. And, no way could I let him live either. But I didn't think ahead, didn't see all the good stuff his death would give me. Billy being dead did more than end a possible problem, it gave me a new identity. Which I needed. It also scared the crap out of every other dealer. Foreign and domestic. I mean, if I was willing to kill my own brother, chop off his hands and head, what the hell would I do to someone who crossed me that I didn't love? No one's tried to cut themselves in or out of my business for a real long time.

"You still look kind of green. Sure you're not gonna puke? This goddamn carpet cost me twenty grand."

The reality of Billy's murder tumbled around in time with the throb from my brain. Another question surfaced. "But if Billy's dead, then what's this all about?"

"What's what all about?"

"This." I gestured at him, at the room and then myself. "Why send the Elf after me? Why send him to snatch me? If it's not to see Billy, then why?"

"The Elf?" Grady smirked. "That's a new one. Don't think I've ever heard anyone call Sean something that warm and fuzzy. I sent Sean after you because you've got something that belongs to me. And I want it back."

Dazed as I felt, a few moments passed before my mind honed in on the eight thousand dollars I'd found after Billy died – died the first time. I stared at Grady. With all the wealth he had amassed, the man cared about the eight grand I took from Billy's room? I shook my head, but stopped as the motion amplified the throb on the right side of my skull. "I can write you a check. But I need to transfer the money. Or I can go to the bank and get it."

"You moved it to your personal account?" Grady took a step forward, his face red. "Are you nuts? When? Tell me you put it in a safe deposit box and not in your account."

"What difference does it make where I put it? Were the bills marked or something? Like from a robbery?"

Grady cocked his head and stared. "What the hell are you talking about?"

A chill grew at the center of my chest then ran down my arms to my fingertips. At least I felt something again. "The eight thousand dollars." Grady continued looking at me, a frown creasing his forehead. "The eight grand I found in a coffee can under the floor at Billy's place," I added. "The coffee can where he kept our money. When I saw all that cash,

I knew it was drug money. But I needed it to get gone, so I took it. I spent a little and put the rest in the bank."

After scrubbing his face with his free hand, Grady pointed the gun at me. "Don't fuck around with me. You think I care about a dinky-ass eight grand?" He sat. "Jesus, you scared the crap out of me. Thought you done something dangerous and stupid. I want the other thing of mine you took."

My thoughts moved in a sluggish and swollen fashion. An image of Billy floated through my brain: He stood in front of a movie theater with someone, the other man's face blurred by motion. Now I knew that other man's identity and why Billy had looked unhappy. "That was you. In the picture. Is that what you want? The photo of you and Billy? Because the name of the movie's visible on the marquee behind you? Are you worried the cops might figure out you didn't die in Viet Nam if they ever get ahold of that picture? Don't bother. Your face is all fuzzy. No one would recognize you."

Grady leaned back. "You're still messing with me, right? I don't give a crap about some old photo."

"Then what?" I felt the fingers of my right hand mime rubbing my good luck charm. "Oh." I felt like an idiot. But I always thought of the dog tag as Billy's not Grady's. My stomach lurched when I remembered the way I had rubbed that piece of metal to give me comfort over the past ten years. "I don't have it." I pictured my keychain dangling from the Elf's injured balls and fought an inappropriate urge to laugh.

"The hell you don't."

My earlier bravado vanished. Deep down I had counted on Billy getting me out of this mess. Would telling Grady the truth prolong my life or hasten my death? The gun's safety released with a click that echoed inside my chest and helped me decide. "Your guy took it when he grabbed my car keys. It was on my keychain. The Elf, I mean Sean – he's got it."

"You gave it to Sean? Sean's got the tag?"

"Yes."

"Well, this changes things." Grady narrowed his eyes. "I should've known. Dammit." He stood then hurled his chair against the wall.

Pulse racing, I tensed, waiting for Grady to strike out at me.

He swirled around to face me. "The way he hated you so hard right off the bat, that was weird." He shook his head. "I should've seen through it. The bastard was trying to throw me off the scent, right? Pretending to hate you. You both must think I'm a goddamn fool." He crossed the few feet of carpet separating us and grabbed a handful of my hair and yanked me to my feet.

Tears filled my eyes. My scalp wound tore open. Hot blood trickled down my temple.

"How long have you two been working together, huh?" Grady gave my hair another sharp tug. "Since that first night when I had him hitting on you at The Deuce? You fall for his snake charmer act and decide to partner with him? What's the plan? Sean stays put, pretends to keep working for me, hoping I'll believe the tag got lost years ago? What'd the bastard promise you? How much?"

"Nothing. We didn't team up." I tried to pry Grady's hand loose. In response he wrenched my head upward until I stood on my toes. "He took my keychain. I don't think he noticed the dog tag."

Grady raised the gun to eye level and pressed the barrel against my forehead.

The cold mouth of metal dug into my skin. I tried not to picture what would happen if he pulled the trigger.

Grady's breath grazed my ear as he spoke. "That better be the truth. And you better hope the sonofabitch still has it." He pulled the gun back from my forehead.

I could breathe again. Grady hustled me from the room, using my hair as a rudder.

Stu looked up from his paperwork when we entered the office. His lips formed an 'O' of surprise. He half-rose. "What's going on?"

"Where's Sean?" Grady pulled me to a stop.

Stu shrugged. "I dunno. Upstairs maybe. Or checking on the old guy."

"Got your gun?"

"Right here." Stu patted the desk.

"Get it. If Sean shows himself, shoot him."

"Shoot- What's going on?"

"Sean's trying to screw me. And you know

how I feel about that." Grady jerked my head back and twisted until we made eye contact. "You're gonna learn you messed with the wrong guy."

My scalp felt like it might tear loose. "I didn't. We didn't."

"Shut up." He turned back to Stu. "I'm not screwing around here. Get your goddamn gun out of the goddamn desk."

"Right." Stu wrenched open a drawer then held up a nickel-plated handgun. "I'm on it."

"Good. We'll check upstairs. You stay here. And if you see Sean, shoot him. He's not leaving this house. Got it?"

Stu nodded.

Grady pulled me forward, quick-marching us into the mansion's wide foyer.

I glimpsed the dark archway to what had been the game room ten years ago, the room where I found Billy's butchered body. In spite of the pain from my skull, my head felt like it might float away.

"I'm giving you a chance to make things right." Grady gave me a shake. "You listening?"

I tried to nod, but his grip on my hair prevented me. "Yes."

"Good. We're gonna climb these stairs, go to Sean's room. Then we're gonna look for your goddamn keychain. If my dog tag's still on it, I might change my mind about you and Sean trying to screw me."

Right. It didn't matter whether or not I convinced Grady that Sean and I weren't working together. Not after telling me what he had done to his brother. Once we found the dog tag, I was as good as dead. But what if I found it first? My Swiss army knife was on the key chain, too. If I got my hands on that, I would have a weapon. My half-second of hope crumbled as reality crashed in. Who was I kidding? A three-inch Swiss army knife against a gun? I'd probably do as well to get a running start and jump out one of the second story windows. At least that way I would die outside this house of horrors.

We bounded up the stairs in unison, my head throbbing with each step. At the top, Grady flattened himself against the wall. He pulled me to him like a shield, his arm clamped against my windpipe. I clutched at his arm, trying to free my airway. He extended his free hand and opened the door to our right. He pushed me ahead of him into the Elf's room.

The high-ceilinged room was empty, the bed unmade, clothes scattered across the floor, chair and dresser. "Call his name," Grady whispered in my ear, his hot breath like a fever on my skin. He loosened his grip on my throat.

After sucking in two deep breaths, I called, "Sean?" My voice sounded reedy and weak. I tried again. "Sean? You in here?" No response.

Grady shut the door behind him. "Check the bathroom." He shoved me to the closed door on the left side of the bed. "Open it."

I grabbed the cut-glass knob, the faceted planes cold against my skin. My sweaty palm slipped. I tightened my grip, turned the knob then shoved the door open. The room smelled of damp towels, mold and Irish Spring soap. Fitting. Grady pushed me forward until we both stood inside. No way the Elf could hide his huge body in this small room.

"Check the shower." Grady nudged me forward.

My hand trembled when I ripped back the plastic curtain. The stall was empty.

"OK. Let's find this keychain of yours." Grady pulled me back into the bedroom then pushed me at the dresser.

There had to be a way out of this. While my brain churned, I removed the layer of sweat-marked shirts the Elf had left atop the chest of drawers. Once I cleared away the Elf's laundry, I saw the dresser held a collection of loose coins, a blue plastic button, a tube of antibiotic ointment and a pair of nail clippers. But no keychain. Also no plan of escape. I turned my attention to the drawers.

The top one held a huge collection of skin magazines. I lifted them out and told myself not to think about why or how the magazine pages got to their curled, soiled condition. The bottom of the drawer revealed more loose change, two ticket stubs from a recent action-adventure movie, and a cat's-eye marble.

I peeked at Grady then pushed back my disappointment. The gun stayed tucked in the waistband of his jeans while he tore apart the Elf's bed. Grady stood between me and the door – running wasn't an option. I pulled out the second drawer, then repeated my search on it and the next one without success. After I checked all the drawers, I moved on to the nightstand. The single drawer held a stack of magazines, a pack of gum and more loose coins, but on the shelf below, I hit pay dirt. Beneath a grimy wife beater T-shirt, my keychain glinted in the afternoon sun. My car keys and house key remained hooked to the silver loop. But the dog tag no longer dangled there.

I was in real trouble now.

Twenty-five

I didn't understand. The Elf hadn't 'taken' Grady's dog tag – he got it as bonus when I stabbed him. Why take the tag off the key ring? Did he know Grady wanted it? And why was Grady so hot and heavy to get the thing back? Everyone already thought Grady was dead, so what did it matter who had the damn tag?

What should I do? Bury the keychain under the Elf's dirty T-shirt? Pick it up and tuck it in my pocket? Or show it to Grady and admit the dog tag was gone?

My brain still felt slow and soggy. No clever plan was going to jump out. It was probably best to stick with the truth and see where that led – after I removed the Swiss army knife from the keychain. It wasn't a big blade, but any weapon was better than nothing. Jaw clenched, I released the catch for the ring, slid the knife free then tucked it inside my back pocket. "Found it." I raised the key ring. "But the dog tag's gone."

Grady lunged across the room.

"Wait." I held up my free hand like a traffic cop. "I never gave this to Sean." Grady continued towards me in a rush. I scurried back until I ran out of room for retreat. "He took it. He must've taken off the tag. It's got nothing to do with me."

He wrenched the keychain from my hand, hurled it to the floor. "God dammit. You better hope he took it. Because if that tag's gone, you're gonna pay." Grady's fingers encircled my throat. He stepped in until we stood inches apart. He leaned forward, his forehead touching mine as he tightened his grip on my windpipe. "If that dog tag is lost," he said, his voice low, like a lover promising passion, "I'll cut out your tongue for lying to me."

Sweat coated my hands as I stared into his bottomless eyes and tried to pry his fingers loose from my throat.

"That's how I'll start." With his free hand, he raised the gun and pressed it against the side of my head. His breath landed hot and swampy on my cheek. "The big finish comes when I get out my saw and cut off your goddamn head."

The expression in his eyes sent sparks of dread down my spine. When I looked into those poisonous pools, I saw who he was. Grady released my throat. A sob escaped across my bruised larynx before my knees gave out. I doubled over, bumping my head against his chest. Tears blurred my vision. I forced my knees to hold firm. Grady had told me a truth I didn't want to know. But he wasn't a man who spared others. He wasn't someone you could soften with pleas. I didn't care why he wanted the damn dog tag. He had shown me the evil inside him. And given me the broad strokes of what he'd done to Billy.

He looked eager to do the same to me.

A shot roared through the mansion. Grady jumped back then spun, gun pointed at the closed door to the landing. I stared at the door, too, but saw no threat except Grady. He reached back, grabbed a handful of my hair then pulled me across the room. At the door, he released my hair and clutched my shoulder, positioning me in front of him before he wrenched it open. Once again using me as a shield, he shoved me through the doorway and onto the landing.

Another gunshot boomed. My heart jackhammered. I felt like my whole body was vibrating. Grady pushed me forward to the staircase. In lockstep, we began our descent. Silence once again blanketed the first floor; our footfalls on the carpeted steps were the only noise I heard above my pounding pulse. Halfway down, a faint moan drifted from below. A big part of me wanted to collapse, curl into a ball. But I wasn't going to give in to that impulse. I wouldn't offer my neck to Billy's killer. I didn't know how I was going to get through this – or if I could. But, if death came for me, I was going to do my best to take Grady with me.

When we reached the ground floor, the smell of cordite and burning wool filled my nostrils. Grady yanked my hair, directing me to the office where we'd left Stu. When he pushed the door open, the smell of blood and shit filled the air.

"Damn it." Grady shoved me away.

I stumbled then caught myself.

Gun raised, Grady scanned the room. He lifted his eyes to the ceiling. "Sean! You're fucking with the wrong guy." He moved forward and I saw what Grady's body had hidden from view. Stu was crumpled against the desk, forehead touching the paper-covered surface. Red splotched several of the white sheets. Grady charged past the desk, toward the sitting room.

No one clutched at my throat or bloody scalp any more. This was my chance to get out. My gaze landed on Stu again and everything seemed to shift. I flashed back to how the place looked a decade ago: This had been the living room. The room where I found three of the bodies. I stepped away from their imagined forms sprawling on the floor.

Stu gave a bubbly-sounding cough. My reverie shattered, I turned toward the desk. He struggled to push himself upright, grunted then sank back against the burgundy leather. With another grunt, he tried to stand, but landed in the chair, his face white and waxy like an orchid. His eyes appeared dull and confused. With his creased forehead and pasty skin, he looked ancient. Strange to think we were almost the same age. Stu grimaced. I tried to mask my revulsion at the sight of his blood-covered teeth. Death was wrapping its arms around him. There was nothing I could do. One of his hands clutched at his chest over the Rorschach of blood staining his sweatshirt. His other hand scrabbled through an open desk drawer.

Stu's struggle for breath mesmerized me. My feet felt Krazy Glued to the thick carpet and I stared at the dying man without moving. Light bounced off his bald scalp, creating a halo. But Stu was no angel. He had climbed into bed with the devil. For all I knew, he helped kill Billy. He looked at me, bared his teeth again then his eyes widened. He lurched forward, his hand flopping onto the desk with a slap. With a muddy-sounding grunt, his other hand landed on the desk gripping the nickel-plated handgun.

He moved his lips, but no sound came out. My gut said to run, but I stared at his blood-coated teeth. He took a rattling breath then let go of the gun. It clattered onto the wood surface. Stu and I stared at one another. Before Grady dragged me out of the room by my hair, he had ordered Stu to get out his gun. I saw him set it on the desk. Why had he put the gun away?

"Ramona," Stu whispered.

The name broke the spell. I retreated a step. Whether or not Stu survived was out of my hands. My survival hinged on the choices I made right now. I dashed to the desk and grabbed the handgun. Stu didn't try to stop me. I didn't know why he had left himself open to the Elf's attack, but I didn't plan to make that same mistake. I took another step back then one more. There were three doors to choose from: The door Grady rushed through, the one that went to the foyer and the front door, and one that remained closed. For all I knew, the last door led to freedom. Or disaster. I chose the path I knew. With one last look at the dying man, I ran. Again.

I dashed across the slippery stone floor of the foyer. As I headed for the front door, Grady's words flashed through my mind. He had said the old man threw-up on the guest room carpet. That meant Trevor was alive and somewhere inside this house. I didn't like him and Trevor didn't like me, but he'd wound up here because I stole his wallet. I spun and ran along the wide hallway to my right, head throbbing. The thick carpet muffled my steps.

Open doors lined the corridor. I raced on. What I was looking for wouldn't be left in plain sight. Another gunshot echoed through the house. I froze as my heart did the can-can. It sounded like the Elf and Grady hadn't worked things out yet. The shot had come from somewhere behind me – maybe the other wing? With a shaky breath, I resumed jogging, my headache keeping time with my steps. Near the end of the hall, the light became dim. The last door remained closed. I pegged that as the place where Grady had stashed Trevor.

The doorknob refused to turn no matter how hard I twisted. I wanted to weep. In this type of situation, in the movies, people shot off the lock or kicked in the door. But if I fired Stu's gun, wouldn't that bring Grady and the Elf running? I tucked the gun into my jeans at the small of my back. Maybe shooting out the lock wasn't wise, but kicking in the door was worth a try. In a house this big, the risk seemed small that I would make enough noise to draw Grady's attention and wrath. I backed up then kicked with all my might. Too far from the door, my foot barely connected. After taking a step closer, I tried again. The shock of hitting the sturdy wood reverberated through my leg and up my spine, making my head wound throb and rattling my teeth. But the door didn't budge. I strained for sounds of reaction from the other end of the house or the opposite side of the door, but heard nothing. I kicked the door again.

A well-built home, the door neither shook nor cracked. I stood panting, hands on hips, assessing the situation. My fingertips brushed the bulge made by Trevor's wallet in my back pocket. I pulled out the billfold and rooted through the plastic sleeves for a credit card. Though I had never jimmied a lock, I watched Billy do it more than once. Trevor's American Express card would do the trick. I crouched, picturing the way Billy used to hold his hand as he slid the card between the door and the jam. I inserted the plastic rectangle where the tongue of the lock met the door frame. The card jammed against something. I wiggled the card then shifted my angle of approach, but couldn't get it to slide in deeper. Mimicking Billy's stance and motions wasn't going to get me very far; I had no idea if the card was in the right spot or if I was using the right amount of pressure. I pulled out the card, took a deep breath and tried again, this time a quarter of an inch higher. The card stuck again. Was it something about the card? Would Mastercard or Visa work better? I stared at the credit card and Trevor's full name jumped out at me: Trevor Hamilton Marlowe.

"Sonofabitch." Trevor was Hamilton? Mom's mystery man?

No time to stop and think about that now. A new plan came forth, Venus-like from my churning brain waves. I ran to the nearest open door on the same side of the hall then rushed through the vacant bedroom to the window. The latch stuck, but after a few choice swear words and a lot of shoving, I got it to move. I heaved up the sash then climbed over the sill and dropped four feet to the dying grass of the back lawn. Years of grime obscured the view through the neighboring window, but not so much that I couldn't see Trevor bound to a desk chair. My unzipped overnight bag lay by his feet. I hoped the treasures my father had saved for me were still inside. It took less than twenty seconds to pull a brick from the decorative edging of what had once been a flower bed. With a glance around the yard to make sure Grady and Sean hadn't brought their fight outside, I hurled the brick through the window. Glass shattered, the noise way too loud. I dug out another brick, tucked my hand inside my sleeve then used the brick to knock the remaining shards of glass away from the frame. Once the path was clear, I pulled myself across the rotting sill.

The smell of vomit filled the room. Bile splotched Trevor's shirt and pants as well as a small section of carpet. I ran to him and crouched by his side. For once, his face didn't register contempt when he saw me. I lifted one edge of the duct tape sealing his mouth. "This is going to hurt." He nodded his understanding. I ripped off the tape.

Trevor grunted and closed his eyes. When he looked at me again, his anger showed. "What in blue blazes is going on? What kind of mess did you get me into?"

I stared at the man who might be my father and felt tears burn my eyes. But crying now wasn't an option. "Don't." I held up a hand in warning. "Just don't." Using the Swiss army knife, I cut the tape from his right arm, his long-sleeved shirt protecting his skin from possible nicks. "You've got no idea what's going on. I didn't invite you to tag along. And I didn't have to come looking for you." After freeing his left arm, I turned my attention to his ankles.

"You're right. Sorry." Trevor flexed his hands to get the circulation going. "You have a plan to get us out of here?" When I cut the final piece of tape, Trevor bolted up then wobbled. I grabbed him, helping to keep him upright. He swore as he shook out his right leg, then his left. He pulled away. "I'm okay now. Where do we go?"

Though he looked fit, I wasn't sure he would be able to climb the seven-foot-high back fence if I took him out through the window. The way my head felt, I wasn't sure I could do it either. And I had no idea if there was a back gate. If we weren't able to get out, we could get trapped in the backyard like a pair of mechanical ducks in a shooting gallery. A shudder ran down my spine.

The front door held its own risks, but seemed the best option. "This way." I unlocked the door and peeked out. No shouts of alarm sounded. The hall remained empty. "Come on." I guided Trevor down the passage. No gunshots had rung out for a while. While that cut the risk of us getting hit in their crossfire, it also left me with no clue as to where Grady or the Elf lurked. My bladder shrank to the size of a walnut. Each open door we approached offered the threat of attack. One after another, I peeked into the rooms that branched off the hall but saw no one.

When we reached the entry to the foyer, I flattened my back against the corridor wall. I leaned close to Trevor, speaking into his ear. "The front door's our best way out. I think Grady and Sean are in the other wing. I say we tiptoe to the door and, once we're outside, run like hell. Sound good to you?"

Trevor nodded, his face pale, but determined.

"Okay, let's go." I took a deep breath then stuck my head around the corner. A bullet tore through the foyer wall to my right. With a yelp, I ducked back, grabbed Trevor's arm and pulled him into the shelter of the hallway. Heart racing, I looked at the man who might be my father. His mouth hung open and his eyes lacked focus. "Trevor, listen to me." I shook his arm, willing him to stay strong. With a loud intake of air he seemed to pull himself together and zero in on me. "I want you to go back the way we came. Go back down the hall. Understand?" I waited until Trevor nodded his comprehension. "Climb out the broken window and find a way out of the yard. Then go for help."

He took two steps then stopped. "Aren't you coming?"

"No. Whoever's out there saw me. He knows I'm here. If I stay, he'll keep fighting. If I go with you, he'll follow." I looked at Trevor, trying to hide my despair. For the majority of my life, the man I called father had viewed me with disappointment. Now, I might be looking at my birth father, and – hard to believe – my relationship with him was even worse. The thought of watching him die was more than I could bear. "If we run and he follows, no one gets away. Having your death on my conscience would mess me up in ways you can't begin to imagine. Go."

Trevor nodded. He moved toward me, gave my shoulder a light squeeze then slipped down the hall. When he reached the shadowy end of the corridor, I turned my attention to the foyer, once again edging toward the opening.

Twenty-six

The Elf hunkered behind the stairway's newel post. A large swath of blood stained his left sleeve. Impossible to tell from this far away if it was his own blood. He lifted the gun and fired again. I flinched and tried to meld with the wall. Whoever's blood was on the Elf's shirt, it didn't seem to have dampened his enthusiasm for the attack. But he stayed where he was and didn't come charging across the foyer. Maybe he suspected I had grabbed Stu's gun and wrongly thought I knew how to use the thing. Or maybe the blood on his sleeve was his. I hoped for the latter.

With a shaky breath, I pulled the gun from my waistband then backed down the hall. I needed to figure out if the gun's safety was on or off. And whether or not I had any bullets.

Palms wet with sweat, I stared at the gun. I recognized the trigger. But where was the damn safety and how could I tell if the thing was on or off? The gleaming piece of metal provided no answer. But there was one way to find out. I stole to the foyer entrance, pointed the gun barrel in the Elf's general direction and pulled the trigger. My arm jerked up. I stumbled back a half step as the gun recoiled. Now I knew: The gun was loaded and the safety off. Jesus. Lucky thing I didn't shoot off my ass earlier when I climbed out the window.

The Elf returned fire. A bullet pierced the plaster less than a foot from where I stood. I crouched, covered my head and hoped my body stopped shaking long enough for me to fire another round. I wished for the know-how and time to figure out how many bullets the gun held. From my position near the floor, I couldn't see the Elf. I closed one eye, focused on the gun sight, aimed at the newel post on the bannister then pulled the trigger. The recoil knocked me onto my back, which wound up being a good thing when the Elf responded with a volley of bullets that cut the lath and plaster three feet above me. When the shots stopped, I crab-walked farther down the hall then sat with my back against the wall. Maybe I should retreat, climb out the bedroom window. Maybe Trevor had gotten trapped in the backyard and needed a boost to make it over the fence. Maybe the Elf was injured and unable to follow, unable to gun down Trevor and me.

Undecided, I leaned forward and peered

toward the front door. Shit. The Elf was moving across the foyer, his gun pointed toward the hall. I shut my eyes and shot, pulling the trigger again and again until it clicked instead of fired. Empty. I looked to see if I had hit anything. The Elf towered, a giant shadow blocking the opening between the hall and freedom. Backlit, I saw only his silhouette, but he seemed to be clutching his stomach – which meant his gun was no longer pointed at me. It also meant I had hit him. What were the odds?

Another shot sounded. The Elf half-spun, blood spraying from his chest, like a weird magic trick. But the look of surprise on Sean's face told me this was real. He lurched against the wall then collapsed to his knees. Crouched behind him was Grady, his gun arm raised. Sean tumbled onto his side and Grady stood, shifting his weapon to point at me. "Come here."

I hadn't hit Sean at all, Grady had. I pushed myself up and leaned against the wall.

"Drop the gun. Kick it over there." He gestured with his head at the open foyer behind him. I followed his instruction, the gun clattering onto the stone floor. I stared at the Elf, his body sprawled a few yards from the spot where I had found Billy's blood-encrusted jacket a decade ago. Grady kicked Sean's gun away, though it didn't look like the Elf would shoot anything ever again. The gun skittered toward the front door.

"Search him." Grady waved me over to the Elf. "Find my goddamn dog tag."

"Right." I stared at Sean's blood-drenched chest and at the cavity created by the bullet that tore through him. The smell of blood mixed with urine. A wave of nausea hit. I looked away.

"Searching him should be nothing to you. If you weren't partners."

"Jesus. I don't have to have liked or cared about the guy to feel grossed out by his bloody corpse."

Grady laughed. "This is nothing. Until you've seen a guy chewed into pieces by enemy fire... But what the hell do you know? You're one of the lucky ones."

My mouth dropped open. "What?"

"A princess like you? You're never gonna see war. Never go hungry. You've led a charmed life." He snorted. "You've even survived your worst nightmare. You told me so. Like in *1984*. You're never gonna come up against anything worse than what you already have." Grady pointed his gun at my head. "Pat him down. Now."

I ran my trembling hands along the Elf's right leg, the one closest to me, starting at his ankle.

Grady laughed. "You've got no idea what you held onto for the last ten years. Sean didn't fill you in, did he?"

I shook my head before reaching inside Sean's right front pocket and pulling out the contents: loose coins, a used tissue. I leaned across his body, feeling my way up his left leg, doing my best to avoid the blood and gore splattered across the front of his trousers.

"Tell me, Ramona, were you this squeamish when you ripped the dog tag off the stump of Billy's neck?"

I sat back on my heels and stared at Grady. "Jesus. Billy was your brother. Don't you have any feelings for him?"

"I got plenty of feelings. Most of them pissed off. He should've stuck with me. And I don't hear you denying you stole my goddamn dog tag."

"I didn't steal it. I slipped on the thing. The chain must've broken when you attacked him." I needed to shut out the images Grady's words prodded to life. Images of Billy's face. How his eyes must have looked when he stared at his beloved brother and saw betrayal. I hated to know Billy died feeling abandoned and alone.

"Not that you'll get it, but I took the dog tag because Billy always wore it. I took it to feel close to him. That's all." My fingers brushed the familiar rounded edges of the metal rectangle inside the Elf's left pocket. I pulled out the dog tag.

Grady snatched it from my hand and rubbed the metal as he smiled. "I still can't believe you didn't know what you had. All those years. This thing could've made you a rich woman. See here?" He held the dog tag out so his name and the series of numbers faced me, a look of pride on his face.

I shrugged. It was nothing I hadn't seen before.

"The first two lines, they're part of the tag, the way it came. But this bottom line of numbers I had engraved special."

"Okay."

Grady shook his head. "This little tag holds the key to over $6 million in cash. Tax-free. My money. It's been a bitch-and-a-half getting it back. Thanks to you and Billy."

Billy. God, I was going to wind up as dead as him. As dead as Sean if I didn't figure a way out of this. My brain felt less cluttered than when I first came to, but still not sharp. But as long as I stayed alive, a chance remained Grady might screw up and I would get away. "What do you mean?"

"When I was in country, I set up a Swiss bank account. Me, a poor kid from the Bay Area. Can you believe it? My old man never would've thought it possible. Once I got that in place, I needed somewhere safe to keep the account number. That's when I got the bright idea to have it added here. When I saw my chance to trade tags with my platoon mate, everything was set. And it should've been a piece of cake when I came home. New identity, no one looking for me, several million bucks just waiting for me. So I snag the spare house key my folks kept hidden in the yard and went inside. Perfect plan, right? But my goddamn tag's not there. I tore the place apart looking. Even went so far as to call my dad. Pretended I was Billy and asked if I could have my brother's dog tags. Dad called me a drug-addled idiot. Said I couldn't even remember stealing my own brother's dog tags and punching out my old man's lights. News to me that Billy had my tags. And that he decked the old man."

"I don't get it. He had the dog tag when he started working for you. Why didn't you take it back then?"

"Seemed like a good idea for him to keep charge of it. Hell, he didn't know what it was worth. So I felt safe with him guarding the thing. But, after I chopped off his head, I couldn't find the damn dog tag. And it wasn't like I had a lot of time to mess around looking for it. I had to get my little homecoming surprise ready for the Escalante family."

Grady stared past me with a smile cold as a scythe. I suspected he was picturing the bloodbath he created inside this house ten years ago. I closed my mind against those images. "Why didn't you just ask him for it?"

"The tag always hung around his neck. I figured getting it back would be easy. But before I found it, the Escalantes came home and I had to take care of them then set the scene for the cops. You know, write the slogans on the wall. I wanted the cops to think a crazy person killed everybody. By the time I was done, too much time had passed. It was way too risky to stay longer looking for my dog tag." Grady still held a dreamy look as if the Orwell Massacre remained a treasured memory.

I rose on my knees. Though I had no plan, I wanted to be ready if an opportunity appeared. Maybe if I kept Grady focused on the past, he would relax enough for me to find a way out of this. "You left here, thinking the account number was lost?"

"Nah, not lost. Out of reach. But there was no need to panic. I figured the cops would find the tag and I'd get it back. Even then I had contacts. But my guy on the inside told me the cops never found any dog tag. They searched the house, bagged everything. But the tag wasn't here. That left only one other possibility – that Billy's sweet little girlfriend Ramona took it." His gaze turned back to me.

My intestines twisted. "I–"

He held up his hand and I froze. "But here's the real kicker: When I had one of my guys talk to Billy's friends, I find out nobody knows your last name. Or where you live. Or anything about you. No one's got any idea where you went when you blew town." He waggled the gun at me.

"That smelled bad. I don't mind telling you, I started to sweat. So I rounded up Stu and questioned him. Hard. He remembered driving you and Billy to your neighborhood one time. He found the general area where he dropped you, but didn't know any more than that. When I offered his girlfriend a healthy supply of coke, she narrowed things to one street. She thought you lived on the north end of the block, but wasn't sure. Let's face it, a cokehead's not what you'd call a reliable source."

I closed my eyes for a moment. How had Janelle known the name of my street? Or what end of it I lived on? I had never brought her to my house and was sure I never told her my address. "Billy must have told her where I lived."

"Yeah well, she helped, but not enough. Turned out nine families with daughters lived at that end of the block. Nine, can you believe it? One had a girl named Roberta and another a girl named Rowena. But no Ramona. Of course, neither of them was who I wanted. Were you friends with the Duffys?"

The bizarreness of conversing across the Elf's bullet-torn body made my vision swirl. I touched the wall for support. My mouth felt dry. I swallowed twice before answering. "Who're the Duffys?"

"They lived on the same end of the block. Had four girls, all good candidates."

I remembered the couple from Dad's funeral. They'd mentioned a daughter named Rhonda and one named Rachel. I nodded my understanding.

"Catholic family. Four girls born in a six-year period. Two of them were off the map. Found out one was hitching her way through Europe and that the other had given her parents the bird and moved out of state. The P.I. I hired couldn't find her. But when the grandma died, the kids all came home. Don't look at me like that. She died of natural causes. And all four girls came to the funeral. But," Grady shrugged, "obviously none of them was you. Right then, I thought the money was gone forever. I made the P.I. go back to the beginning. Check everyone again. The guy still couldn't find dick. He even did a door-to-door in your neighborhood. Talked to everyone, including your old man. Course I didn't know he was your old man at the time. But he told my guy his daughter died of a drug overdose. Came across very believable. Neighbors said the same thing. My guy believed you'd snuffed it. He convinced me you couldn't be the girl Billy loved." Grady shook his head.

That explained the weird vibe I had gotten from a lot of the people at my dad's funeral. Though I suspected my parents failed to mention my existence to their new friends, I never would have guessed they told their long-term friends I was dead.

"But, the Duffy funeral gave me an idea. The way those girls came home to see their dead grandma. I told Stu to watch the obits on anyone who lived on that end of the block. Just in case. When anyone on the block died who had a daughter, I sicced Sean on the situation. I didn't get too excited when Stu told me your old man kicked it. But, I was out of leads, so I had Sean watch your folks' house and talk to anyone who came and went. And surprise. You weren't as dead as your daddy claimed. I gotta say, my old man was a piece of work, but he never denied my existence. That's a real slap in the face. I'm kind of surprised you came home to pay your respects. But, I'm glad you did. If you hadn't..." Grady shook his head.

I fisted my trembling hands. "Ten years is a long time to wait."

"Explains my bad mood. But, I been doing a helluva lot more than sitting on my ass and waiting. I've been growing my business, keeping the wannabe wolves at bay. But, even though the money's been rolling in, I gotta admit, there was a time when I thought about popping a couple people on your block. Just to see if that might move things along." He shrugged. "But it's different when you kill someone who's not in the trade. Cops gotta get all over that kind of situation. Seemed smarter to wait." Grady crouched, talking over the Elf's chewed up body like he chatted with me across a grotesque coffee table. "Now, I think that I've been pretty honest with you. Opened up. Shared. Whatever the touchy-feely name is for that kind of crap these days. And I think you owe me."

"I owe you? You..." I wanted to tell him he'd ruined my life. The man had taken Billy away from me. Given me nightmares for a decade. Made me run for cover. And, since my return to Mill Valley, the Elf had terrorized me on Grady's say-so. But my anger sputtered out. Billy's death had changed my life. Scarred me. But it hadn't ruined me. Did Grady see that truth? I closed my eyes and took a deep breath. "What do I owe you?"

"An explanation: Why'd you lie to him? To Billy? Why give him a fake name? Were you slumming with the poor boy punk rocker? Holding out on him, knowing one day you'd slip back to your rich bitch life?"

I didn't want to give Grady any pieces of Billy. He didn't deserve them. But I didn't want him to think I had been out to get his brother, too. "Billy knew that wasn't my name."

"No way."

"It's true. He knew because he's the one who named me."

"That little peckerhead." Grady straightened, pointing his weapon at me. "He told me your name was Ramona. No last name. Just Ramona. I can't believe the little shit lied to me. About something he didn't even know was important."

"He didn't lie. When he named me, that's who I became. Ramona. No last name. No family. Except for Billy."

"Yeah, right." Grady shook out his legs. "Get up."

I followed his order then shifted onto the balls of my feet, ready to run. Like I could really outrun a bullet if he pulled the trigger.

"You sure as hell vanished. Erased yourself from the map. So, don't tell me you weren't always planning to take off on Billy. If that itch wasn't lodged somewhere in the back of your mind, you wouldn't have been able cut and run the way you did."

I opened my mouth.

He waved me silent. "You can argue all you want, but you know I'm right." Grady glanced past me and down the hall. "Where's my other prisoner?"

I shrugged.

He could see as well as I that the door to the room where he had left Trevor tied up stood open. "You stupid bitch. It's not like the guy wanted to help you. Now I gotta track him down." He grabbed my arm and dragged me along the hall then pushed me inside the vacant room. His gaze moved from the swaths of duct tape on the floor, to the empty chair, to the broken window. He lifted the gun and once again pointed it at me. "Who the hell is this guy and how do I find him?"

If I didn't give him something, Grady might think to search me and find Trevor's wallet tucked in the pocket of my jeans, complete with his name and Mom's address. I stalled. "How should I know? The Elf called him a Good Samaritan."

Grady shook his head. "Nice try. I know the guy came here because you stole his wallet. I'm sure you snatched it because you wanted the green stuff. But Billy told me how you remembered the stuff you read. I'm betting you know the guy's name. So give."

"The name's Trevor."

The deep voice made me jump.

Grady spun towards the open door. A gunshot blasted. Grady's side erupted. Hot blood spattered my forearms and chest. My mouth dropped opened. I scurried back. Grady struggled to raise his gun arm. He managed to lift his hand a few inches before another shot hit, knocking him backward. He staggered against me. We tumbled to the carpet. I shoved him off and scrambled away from his bloody body. Grady stared at me, still trying to raise his weapon. I wrenched the gun from his hands, scooted back another foot then looked at my savior.

"You came back."

Trevor nodded, Sean's discarded gun dangled from his right hand. Trevor no longer looked like a tidy major domo, his white shirt torn and dirt stained, bits of greenery tangled in his hair. "I came back. You didn't have to help me, but you did. Seemed right to return the favor."

"By now someone's got to have called the police."

He nodded toward the hallway and the front door. "I've got a feeling you shouldn't be here when they arrive."

"Neither should you. This thing... This is old, old business. Old and over now." I pointed at the door. "You wipe down the door knobs – both sides of the door – and anything else you touched. I need to wipe down the study and the office and a room upstairs so it'll take me a little longer. When you're done, wait for me in the car."

Trevor surprised me by wiping Sean's gun with his sleeve before setting it on the carpet. I followed his example and used the hem of my shirt to wipe my fingerprints from Grady's gun.

Trevor straightened. "I'm going out the front door this time."

I looked at his disheveled hair and clothes and nodded. "I don't blame you."

"Better hurry. From Mill Valley to here – I'm guessing we've got five or six minutes before the police show. Tops."

"OK." I ran out of the room and down the hall, stopping next to the Elf's bloody body to wipe down the wall where I thought I might have touched it. In the office, Stuart slumped face down on the desk. I tried to stay focused on the Eames chair where I had been bound as I wiped down its arms. With the way the duct tape had been wrapped around my wrists, part of me doubted I left any prints but why take chances? I trotted into the next room and wiped down the arms of that chair as well. I didn't think I had touched anything else, but used the hem of my shirt to wipe off the door knob, too. When I re-entered the office, I stared at Stu. There was a good chance I leaned a hand on the desk top when I reached for his gun. I repressed a shiver and stood by the desk. Stu's body remained still, no longer breathing. "I'm sorry." I took a deep breath then starting wiping the surface areas of the desk where Stu's blood hadn't pooled. "I'm sorry," I said again then ran from the room.

Upstairs I wiped down door handles, drawer pulls and the surface of both the Elf's nightstand and dresser. I didn't care what kind of mess I made, just as long as my prints were gone. Racing down the stairs, I reassured myself that I never got a chance to touch the railing. When I reached the foyer, instead of running for the front door, I turned and ran back down the hall. No way was I leaving without my bag, without that letter Dad wrote to me.

The Elf's body somehow looked both bigger and smaller than before. I edged around him and ran. Breathing hard, I entered the last room. Grady half-sat, propped against the wall. With each breath, blood bubbled from his mouth. Trevor had shot a chunk out of Grady's side and another from his chest. Keeping out of reach, I grabbed my overnight bag. "Can you hear me?"

Grady's gaze found mine. The look in his eyes told me he heard and understood. He knew the end was coming for him.

"Good. I want to make sure you know that right now, you're living your worst nightmare. Your face may not rot off, but your insides rotted away years ago. You're dying alone in a jungle. And no one knows who you are. Or cares."

Twenty-seven

At the front door, I turned and glanced into the foyer, past the Elf's bloody corpse. I had carried Sean's gun with me from the back room and now set it on the cold stone floor beside him. This house remained the last place I saw Billy alive. This house, the birthplace of my nightmare. The place where, like a fool, I dreamed I would see Billy again. I should have known better. Long ago I learned that though nightmares came true, dreams didn't.

The wail of a police siren sounded in the distance.

Time to go.

With a final goodbye to Billy Bang, I wiped down the door knob then slipped outside and jogged across the sloping front lawn. There was no way to know for sure if the siren was racing to this address, but why take any more risks? The cab driver I had paid to wait for me was gone. The guy had probably taken his extra ten bucks and took off the moment I walked out of sight. Trevor sat behind the wheel of his car, motor running. A part of me still couldn't believe he had re-entered the house for me. Or that he sat waiting for me out front. I climbed into the passenger seat and nodded. Trevor floored it. He didn't want to get caught at the house any more than I did.

After swinging a broad U-turn and barreling down the hill, Trevor made eye contact. His face looked ashen, but he appeared in control. "Those guys back there were maniacs. I swear I had no idea what they were like when I told them you..." He shook his head. "At the grocery store, when I couldn't find my wallet, I knew something was wrong. I was sure I brought it with me. I checked the car. Checked the store aisles. Then it hit me: You took it.

"I was the one who booked your room at the Inn. I knew you'd show up there eventually so I waited out front. And when you climbed into that cab, I followed. I didn't know where you were off to or why. But when I saw you on that wall, I figured you were planning to steal from them, too."

"I don't blame you."

Trevor grimaced. "I don't care why you went to that house. I never should've told them you were there. I'm sorry."

"You couldn't know. Hell, I didn't know. I thought I was going to meet an old boyfriend. Instead I found his psychotic brother. The psychotic brother who killed my boyfriend ten years ago. In that same house." I grabbed the door handle as Trevor two-wheeled it around the corner at the bottom of the street. His jaw tightened, the structure of his knuckles became visible as his hands gripped the wheel. But he didn't slow. Trevor came across as the man you wanted driving in a crisis.

The sirens grew louder. I touched Trevor's hand. "Slow down. We don't want to look guilty."

"Right." He brought us to within the speed limit before a cruiser rounded the next bend in the road below. The black and white whizzed by, lights flashing, speeding toward the site of the Orwell Massacre.

When the story got out about the place being the site of a second killing spree, would someone finally tear down that haunted house?

Trevor maintained an inconspicuous forty-five miles per hour as we wound our way back toward Mill Valley. I looked down; gore from Grady and the Elf dappled my arms and shirt. "Pull over."

"What?" Trevor said without slowing.

"I need to get this stuff off me." I gestured at the bloody splotches.

"Not here. When we get somewhere safe."

Right. Listen to Trevor. I tried not to look at the penny-sized spots that smelled of copper. Tried to ignore the sensation of the blood of two dead men drying on my skin. I closed my eyes, wishing I could block out the image of their bodies sprawled on the floor, dead and dying. All so senseless.

I opened my eyes then looked at Trevor. "I'm sorry about your wallet. About taking it. There was probably a better way to handle things, but at the time, I couldn't see it. Those men trashed my car, stole my purse, my wallet. They took the boxes of mementos Dad left me. I needed food and a roof. I didn't have anywhere to go." I shrugged. "I know that doesn't excuse what I did. But I want you to know why I did it."

Trevor didn't respond right away. We continued in silence for several minutes, the rumble of the car's engine filling the quiet. Every mile we covered increased our safety zone but the feeling of dread lodged in the pit of my stomach remained. I turned my attention to the surrounding countryside in an attempt to ignore the blood dotting my skin. The open landscape appeared serene. It was hard to reconcile the beauty of the hills with the horror and death we had narrowly escaped. The mustard and tall grasses covering the slope had already browned at the blade tips. By mid-July, this area would be cleared to prevent wildfires. But now the earth looked ripe. As a child, I had loved this time of year. Released from school, the sky sunlit until bedtime. I had felt free, on the verge of adventure, the promise of a new beginning always waiting in the wings.

Another foolish dream.

Trevor cleared his throat, pulling me back to our situation. "Nothing excuses you stealing from me. True." His voice sounded raw. "But you might have had somewhere to turn to if I hadn't kicked you out of your own home."

His generous response surprised me. I blinked and continued to look away. "No, not mine. Mom's home. That place never felt like home to me."

"Still, your mother might've acted more welcoming if I hadn't gotten starchy about you."

Trevor's choice of word made me smile. "Maybe. But she's never been the lioness who protects her cub."

"Careful there. I'll cut you some slack because you saved my life. But don't disrespect your mother to me."

"You love her." I turned to look at him. "Right?"

Trevor's spine became arrow-straight as he signaled for a turn. "I work for her."

"Please. Don't insult me. Not after what we've gone through. You love her. I can see it in your face. I think you've loved her for a long time." I stared again at the white bulges of his knuckles as he gripped the wheel, guiding us around another bend in the road. We were a few miles from my mother's house. Soon Trevor's car would become part of the recognized scenery, blending us into anonymity. "You've known her a long time, right? Even before my dad."

Trevor licked his lips, but he didn't respond to deny or confirm.

"Why did you two break up? Or stop seeing each other. Or whatever you call it. All those years ago."

Maybe the rush from shared danger influenced him, or maybe Trevor still felt spurred by gratitude. Whatever the reason, he began to talk. "I wanted to marry her. She turned me down. Marion needed more security than I could offer. I'd planned for a career in the military. Can you imagine your mother living on an army base? Shopping at the commissary?" He shook his head then gave a sad-sounding laugh. "She got that part right. As much as I loved her, that life would have made her miserable. All those years living abroad. But not in the kinds of places she wanted to live. She would have been miserable in the hot, dusty locales where I wound up stationed." Trevor spun the wheel to the right, pulling onto the long incline of the gravel drive, toward safety. At the top, he parked under the white porte cochere. He turned in the seat to look at me, his expression earnest. "After I retired from the service, I contacted Marion. I want you to know that I never... We never..." He frowned at his hands, now knotted together in his lap like the roots of a plant kept too long in small pot. "I respected your father. Del was a good man. In a bad situation. Your mother... Her condition had gotten out of hand. Del saw how much happier she was when I was around. That she seemed less... Less unwell when I stayed by her side." Trevor cleared his throat before continuing. "He asked if I wanted a job. As Marion's companion, driver, escort. The last person hadn't worked out. Of course I said 'yes.' But Marion and I never behaved in any way that could be called improper. I would never have betrayed your father's trust in that way."

The devil in me raised its head. "But that was then and this is now?"

Trevor's face reddened but he didn't turn away. "That's one way of putting things."

I nodded. "Thank you. I know you didn't have to tell me." I leaned forward and pulled Trevor's wallet from my back pocket. "Here. I spent most the money for a room at the Inn. You can drop me off there, instead of me staying here. I promise I'll get your money back to you."

"We'll work out where you're staying later. First let's get you inside and cleaned up."

Inside the shower, I stood under the hot needles of water and scrubbed until my skin looked raw. While I washed away the lingering feel of blood on my face and arms, it hit me. My long-held dread that I had somehow failed the victims of the Orwell Massacre was wrong. Billy drugged me. I couldn't have helped myself, let alone the others. But Billy and I had both been in the dark about what was to come. Billy didn't abandon me. Nor did he sacrifice me to save himself. He wasn't the one who brought my Orwellian nightmare to life.

Head lowered, I let the water pound along the back of my neck as I tried to absorb this new reality. I had carried the guilt for so long, shaking it off wouldn't be the work of a day. Maybe in time, the weight would lift from my heart.

When my fingers started to prune, I rinsed one more time and turned off the tap. I re-checked my arms and hands: no blood or gore. Yet I still felt dirty. In time, the stain of violence would fade and I would find a way to weave today's revelations and revulsion into memory. I would learn to live with the defects and tears in the fabric of my life, along with the treasured patterns. I had done it before, I could do it again.

I stepped out of the tub. My blood-spattered jeans were gone, replaced by the rumpled and grubby pair from my overnight bag. Less than desirable, they were better than nothing. I pulled on my spare T-shirt. After scrubbing my tennis shoes in the sink, I slipped into them, squishing with every step. I stared at my reflection in the floor-length mirror hanging from the back of the bathroom door. They were going to love me at the Inn.

Trevor's earlier candor led me to suspect he had no idea he remained the likeliest candidate for my birth father. I felt pretty sure Mom would refuse to talk to me about it. After what Trevor and I had endured together, sharing my suspicions with him felt wrong. I didn't want to risk telling him one more thing that might not be true. I considered stopping in to see Mom before heading downstairs, but decided I had experienced enough turmoil for the day.

Trevor waited in Dad's study, sipping something tan-colored and alcoholic. He had cleaned up, too. His hair was once again free of flora, the vomit-stained shirt replaced by a gleaming white one with a crisp collar. "I checked on Marion. She was angry I didn't come when she called. But it sounds like she slept through most of our adventure."

I swallowed the urge to roll my eyes and say, "You mean was passed out." Instead I nodded at his description of my mother's day. The pretense that I agreed with his assessment seemed a small price to pay.

"She's resting now. Drink?" He raised his glass.

"No thanks. I better get going."

"You know you can stay."

"Yeah. But I think it's better if I don't. Thanks though." Hesitant about how best to continue, I picked at a spot of dirt on the front of my jeans. "Uh, I know this is a hard time for Mom, but maybe you could talk her into getting some kind of treatment. I'd try, but she and I... We're like oil and water. I don't think she'd listen to me. She respects you. I can tell your opinion counts."

Trevor nodded. "I'll try. But why don't you stay? The Inn's nice. But you're with family here. I'm sure Marion would be happy to have you spend the night."

Family. He had no idea how close to the truth he might be. I shook my head. "I'm not as sure about that as you are. I love Mom. I do. But she brings out the absolute worst in me. Behavior-wise." I shook my head. "That's not fair. She doesn't do it to me. I do it to me. Until I get my reactions to her worked out, it's probably better if I'm not her houseguest."

"If you're sure."

"Maybe, down the road, I can come back for a visit. If it's okay with you guys."

"That would be nice." Trevor set his glass on a side table and stood, pulling a key ring from inside his trouser pocket. I hoisted the bag of treasures Dad had saved for me and followed Trevor out to the car. He opened my door then waited until I got settled before he closed me in.

When he slid behind the wheel, he turned to face me. "Will you stay in town a few days or...?"

"I think after a good night's sleep, I'll head back to L.A. That's what I'd planned to do. Before things got crazy."

"Uh-huh." He drove down the gravel drive and turned toward downtown Mill Valley. "The police... We could get into trouble for leaving the scene of a crime. If anyone saw us."

I suppressed a smile. Already Trevor was rewriting history, his sin now leaving the scene of a crime, not shooting Grady. "True.

But in that kind of neighborhood? People live in places like that to safeguard their privacy. That's why the walls are high. Someone must've heard the shots – or the cops wouldn't have got there so fast. But I didn't see anyone out on the street when we left. Between the walls, those hedges and the size of the lots, most the neighbors wouldn't be able to even see your car. And the possible one or two who could do that would've needed to have binoculars at the ready to read your license plate.

"There's nothing connecting you with those men. Nothing to connect you to that house. Except me. And I knew one of them a decade ago. We were thrown together by circumstance, but we didn't hang out. We weren't friends." I didn't need to close my eyes to picture Stu plucking another starry-eyed girl from the audiences that came to see his and Billy's band a decade ago. To see Stu lead another nameless girl out into the alley for a quickie between sets while Janelle pretended not to see and coked herself into buoyant oblivion. "We weren't friends," I repeated. "No one around here knows we knew one another even for that brief period." True for the most part. Except for Janelle. But from what I had seen, she wasn't really Janelle anymore. Besides, I doubted she kept up on current events – other than what drugs were slated to arrive and when. "No one will connect us to what happened."

"What about your car?"

"What do you mean?"

"The police have it. No matter how burned it was, they'll track you through the license plate or the VIN."

"Yeah, but my car's got nothing to do with... Oh shit. Can they retrieve fingerprints after a fire? The guy that hit you? He's the one who took my car and torched it."

Trevor shook his head. "Guess that depends on where he touched the car and what parts got burned. Even if they don't find his prints, you'll look guilty of something if you don't claim the car."

"You're right."

Trevor pulled over opposite the Mill Valley Inn and cut the engine.

I stared at the tall windows and wrought iron demarcating each balcony. "Got it. I'll go in, collect my stuff from the desk and check-in. Then I'll call the cops from my room and tell them my car was stolen." I nodded as my story gelled. "I can say that, after a visit with my mom that didn't go well, I had too much to drink and left my car in Lytton Square. Tell them I spent the day nursing a hangover and didn't go looking for my car until now. How's that sound?"

"Not bad. A little scary how quickly you came up with it." Trevor smiled.

"The thing is, I'm in no shape to talk to the cops in person. If they want me to come in and fill out paperwork..." I shook my head. "But, you're right. I need to take care of it. Once the car thing's handled, I'll catch the bus to San Francisco and take the train home. Anything else I need to deal with, I'll do by phone. Long distance feels safer."

"I take it you won't be coming back for a while."

"Probably not." I reached across the center console and took his hand. "Thank you. For coming back for me. For saving me."

"Like I said before, I was returning the favor."

After I climbed out of the front seat, I leaned back in through the open car door. "I could be wrong about this, but I got the impression Mom needs to tell you something. Like something's weighing on her mind. Maybe if you can get her to complete some kind of rehab, she'll be ready to tell you what it is."

Trevor cocked his head.

I shrugged. "It's just a feeling I got from her. It seemed important."

That was the best I could do for now. If Trevor wasn't my birth father, I would live. My mom, my dad, me – there was no way to alter our past. But room for change existed. Didn't I know better than most you could always shake things up, find a new way to live? For the first time in a decade, I was ready to move forward instead of hide.

A young mother trundled along the sidewalk, a tow-headed boy gripping her right hand. The boy pointed across the street at a gray-hair woman walking a dog. "Lassie!"

The mother smiled. "Yes, that's a dog like

Lassie. A border collie. Can you say collie?"

"Collie." The small boy laughed. "Collie, collie."

His happy chant brought to mind the old cry of olly olly oxen free. My decade-long game of hide and seek was over. A feeling of peace settled in my chest. I hadn't done anything to hurt those people at the Orwell Massacre. No one was chasing me anymore. From here on out, I didn't need to run, didn't need to feel burdened by the weight of my past.

Inside the Inn, classical music played and jasmine scented the air. As I strolled to the front counter, a simple truth popped into my head. I stopped in my tracks and laughed out loud. The stuck-up desk clerk from my morning check-in eyed my rumpled jeans and T-shirt, his upper lip curling with distaste. Dear God, if that jerk knew how rich a woman I was, the guy would crawl through broken glass to compliment me on my ensemble.

Like that other day when I was seventeen, this one would haunt me for a long time. Maybe forever. A depressing, awful day. Horrifying and bizarre. The stuff of nightmares. But because of this day, I felt free. For the first time in years.

And I was rich. Filthy rich. If I wanted to be.

Grady said Billy told him I remembered 'the stuff I read.' But Billy must not have told him I retained everything I read with exactitude. For years. Grady would roll over in his grave if he knew I didn't need his dog tag to get the number for his Swiss bank account. I had rubbed that medallion like a good luck charm for a decade and knew the number by heart.

The question remained: What was I going to do with that knowledge?

Billy once labeled me a brilliant screw-up. I did tote more baggage than I liked to admit. Yet I had always harbored dreams of doing something meaningful with my life. I didn't know what the hell I was going to do when I got home – other than have a long, honest talk with Rob and hope for the best. But with over $6 million in a Swiss bank account, I could afford to help a lot of people. Like my neighbors, the Stegmans. A smile spread across my face. There wasn't a helluva lot I couldn't afford to do.

But first things first: When I got home, I would call Rob and ask him to come over. Once he got there, I'd tell him everything. My real name, what had happened ten years ago and what happened today. I would take a chance and trust him. Trust him with my future.

Thank you for reading Erasing Ramona.

For notices about new releases, please join my mailing list or follow me on Facebook. I love hearing from readers!

https://www.facebook.com/ peggyrothschildauthor

peggyrothschild.author@gmail.com

http://www.peggyrothschild.net

You can also find me on Twitter @pegrothschild

Reviews on Amazon are always welcomed!

9 781512 013580